In the process of tracing her Canadian family to their origins in eighteenth-century Britain **Deborah Hale** learned a great deal about the period and uncovered plenty of true-life inspiration for her historical romance novels! Deborah lives with her very own hero and their four fast-growing children in Nova Scotia—a province steeped in history and romance!

Deborah invites you to become better acquainted with her by visiting her personal website, www.deborahhale.com, or chatting with her in the Harlequin Mills & Boon online communities.

Novels by the same author:

A GENTLEMAN OF SUBSTANCE
THE WEDDING WAGER
MY LORD PROTECTOR
CARPETBAGGER'S WIFE
THE ELUSIVE BRIDE
BORDER BRIDE
LADY LYTE'S LITTLE SECRET
THE BRIDE SHIP
A WINTER NIGHT'S TALE
 (part of *A Regency Christmas*)
MARRIED: THE VIRGIN WIDOW*
BOUGHT: THE PENNILESS LADY*
WANTED: MAIL-ORDER MISTRESS*

Gentlemen of Fortune

This book is dedicated to my agent,
Pam Strickler, whose support
and wise advice helped me
rise to the challenge of this story.

'There.' The mellow murmur of Bennett's voice went straight to her heart in that vulnerable moment. **'That's better.'** He raised his hand to her cheek in a featherlight caress. Then an irresistible magnetism seemed to draw their lips towards one another.

The first warm, tremulous contact after such a long absence made Caroline's senses crackle with suppressed desire suddenly reignited. It flared and spread swiftly, until it felt as if wildfire raged through her veins.

The blaze swept through Bennett too. His embrace tightened, as if to claim her. His kiss grew deeper and more demanding, while she ached to give him everything he wanted and more. Her lips parted to invite the hungry thrust of his tongue.

Old desires fused with strange new emotions to make this kiss sweeter and more satisfying than any they had shared before. Caroline savoured it like a serving of her favourite food after a long fast. She sought to hoard the feel and taste of it, knowing this would surely be the last time Bennett ever kissed her. While his lips moved over hers with such thrilling fervour she could pretend that he cared for her in the way she'd once longed for.

AUTHOR NOTE

In most Regency romances the wedding of the hero and heroine is the beginning of their *happily-ever-after*. But for the Earl and Countess of Sterling it is the beginning of their problems. Wed too quickly, for too many of the wrong reasons, they grow further and further apart—until scandal rocks their marriage, forcing them to choose whether to walk away or fight for a happier future together.

In HIS COMPROMISED COUNTESS the last person with whom Bennett wishes to share a small house on a remote island is the wife he believes has betrayed him with his hated rival. Caroline feels the same about her husband, who threatens to destroy her life of pleasure and part her from her young son. Only when they are thrown together under the most difficult circumstances can Bennett and Caroline begin to confront the problems that have beset their marriage and rekindle the spark of attraction that never quite went away.

I hope you will enjoy visiting the fascinating Isles of Scilly with Bennett and Caroline as they learn the true meaning of love.

HIS COMPROMISED COUNTESS

Deborah Hale

First published in Great Britain 2012
by Mills & Boon, an imprint of Harlequin (UK) Limited.
Harlequin (UK) Limited, Eton House, 18-24 Paradise Road,
Richmond, Surrey TW9 1SR

© Deborah M. Hale 2012

ISBN: 978 0 263 22908 0

Harlequin (UK) policy is to use papers that are natural,
renewable and recyclable products and made from wood grown in
sustainable forests. The logging and manufacturing process conform
to the legal environmental regulations of the country of origin.

Printed and bound in Great Britain
by CPI Antony Rowe, Chippenham, Wiltshire

Chapter One

With a flourish, someone pulled back the blue damask curtain from the alcove of Almack's card room, as if it were the stage at Drury Lane. The scene it revealed might have come from any of a hundred sentimental plays—a pair of lovers stealing a passionate kiss. But instead of sighs and murmurs of approval that might have greeted such a sight at the playhouse, this one provoked scandalised gasps followed by brittle, breath-baited silence.

They were as handsome a pair as any actors, the man well built with a full head of auburn hair and fashionable attire that might have won the approval of Beau Brummell himself. The lady wore a silvery-blue gown of the finest silk. Though her face was turned away from the audience for that first instant, her beauty was as obvious to them as her identity. Golden curls were swept up off her long, graceful neck, adorned with the famous Sterling sapphires.

Everyone who caught a glimpse of her must have immediately recognised Caroline Maitland, Countess of Sterling, one of the most celebrated toasts of the *ton*. They must also have recognised that the man with his arms around the countess, and his lips upon hers, was not her husband.

Surrounded by several of the most voluble gossips in all of London, Bennett Maitland, sixth Earl of Sterling, stared into the alcove, fighting a rising tide of rage and humiliation that threatened to demolish his iron self-control.

He had stubbornly refused to heed Fitz Astley's sly barbs about his wife's fidelity, just as he had once tried to deny another of his enemy's sordid revelations. A revelation that had brought his whole world crashing down. Scoundrel though Astley was, he had not been lying then. Nor was he now. The evidence of Caroline's promiscuity was presently on display for all to see!

Catching his wife engaged in such wanton intimacy with his bitterest foe was like a jagged knife thrust deep into Bennett's chest. The once-passionate physical connection between him and Caroline was the only thing that had held their crumbling marriage together. Now she had thrown it in his face and made him question how many other lovers she might have taken, making him the secret laughing stock of London. Yet he would rather have died in jaw-clenched agony than give the man he loathed, and the woman he had come to despise, the satisfaction of knowing how grievously they'd mortified him.

By the time the horrified silence shattered into poison-tipped shards of whisper, Bennett had clamped his gaping mouth into a rigid line. Battling back a suffocating wave of humiliation, he forced himself forwards to seize control of the situation.

By this time, his wife and her paramour had realised they

were discovered. Though it was far too late to save her tattered reputation, Caroline pulled away from the scoundrel's embrace and shrank back, as if hoping she might somehow hide from her husband's righteous wrath. Fitzgerald Astley had no such scruples. He continued to stand there in a lounging, insolent pose, his mouth twisted in a gloating smirk that Bennett longed to thrash off his face.

'Bennett, I'm so sorry,' Caroline murmured as he stalked towards them. 'I can explain if you'll only listen. Please don't make it any worse.'

Her face had paled to a hue of alabaster purity—most ironic, that. Her pallor might have given his wife a deceptively innocent look, except that it made her lips appear even larger and redder than usual, swollen perhaps from the kisses of that despicable cad!

Bennett wished the sight would quench the last stubborn embers of desire he felt for her. Instead he was doubly betrayed by the traitorous stirring of lust in his loins. Part of him longed to seize his errant countess and sear away any memory of Astley's kisses with the legitimate demands of his own lips.

He managed to resist the temptation.

'Nothing I do,' he growled, 'could make *this* any worse.'

That was not quite true, but he had no intention of acting as if nothing had happened, simply to spare her the shame she had brought upon both of them.

Astley's smirk curled into an outright sneer, making his too-handsome countenance as loathsome as Bennett had long regarded it. 'I suppose you will want to call me out, then, Sterling? Where shall we duel, then? St. James's Park? Hyde? I do think it rather unjust that I should be singled out when you have turned a complaisant eye upon all your lady's previous *amours.*'

'What are you talking about?' Caroline cried. 'I have never been unfaithful to my husband! I didn't even mean to… You took me by surprise. I only wanted…'

Astley chuckled and wagged his finger at her. 'I sympathise with your desire to salvage your reputation, Lady Sterling, but I fear our secret is out. I doubt anyone who saw us kissing just now would ever believe you were unwilling. Quite the contrary. Another minute and I vow you would have had the buttons of my breeches undone.'

'Viper!' A shriek of tormented rage burst from Caroline as she hurled herself at Astley.

Bennett would have loved to see her scratch the scoundrel's eyes. But such a spectacle would besmirch his cause even worse than it had been already. Perhaps irreparably.

As Caroline sprang towards Astley, Bennett caught her by the wrist and pulled her back, flaying her with his blistering glare. 'If you cannot exercise a little discretion, madam, at least do me the courtesy of holding your tongue!'

His words appeared to quench her defiant anger with a deluge of shame. Her body went limp and her free hand flew to her mouth as if to stifle a sob.

Unable to abide any further contact after what she'd done, Bennett let go of his wife's arm with all the revulsion he might have dropped a wriggling rat. He turned his attention back to Astley, to address his enemy's assumption that they would duel.

'You expect me to risk my neck defending my wife's honour?' He infused his question with years of accumulated disdain for the pair of them. 'I would sooner call you out for implying I am such a fool. Even for that, I prefer to strike where it will do you greater injury.'

Though Astley arched a contemptuous eyebrow, Bennett had the trifling satisfaction of glimpsing a quiver of alarm in his enemy's pale-blue eyes. 'Indeed? And where might that be?'

'In your purse, of course.' Bennett kept his voice low and menacing, but loud enough to carry to the roomful of breath-bated onlookers. 'I hope this dalliance was worth the damages it will cost you.'

For a moment, the threat seemed to strike Astley dumb.

Instead it provoked a sound from Caroline. Her eyes widened in horror as if she had only now realised all she stood to lose. A whimper like a wounded animal's broke through the hand she still clamped over her mouth. Fortunately, his earlier warning kept her from trying to speak.

Astley found his voice at last. 'Sue me for crim. con.? You wouldn't dare!'

Crim. con. meant a criminal conversation suit brought by a husband against his wife's lover for monetary damages—a necessary step toward obtaining a divorce. Bennett despised the vulgar colloquial term, which trivialized such a devastating betrayal.

Now it was his turn to sneer. 'Pray what is to stop me? Given what you just confessed in front of all these witnesses, I believe it would be an easy case to win.'

Leaving Astley to reflect on just how deep a hole he had dug for himself, Bennett turned and strode away through a crowd that parted before him like the Red Sea before Moses. He was not certain whether Caroline would follow or remain behind with her paramour. Indeed, he was not certain which he would prefer. But when he heard the faint rustle of silk and the soft patter of kid slippers behind him, the sounds stirred a flicker of satisfaction from deep within the bitter ashes of his humiliation.

Stalking down the grand staircase, he fixed his eyes straight ahead and set his mouth in a grim line to warn anyone he met against the folly of speaking to him. He was aware of heads turning as he passed, furtive whispers dogging his footsteps.

Gossip travelled fast. By breakfast the tattle would be all over London. By the end of the week the scandal sheets would be lampooning him; the print-sellers' windows would be papered with vicious caricatures. Though he had striven to lead a blameless life of public service, he would now be pilloried alongside the likes of the Prince Regent and his disreputable brothers!

Was that what Caroline wanted?

Though Bennett could not deny their marriage was an egregious mismatch, they had been happy enough once. Gradually, however, their differences had multiplied and the gulf between them had widened. But when and why had his wife grown to hate him enough to do this? After all he had given her and how little he asked in return, did she not owe him a single scrap of gratitude or loyalty?

A raw April wind blew Bennett's hair about as he emerged on to the street. Damn! He had left his hat behind.

Well, no matter. He might send a footman to fetch it tomorrow…or not. He had plenty of others, after all. And he'd be hanged if he would darken the door of Almack's again!

Striving to ignore his wife's presence, Bennett was relieved when his carriage appeared promptly, in spite of the early hour and their precipitous departure.

'Back to Sterling House, my lord?' the coachman called down from his perch.

Bennett gave a curt nod as the footman helped Caroline into the carriage box. 'Stop by my club first, Samuel. I will provide you with further instructions there.'

Before the coachman could reply, Bennett climbed in after his wife.

The vehicle had scarcely begun to move when Caroline's voice emerged from the shadow-wrapped depths of the seat opposite him. 'Please, Bennett, I know you must be as angry and embarrassed as I am by that dreadful scene, but surely you know I never had any intention of kissing Mr Astley.'

Clearly the woman had no idea of his feelings in the matter or she could never make such a ludicrous claim. Bennett leaned back in the carriage seat and crossed his arms over his chest. Did she truly expect him to believe she hadn't invited and enjoyed that kiss and how many others before it?

Bad enough she had made him a cuckold—he would not let her play him for a fool as well! 'Are you saying you tumbled into Astley's arms by accident?'

'Of course not.' The pretended remorse in her tone took on a hint of exasperation. 'When I told him you'd ordered me not to have anything more to do with him, he suggested we slip into the alcove so you would not see us.'

They'd had a bitter quarrel earlier in the evening on the drive to Almack's, which now felt like a lifetime ago. Spurred by Astley's thinly veiled accusations against Caroline, Bennett had forbidden her to continue associating with the bounder. She'd had the temerity to flare up at him, demanding to know why she must snub a man who appeared to enjoy her company when her husband did not. She'd extolled Astley's wit and amiability, bringing Bennett's temper to the boiling point. When the carriage arrived at Almack's, she had flounced in, having given her husband no assurance that she intended to do what he'd asked.

Now she had the gall to use his reasonable request as an excuse for her folly? Bennett's head pounded until he feared it would explode.

'No sooner had we got in there,' Caroline continued, 'than he seized me and began to kiss me. I was so taken by surprise I could not think what to do. Nothing like this has ever happened to me before...at least not in a very long time.'

Like a slap in the face, her words reminded Bennett of the long-ago evening when he'd first kissed her and insisted she must marry him. On that occasion Caroline had not protested or even feigned reluctance, but returned his ardour with an answering passion he had not expected from an innocent young lady. At the time, her fiery desire had not troubled him—quite the contrary. Now he chided himself for not seeing where it might lead one day.

'So when you say you're sorry,' he rasped through clenched teeth, 'you do not mean you regret what you did. Only that you got caught red-handed this time.'

'No! I mean...of course I'm sorry it turned into such a scandalous spectacle and embarrassed us both. But I'm also sorry I did not behave with more prudence and propriety.' Each word sounded more forced than the one before it.

It was clear she didn't mean a word. His errant wife was only spouting whatever she thought might save her from ruin.

Bennett shook his head. 'That is the most improbable tale I have heard in a great while. You must take me for a perfect idiot. Though perhaps I encouraged you to think me an easy dupe by not suspecting your prior indiscretions.'

'What *prior* indiscretions?' she demanded. 'I never committed adultery with Mr Astley, let alone any other man!'

He resisted the temptation to believe her. Now that the wool had been ripped from his eyes, like that curtain at Almack's, so many incidents that had seemed innocent at the time took on much more ominous significance. Their marriage had long since lost its original enchantment for him. Now he wanted nothing more than to be rid of the wife who had brought further shame upon the family honour he'd worked so hard to restore.

Bennett gave a harsh, mirthless chuckle. 'I would hardly expect you to admit such a thing, though the truth would make a refreshing change.'

'But it *is* the truth!' She had the devil's own gall to sound offended by his doubts. 'I cannot deny I have been admired by other men, but this was the first time matters went so far.'

He did not want to have this conversation with her. It served no purpose but to further inflame the feelings he was struggling so hard to control. 'Do you reckon anyone in the Doctors' Commons would believe that after what was seen and heard tonight by so many unimpeachable witnesses?'

His reference to the ecclesiastical court brought a gasp from Caroline. 'Did you mean it when you threatened to seek damages against Mr Astley?'

Finally the full consequences of her actions seemed to dawn on her.

'You should know by now, I am not in the habit of saying things I do not mean. Insincerity is Fitz Astley's forte, not mine.'

Caroline did not bother to defend her paramour, being much more concerned with her own interests. 'You cannot propose to divorce me over a single kiss I didn't want and the accusations of a blackguard who would take such vile advantage of a lady.'

Did she not realise there were far worse things he could do than divorce her? 'I can assure you, a great many Bills of Divorcement have passed through Parliament on the strength of less damning evidence.'

'But that's not fair!' she cried, as if she were an innocent victim.

'The world is not fair!' Bennett thundered. 'As you might know if you would once look beyond the tip of your pretty nose. Every day innocent children are born or sold into slavery, torn from their families at the whim of cruel masters. Have you any idea how much damage you may have done to the Abolition Movement with your wanton, wilful behaviour? Or do you not give a damn?'

'Of course I do! I have heard and seen and breathed Abolition ever since I was young enough for Mr Wilberforce to bounce me on his knee. But how can I have hurt your cause?'

It galled him to have to explain to her. 'I have made great progress, rallying support for an Abolition Bill in the House of Lords, which has always been a stumbling block in the past. How effective an advocate do you suppose I will be when it becomes known my wife has been bedded by my most vicious opponent? No one respects a cuckold.'

'But you aren't! That's what I am trying to tell you, if you'd only heed me.' She leaned towards him, emerging from the shadows into the faint light shed by the street lamps, her arm outstretched.

Bennett resisted the urge to pull her into his arms and reassert his claim upon her, as another part of him longed to do. That was dangerous weakness to which he must not succumb.

Perhaps realising she had exhausted all other means of saving herself, Caroline marshalled her final-line defence. 'If you divorce me, I may never see Wyn again!'

'See him again?' How dared she try to use their son that way, after what she'd done? Her behaviour was a betrayal of the child as much as him. 'You do not see much of him now that I can tell. You swan into the nursery for an hour or two to amuse yourself. Once you've got the boy overexcited and fractious you leave Mrs McGregor to manage him. Wyn would be far better off without a mother who treats him like a plaything to be picked up and cast aside again at a whim.'

Before Caroline could attempt to defend herself from his charges, their carriage came to a stop in front of his club.

'What are we d-doing here?' she asked in a dazed, plaintive tone against which Bennett steeled his heart.

The earlier fight seemed to have gone out of her. In a splash of light from the street lamp, Bennett glimpsed her bare arms wrapped around her torso and realised she was shivering.

'I intend to stay here tonight,' he announced, then added, 'You left your cloak.'

'I d-didn't think of it until w-we were outside. And I didn't d-dare go back for fear you'd leave me b-behind.'

He would have been well within his rights to do just that, Bennett mused bitterly. Yet a deeply ingrained code of gentlemanly conduct compelled him to remove his coat and thrust it towards her. 'Take this.'

Caroline only hesitated an instant before pulling the garment around her.

Now Bennett had one thing left to say to her. Ever since they'd quit Almack's, part of his mind had remained detached, pondering how best to handle this beastly situation. One step was imperative. 'You must get out of town first thing tomorrow and stay away until the worst of the tattle dies down.'

Expecting her to object, he was surprised when she replied, 'Where shall I go? Brighton? Bath?'

'Good Lord, no! The gossip will spread there in no time and word of your whereabouts would get back just as fast. You must retire to some place as far away as possible from society.'

He'd considered and discarded a score of options. Now, suddenly, the ideal destination occurred to him. 'The Isles of Scilly. I have a house there, on Tresco.'

He hadn't thought of the place in years. Now that he had, it seemed a perfectly fitting destination for his adulterous wife.

How could she have been so foolish and unguarded as to place everything she cared about in jeopardy? As the carriage sped through Kensington towards Sterling House, the harsh tribunal of her conscience chilled Caroline worse than the damp cold of the windy April night.

After all, she was not some green girl fresh from the country in her first Season. Over the years she had seen enough scandal to recognise the impropriety of slipping into that curtained alcove with a man other than her husband. She should have known how incriminating it would look if they were discovered there, even without the kiss.

That damnable kiss! How could she have let it happen? She still found it difficult to reconcile the scoundrel who'd taken such a liberty, then callously dragged her name through the dirt, with the charming gentleman who'd traded witty banter with her over the card table and cast admiring glances at her on the dance floor. She'd thought it was only a harmless, flattering flirtation, like a number of others she'd enjoyed in the past without ever compromising her reputation.

When her husband angrily forbade her having any further contact with a man who looked at her in a way he had not in years, her long-simmering resentment had suddenly come to the boil. She could not simply turn her back on her ardent admirer without a single word of explanation or apology. The last thing she'd expected when he beckoned her into that alcove was to find his arms suddenly around her and his lips pressing upon hers.

For an instant, she'd been too shocked to react. Then she'd been further paralysed with uncertainty and shame, fearing she had led him to believe his amorous attentions would be welcome. When she'd finally come to her senses and been about to pull away, the card room suddenly went quiet and she'd plunged into her worst nightmare.

Would Bennett truly go through with his threat to seek a divorce? Until lately, he hadn't seemed to care how much other men admired her. She'd once heard it quipped that every gentleman of her acquaintance was besotted with her, except her husband. Though she'd pretended to be amused at the time, those words dealt a humiliating blow. What did it signify how many men desired a married woman if her husband was not among them?

In the early days of their marriage she had eagerly welcomed Bennett to her bed, deceiving herself that the pleasure he brought her was a token of the love he could not express in other ways. Later she'd faced the harsh truth that his ardour sprang from nothing more than physical desire. He had never felt anything deeper for her and he never would. In recent years, even his desire had waned. Caroline wished she could say the same. She had finally succeeded in quelling the feelings for her husband that had only made her miserable. Yet there were still nights when she lay in her empty bed aching for his touch.

Was it possible Bennett knew Astley was lying, but had seized upon this opportunity to be rid of a wife who had proven such a disappointment to him? Hurt and angry as that thought made her, Caroline was far angrier with herself for giving him such a fine excuse to cast her off.

Her husband was right about one thing, unfortunately. If he wanted a divorce, he could likely get one even though she had never committed adultery. Her single public indiscretion would be taken as proof that she must have done far worse things in private. And Astley's deceitful boasting would be taken as fact, even if he later recanted.

After that, life as she knew it would be over.

As far as society was concerned, she might as well be dead. She would be exiled to the dullest depths of the country, forced to live on whatever pittance Bennett chose to give her. No lady who valued her good name would ever be permitted to associate with such a scandalous outcast. But by far the worst deprivation was that she would never be allowed to see her little son again.

The prospect of losing Wyn battered Caroline's heart. Bennett had accused her of not caring about their son, but he did not understand.

The moment the carriage came to a halt in front of Sterling House, she hurried inside, throwing off Bennett's coat. The whiff of his clean, bracing scent that clung to the garment roused a gnawing hunger within her that she'd spent years striving to subdue.

Stopping by her rooms, she bid her maid pack a trunk for the journey on which they would set out the next morning.

'The Isles of Scilly, my lady? Why in the world are we going there?'

'It was the earl's idea, Parker.' Caroline hoped that excuse would forestall any further questions. 'We must leave at first light and I'm not certain how long we'll be gone, so get to work.'

'Very well, ma'am.' Parker set about her task with a sulky air.

Leaving her maid to pack, Caroline rushed to the nursery. Though she'd arrived home much earlier than usual, Wyn was already asleep. She crept to his bed and perched on the edge of it, listening to his soft, even breathing.

'Your papa thinks I don't care about you,' she whispered, not wanting to wake her sleeping child, yet hoping some part of him might hear and understand. 'But I do love you very much and have since long before you were born.'

At first she'd wanted a baby as a way to please her husband and prove that she could fulfil her chief duty as a wife. But when she'd finally become pregnant and felt that tiny life grow and move within her, she began to cherish him for his own sake and look forward to giving him all the love and happiness most of her childhood had lacked.

But nothing had turned out as she'd hoped. 'I had such a hard time bearing you. And afterwards, you were a fretful little thing and wouldn't feed properly.'

Caroline heaved a deep, shuddering sigh as she recalled

the shrill, angry shrieks of that tiny creature, his face a raw mottled red. The grave, accusing looks of the doctors still haunted her, as they'd shaken their heads and whispered together. She'd felt like such a terrible mother—rejected by her own child when he was barely out of her womb.

Though Bennett hadn't said so, she sensed he was disappointed in her inability to succeed at something so simple and natural. He'd engaged Mrs McGregor and a wet nurse for her baby, who'd immediately begun to thrive in their care.

The gaiety and admiration of society had helped ease the sting of her failure. But her evening engagements often lasted late into the night, making her sleep the next morning until nearly noon.

'I visited the nursery as often as I could.' Her heart ached with the memory. 'But I was afraid to pick you up in case I dropped you or made you cry.'

His nurse, a brusque Scotswoman who intimidated Caroline no end, had made it clear she wished the mistress would not come to the nursery too often and disrupt the young master's routine. To her shame, she had allowed herself to be pushed out of her son's life.

She could not let his father banish her entirely!

Wave after hot wave of anger seared through her. Anger at Bennett, who had stubbornly refused to believe her. His accusations that Wyn would be better off without such a mother had hurt far more than his charges of infidelity. Anger at the law, which punished a wife's infidelity so harshly while letting a husband take a dozen mistresses with impunity. That same unjust law decreed that children belonged to their fathers—sons especially. A divorced mother was considered an immoral influence, unfit to raise the offspring she had borne. Bitterest of all was Caroline's anger at herself for not realising how much her *harmless* flirtations and one moment of heedless impropriety could cost her.

Just then her little son stirred in his sleep, making Caroline fear he might wake and take fright at her presence. Instead he snuggled closer to her, with a murmur of the sweetest contentment. A warm, brooding ache spread through her chest, cooling the fierce fire of her anger.

'It is not too late,' she vowed to her sleeping son, and to herself. 'It cannot be. I will become the kind of mother I always wanted to be.'

After a pensive moment she added in a whisper so soft she could barely hear it herself, 'At least for as long as your father will let me.'

Chapter Two

The next day, when he judged it late enough that his wife must be on the road to Cornwall, Bennett returned home. He looked forward to a sound sleep in his own bed, having scarcely got a wink the night before.

Every time he'd closed his eyes, the memory of his wife in the arms of his enemy had risen to taunt him. He'd also been besieged by his allies in the Abolition Movement. When word of the scandal reached them with disgusting rapidity, they'd flocked to the club, anxious to advise him. To a man, they looked forward to seeing Astley dragged through the mud. They also agreed it was imperative for Bennett to seek a divorce as quickly as possible. He had assured them that was his intention. But now doubts began to gnaw at his resolve.

Not doubt of her guilt, of course. He was convinced of that, in spite of her desperate protests to the contrary. He had long known Caroline to be a naturally passionate woman. For a time it had been the saving grace of their marriage. Now it had become the rock on which their faltering union would wreck at last.

And yet, seeing her in the arms of another man made him

realise how much he missed their often-tempestuous physical relations. It had been the one area of his life where he'd been able to escape his own rigid self-control. He'd sometimes thought of it as performing the function of a safety valve on a steam engine. Without that occasional release, he could not work at optimal capacity without a dangerous build-up of pressure.

But after everything involved with the birth of their longed-for son had gone so disastrously wrong, he'd been reluctant to risk getting his wife with child again too soon. By the time he might have considered it, they had grown so far apart that it would have been like bedding a perfect stranger.

Mortified and furious as he was over Caroline's betrayal, Bennett could not pretend she was entirely responsible for the failure of their marriage. He was every bit as much to blame for having pursued her so relentlessly and rushed her into marriage before their infatuation had had an opportunity to cool. If he had not let desire overcome his reason, he would have seen they were far too different in far too many ways to be compatible outside the bedchamber.

At the time those differences had only added fuel to the overwhelming passion that had possessed him. Too late he'd realised that something so combustible was apt to burn out just as quickly. Now he knew he should have married a woman with whom he had more in common, one he might have been better able to understand.

Glimpsing the stately turrets of Sterling House in the distance, rising behind a screen of majestic elm trees, Bennett looked forward to seeing his young son. Wyn was the main reason for his doubts about seeking a divorce. He'd experienced first-hand the bitterness of a shattered family. He did not want that for his son.

Not that Wyn was apt to pine for Caroline as some children might for an absent mother. According to Mrs McGregor, his stylish countess spent more time each day resting from the previous late night or grooming for some approaching engagement than she did in the nursery. The odd hours she did spend there only served to disrupt the child's sensible, healthy routine, spoiling him with gifts and sweets, making him overexcited from romping about. And when she'd amused herself and grown tired of his company, or when the little fellow grew fretful, she would simply hand him back to the long-suffering Mrs McGregor.

As long as Wyn had his faithful nurse and one responsible parent, surely the child would manage well enough.

That meant he would have to be an even more constant presence in his young son's life, Bennett reminded himself. From the time Wyn was very young, he had made certain to visit the nursery as often as possible to enquire if the child had slept well, if his appetite was satisfactory, if he was in good health and spirits. When Wyn was old enough, Bennett began to make a point of reading to him or taking him for walks around the estate, both of which Mrs McGregor heartily approved.

One fatherly duty he dreaded was the task of explaining Caroline's departure and the breakdown of their marriage in a way his young son could understand, while sparing him the worst of it. Though Bennett had no idea how he would find the right words, he knew he must try. He would not see the little fellow confused and anxious, left to piece together the shameful truth from the tattle of servants, as he'd once done.

The moment he entered Sterling House, Bennett headed immediately for the nursery to check on his son. He hoped Caroline had not been so thoughtless as to subject the child to an overwrought farewell.

When he entered the large, sunny room on the second floor of the east range, all was quiet apart from the soft click of knitting needles and the faint squeak of the rocking chair. Bennett's gaze skipped over the familiar figure of Mrs McGregor, seeking his son.

'Where is Wyn?' He pitched his voice low in case the boy was sleeping. 'This is not his usual nap time.'

'No, my lord.' The nurse's long knitting needles froze in mid-stitch. 'If he were here, he'd be awake by now. But he's gone away on that wee holiday with the countess. Were you hoping to bid them farewell before they left?'

'Holiday?' Bennett repeated the word as if he'd never heard it before and was trying to grasp its meaning. 'What holiday? Where has she taken him?'

An indignant scowl clenched the nurse's sharp features. 'I thought it seemed most irregular, but her ladyship insisted she was acting on your instructions.'

It was true he had bidden Caroline away. But he had not given her *permission* to take Wyn, let alone ordered it. 'Did she say where they were going? How long ago did they leave?'

'This morning, my lord, earlier than I've ever seen her ladyship out of bed before. She said they were going to your house on the Isles of Scilly.'

Suddenly Bennett found himself teetering on the edge of a precipice. Just because Caroline had told Mrs McGregor they were going to the islands did not mean it was true. What if his wife had run away with her lover and taken his son with them—to the Continent, perhaps, or to Astley's accursed plantation in the West Indies?

The very notion threatened to push Bennett over the edge into a bottomless abyss, but he stifled his panic to concentrate on action. Wherever Caroline had gone, he would track her down and fetch his son home, where the boy belonged.

Five days after their precipitous departure from Sterling House, Wyn Maitland tugged on the sleeve of his mother's pelisse. 'How much longer until we get to that *silly* place, Mama?'

Wyn had asked that question at least once a mile on the three hundred of their journey to Penzance, and even more often since they'd boarded this ship for the islands. With each repetition, his words grated harder and harder on Caroline's frayed nerves. A sharp answer burned on her tongue, demanding to be spit out. Or perhaps it was the bile that rose in her throat every time the ship lurched in heavy seas.

One thought alone kept her from bidding the child to hold his tongue. He had not *asked* to accompany her on this long, tedious, uncomfortable journey. She had taken him from his safe, snug nursery, dragging him into the wilds of Cornwall and out to sea. If either of them had reason to be irritable with the other, it was her son with her, not the other way round.

'Quite soon, now, dearest.'

'I hope you're right, ma'am,' grumbled her lady's maid, who sat on the bench opposite them in the cramped, dimly lit cabin. 'When we boarded, they said it would be no more than eight hours' sailing with fair winds. How long has it been now?'

'Nearly twelve hours.' Caroline heaved a dejected sigh. 'I

hope the servants will still be awake by the time we reach the house.'

It was all that had sustained her for the past few days, as she'd discovered the difficulty of travelling with a young child and caring for him day and night—the vision of a pretty country house with its friendly staff of caretakers to welcome them. The first thing she would order was a warm pot of chocolate for her and Wyn to sip in front of a crackling fire. Once her little son was tucked in for the night, she would soak away the chills and kinks of her journey in a hot bath.

'I don't care if they've gone to bed,' grumbled Albert, the young footman who made the fourth member of their travelling party. 'Somebody had better stir themselves to fix a poultice for my ankle.'

He had taken a fall a few hours ago, when the ship pitched sharply.

'I'm sure they'll be glad to.' Caroline sought to lighten the footman's sullen temper. It was clear both he and Parker were disgruntled about accompanying her on this journey. Once the servants realised they might be in for an extended stay on the island, she feared they would desert her. 'How is your ankle?'

'Getting worse by the hour, ma'am,' Albert replied in a reproachful tone as if he blamed her for his misfortune. 'Swelled up and paining like the devil.'

'How much longer until we get there?' Wyn asked yet again. 'I miss Greggy. Why could she not come with us on this holiday?'

Caroline had asked herself that same question. How much easier would this journey have been for both of them if Wyn's capable nurse were there to look after him and answer his endless questions? But Mrs McGregor's presence would have been a double-edged sword, she reminded herself. How could she hope to make good her vow to become a more attentive mother to her son while his nurse lurked about, always coming between them and subtly criticising everything she tried to do?

'Mrs McGregor is long overdue for a holiday of her own.' It was the truth. Caroline strove to stifle her protesting conscience. The woman did *deserve* a holiday, whether or not she chose to take one.

'What about Papa?' asked Wyn. 'Why didn't he come with us?'

Her son's question tore at Caroline. She wondered if Wyn would ever ask for her after she had been wrenched from his life. And if he did, how would Bennett respond to his son's pleas? Would he even care?

'I'm sure your father would like to be with us.' She uttered that well-meant falsehood with all the sincerity she could rally. 'But you know he is terribly busy in the House of Lords, passing laws for the good of the country.'

That part was true, at least. Unlike some of his fellow peers, the earl took his duties in Parliament very seriously. Because he did not align himself on every issue with one particular faction, he was often able to cast a deciding vote or broker a compromise. But there was one matter on which he would never compromise—the abolition of slavery. Much as Caroline resented her husband's mistrust and feared his threat to divorce her, she could not help but admire his integrity and his devotion to such a noble cause.

'How much longer until we get there?'

Fortunately for Caroline, she was spared the need to answer. At that moment, from the deck above, came the distant muffled call, 'Land ho!'

Those were two of the most welcome words she'd heard in weeks. 'Very soon, my love. Before long we will be warm and fed, with solid ground beneath our feet and no more miles to travel tomorrow.'

Wyn gave a cheer while Parker and Albert exchanged a look of relief.

An hour later, they found themselves ashore on a dark, moonless night. It might not have been so very cold, but the damp wind gusted hard enough to penetrate every layer of clothing, chilling the flesh beneath.

'Where are ye bound for, ma'am?' asked the young man who heaved their luggage into a cart pulled by a small dark horse. 'Dolphin Town? The inn at New Grimsby?'

How large was this island? Caroline wondered. On a globe it had looked like one of a cluster of pebbles kicked into the sea by the long-toed boot of Cornwall.

'We've come to stay at a house that belongs to the Earl of Sterling. Do you know the place? Is it far from here?' She was beginning to sound like Wyn.

'Please?' the carter asked in a tone as if begging her pardon for not having understood. 'There's no earl that lives on Tresco, ma'am.'

'The earl doesn't *live* here.' Caroline shushed Wyn who was dancing about, pestering her with more questions. 'I'm certain he has not been here in the past seven years at least. But he told me he owns a house on this island.'

The young man shook his head slowly. 'Only local folk lives here, ma'am. Unless…you mean the old Maitland place?'

Caroline's sinking spirits rebounded. 'That's it, to be sure! Bennett Maitland is the Earl of Sterling. I am his wife.'

How much longer would she be able to make that lofty claim?

'How far is the house?' she asked. 'Can you take us there?'

'Not but a step, ma'am. Over yonder.' He pointed into the darkness.

Caroline strained for a glimpse of lights shining from the windows, but could make out none. 'Is there a carriage I might hire to take us there?'

'Sorry, my lady, there's only my cart and Steren, here.' The young islander patted his pony on the rump. 'You and the lad are welcome to ride if you can find a perch among your baggage.'

Wyn ran over to the cart and the young man hoisted him in. Caroline was about to climb after her son when a cough drew her attention back to Albert. Even if it was 'not but a step', the footman would never be able to hobble that far on his injured ankle. One look at the brimming cart told her it had room for only one more person.

'Get in.' She beckoned the footman. 'I don't want to be out on a night like this any longer than we have to.'

They were soon on their way. Caroline had never thought the day would come when she would walk so a servant could ride. At least the exertion of trudging behind the cart made her somewhat warmer, while the gusts of salty air helped settle her queasy stomach.

But even they could not blow away the sense of guilt that nagged at her for dragging Wyn off on such a miserable journey. If she'd had more time to anticipate the consequences of her actions, perhaps she might have left him to his familiar nursery routine and the competent care of Mrs McGregor. But the dread of never seeing her child again, and her desire to be a more attentive mother during the time they had left, had overridden every other consideration.

'Are you all right, Wyn?' she called to him.

'Y-yes, Mama.' He sounded cheerful enough under the circumstances. 'I've never been allowed outdoors after dark before and I've never ridden in a cart. It's like an adventure!'

Parker muttered something under her breath that Caroline did not catch.

'Here we are,' announced the islander as his cart came to a halt. 'This is the Maitland house.'

'There must be some mistake.' Caroline surveyed the rustic stone dwelling by the wildly flickering light of their guide's torch. The place was no bigger than the groundskeeper's lodge at Sterling House. All the windows were shuttered and not even the faintest gleam of light escaped through the slats. 'It looks quite abandoned. Are there no caretakers living here?'

'Not for ten years, ma'am.' The helpful reply demolished all of Caroline's hopes. 'Mag and Jack Harris used to keep the place for the lady who owned it. But after Jack passed on, Aunt Mag went to live with her daughter on Bryher. The house has been shut up ever since.'

'Does anyone have a key?' Caroline's voice grew shrill with desperation. 'So we can at least take shelter from this wind.'

'No need for locks and keys on Tresco, ma'am.' The carter assured her. 'Off-islanders think we're all smugglers, but we're honest folk and there's few enough of us that we'd soon know if anybody was making away with what didn't belong to him.'

To demonstrate, he lifted the latch and pushed the door open. The hinges gave a painful-sounding squeal.

Wyn scrambled down from the cart and followed his mother into the house behind the carter, who lit the way with his torch. As her anxious gaze swept around the parlour, Caroline's heartening visions of warm fires, chocolate and a hot bath crumbled into cold dust like the kind that covered every surface in the room. Cobwebs draped the ceiling corners. Dead insects littered the floor.

'What *is* that smell?' Parker fanned her nose. 'Did someone set fire to a load of rotten fish?'

'Oh, no, miss.' The carter inhaled. 'That'd be smoke from the summer kelp fires. I reckon it seeped in over the years and never got aired out properly.'

Just then, Caroline would have given anything to be back at Sterling House—even in the servants' hall, which would be warm and clean. If Wyn had not been with her, she might have sunk to the floor and wept in despair. As it was, it took every scrap of pluck she could muster to shore up her faltering composure.

'We cannot stay here tonight.' She shook her head. 'Everything will need to be cleaned and aired before we take up residence.'

'Not by me.' Parker crossed her arms in front of her flat chest. 'I'm a lady's maid, not a charwoman. I'd sooner swim back to Penzance than scrub all this.'

Caroline was too tired and cold to argue the matter just then. She cast the carter a pleading look. 'Is there *anywhere* we can find lodging for the night? Did you say Tresco has an inn?'

'Aye, ma'am. T'other side of the island.'

Parker and Albert groaned.

'We can be there in half an hour,' added the carter, 'if we step lively.'

Though Caroline welcomed the news that the inn was not far away, it disheartened her to realise how tiny this island must be if it took such a short time to cross from one coast to the other. Tresco would be her remote, rustic prison—as different as it could possibly be from the luxurious, stimulating life she'd enjoyed in London.

How long would she be obliged to stay here? she asked herself as her small party trudged through the dark windy night to the inn. Just until the tattle about her and Fitz Astley died down? Or would she be stranded here for the rest of her life once Bennett divorced her?

Somehow she managed to keep going for another two hours, hiring them rooms for the night, ordering a modest supper and finally putting Wyn to bed. Once he had dropped off to sleep, she slipped out of the room. In the narrow hallway she encountered the innkeeper's wife, a small, neat woman with a ruddy complexion and dark-brown hair, grizzled at the temples.

'Are you ailing, my lady?' the woman asked in a kindly tone. 'Tell me your trouble and perhaps I can brew you a remedy.'

'I'm not ill, Mrs Pender, only tired.' Caroline contrived a poor substitute for a smile. 'It has been a long journey from London and I have not slept well.'

'I see,' replied Mrs Pender. 'Well, if it's nothing worse than that, I reckon a cup of camomile tea would do you a power of good. Would you care to join me in my parlour?'

Caroline hesitated for an instant. What would her friends

in London say if they knew she was keeping company with a rural innkeeper's wife? Some of them might think worse of her for that than for being caught kissing Mr Astley at Almack's.

But she was a vast distance from London now. And none of those *friends* were here to comfort or divert her. Indeed, she doubted any of them would have come to visit her if she'd still been back in London. They seemed to view scandal as some sort of contagious malady that might infect them if they ventured too near.

This woman was the first to have shown her any kindness since that awful night her world had come crashing down. Until this moment, she had not realised how starved she was for a bit of agreeable company.

'That is most obliging of you.' Despite her fatigue and all her worries, Caroline found herself able to smile more sincerely. 'I would enjoy a little refreshment and someone to share it. I don't believe I've ever had camomile tea.'

'It's fine stuff, my lady.' Mrs Pender started down the stairs and Caroline followed her. 'It has a mild flavour and calms the mind to help you sleep. I pick the flowers early in the summer from the meadows around Great Pool.'

There were meadows of wildflowers on this island? Caroline found it hard to believe after what she'd seen of Tresco's rugged, inhospitable landscape so far.

'It's an honour to have you and your son staying here, my lady.' The landlady beckoned Caroline into a snug little parlour, then called a servant to fetch hot water from the kitchen. 'It does my heart good to think of family living in the Maitland house again after all these years. I mind your husband used to come here with his mother when he was about the age of your little fellow.'

'Did he?' Caroline sank on to an armchair by the hearth, gratefully soaking up the warmth of the fire. 'I had no idea.'

'Yes, indeed, ma'am.' Her hostess beamed. 'My auntie cooked for them and I used to help her out. The countess was such a kind lady and Master Bennett…I mean…his lordship was the picture of your son.'

'Was he?' Because Bennett never spoke of his mother, Caroline had always assumed she must have died when he was very young, as hers had. If he'd been old enough to remember, why had he never mentioned her? 'Was my husband close to his mother in those days?'

'Quite devoted, ma'am. And he was all the world to her. She was for ever taking him for walks and picnics. When the weather was bad, she'd play cards with him and read to him by the hour.'

Those were all things Caroline wanted to do with Wyn. But first she would have to get that deserted house cleaned so it would be fit to live in.

'What sort of woman was my husband's mother? I never had the pleasure of knowing her.' Would Mrs Pender think it strange that Bennett had not told her about his mother?

'Well…' The landlady thought back. 'I recall she was always polite to folks, no matter what their station.'

Caroline wondered if that was how Bennett had come by his political principles—his admirable concern for the enslaved and the working poor.

'She was pretty as a picture,' Mrs Pender continued, 'though never very strong, poor soul. She always came here for the climate in the autumn while her husband was hunting.'

The maid returned then with a teapot, cups and a steaming kettle. Caroline watched as Mrs Pender brewed up their tea.

While it steeped, she continued to pump the landlady for information to appease her curiosity. 'I suppose it has been quite a long while since they last came to the island?'

'Laws, yes, my lady. It must be every day of two dozen years.'

'That must have been when his mother died,' Caroline murmured to herself.

In the process of lifting the teapot, Mrs Pender froze. 'No, my lady. She came back once, a few years later, without him. Not to stay, but just for a few days to pack up some things from the house to take away.'

The woman looked as if she meant to say something else, then suddenly changed her mind. Instead she fussed with the tea, pouring it through a tiny strainer.

'Is there something else?' Caroline fixed the woman with a searching gaze as she took the offered cup. 'Whatever it is, I should very much like to know.'

The landlady wavered. 'I don't like to gossip, ma'am. Especially not about her ladyship. She was always good to me.'

The woman's evasive answer only intrigued Caroline more. What manner of *gossip* could she know about Bennett's mother?

Taking a sip from her cup, she savoured the wholesome, mellow sweetness. The fragrance alone seemed to soothe her. 'I appreciate your discretion, Mrs Pender, in not talking over the private matters of my family with strangers. However, since I am a member of the family, perhaps you could make an exception?'

The landlady sipped her tea in silence, clearly mulling

over Caroline's request. 'Perhaps it's no great matter, after all, ma'am. It's just that when her ladyship came back that last time, she brought a gentleman with her. Fine looking, he was, and very agreeable. I can't recall his name, now, but he... wasn't her husband.'

Those last few words, Mrs Pender spoke in a scandalised whisper.

Caroline nearly choked on a mouthful of her tea. Had Bennett's parents been divorced? He had never said so, but then again he'd never spoken of them at all. Could this be the reason—because he was ashamed of the family scandal?

'Perhaps the man was some relative of her ladyship?' she suggested. 'A brother or a cousin?'

'Aye, ma'am. He might have been.' Mrs Pender sounded doubtful.

If Bennett was ashamed of his parents' divorce, Caroline mused, why was he so eager to taint their young son with that same kind of shame?

Chapter Three

By taking flight with their son, his wife had banished Bennett's few doubts about seeking a divorce. He'd pursued Caroline's party relentlessly all the way from London, and might have caught up with them at Penzance if a lame horse had not delayed him. By the time he landed on Tresco, late the next afternoon, he feared he would find no sign of Caroline or his son because Astley had spirited them abroad.

Striding up from the quay at Old Grimsby through a spit of rain, Bennett was struck by an uncanny feeling that he'd journeyed back in time. Nothing about the island appeared to have changed in the past twenty years, from the stone cottages with their thatched roofs to the wheeled barrels for fetching water from Great Pool. As he approached the house, he half-expected to meet his younger self running out the front door.

Perhaps that was what stopped him from calling out, compelling him instead to lift the latch with care and ease the door open almost reluctantly. He found the parlour deserted, the furniture still draped in voluminous dust sheets. The room seemed so much smaller than he remembered it. The floor was covered with a layer of dust, soot and dead flies. Was no one tending to the place any more? Or had they stopped bothering after so many years? Perhaps they'd expected some message to warn them of an impending visit before they went to the trouble of cleaning. The only sign anyone had been there recently was a scattering of fresh footprints on the dirty floor.

Had Caroline come here, as he'd bidden her, only to flee from the place in disgust? He wasn't certain he could blame her if she had.

Unpleasant smells issued from the direction of kitchen, but the faint sound of movement overhead drew Bennett to the stairs, which he mounted quietly. Following the sound, he peered into the bedchamber that his mother had occupied on their long-ago holidays here. The sight that met his eyes quite confounded him.

There was Caroline, down on her hands and knees, scrubbing the floor with violent energy. Though she was turned away from him, he recognised her golden curls and her gown. It was one of the simplest she owned, yet it still looked far more elaborate than any housemaid would wear to undertake such a task.

His elegant countess stooping to common housework? If he had not seen it with his own eyes, Bennett never would have believed it possible.

As he watched Caroline dip her brush into a bucket of steaming water, then drag it back and forth across the floorboards, his gaze was irresistibly drawn to her shapely bottom. Raised towards him and covered only with flimsy layers of linen and muslin, it swayed with a most enticing rhythm as she worked. He could picture it bare, those smooth, firm lobes fairly begging for the attention of his hands. His body responded to the imagined invitation with straining hunger.

He ached to toss his wife upon the cold, musty-smelling bed and purge all the conflicting feelings she provoked in him.

Against his will, a growl of sultry yearning rumbled deep in his chest.

The sound made Caroline glance back over her shoulder. Catching sight of him, she shrieked as if she'd seen a ghost. Trying to rise while keeping as far away from him as possible, she scuttled like a crab, knocking over the scrub bucket. When she sprang up to avoid the gush of water, she struck her head on the steeply sloped gable ceiling.

'Look what you made me do!' She rubbed her head as a stream of soapy water poured over the floor. 'Why did you sneak up on me like that?'

Her furious glare and accusing tone quenched his sympathy for her difficulties.

Bennett's temper flared, fuelled by the volatile desire she'd ignited in him. 'What did *you* mean by sneaking away from London with my son? I never gave you leave to take him!'

'You never forbade me either!' She stooped to tip the bucket upright, too late to do any good. 'This was the only way I could get a final chance to spend time with my child.'

'I *would* have forbidden it,' he snapped, 'if you'd had the civility to inform me of your intentions. Instead I was left to discover you'd made away with him without my knowledge or consent. For all I knew, you'd run off abroad with him and your…paramour.'

Her blue-green eyes blazed with the fury of a storm on the Mediterranean. 'If you mean Mr Astley, he is *not* my paramour. Even if he were, how could you think I would ever steal Wyn away? It is you who are determined to deprive our son of a parent, with your threat of divorce.'

If she had snatched up her scrub brush and hurled it at his head, it could not have hit Bennett as hard as that accusation she seemed to pluck from the depths of his conscience. Never in seven years of marriage had they quarreled with such open animosity. Their preferred weapons had been frosty silences broken by the occasional waspish barb. Much as this raw hostility horrified his deep-rooted sense of self-control, another part of him relished the opportunity to vent some of the resentment that had long smouldered inside him.

'How could I think you capable of absconding with my son?' He hurled Caroline's question back at her, heavy with sarcasm. 'Perhaps because you have recently demonstrated the depths of impropriety to which you are capable of sinking. With Astley of all men—the choice does not speak well for your discernment.'

'Why do you refuse to believe there was nothing worse going on between me and Mr Astley than what you saw with your own eyes at Almack's?' she demanded. 'Is it because you don't want to? Perhaps you have been waiting for a chance like this all along—a pretext to be rid of me now that I have served my purpose by bearing you an heir.'

Did she truly believe he was seeking an *excuse* to divorce her? Or was she only trying to deflect attention from her infamous conduct by casting aspersions on his motives? Beneath the passionate hostility that crackled between them, Bennett sensed the other kind of passion. In a plain gown, with her hair tousled by her exertions and a dewy glow in her cheeks, Caroline looked less like the pampered diamond of society and more like an earthy, sensual woman who appealed to him in far too many ways. Did she suspect what power she might hold over him if he let down his guard?

He must take care she did not.

Refusing to dignify her preposterous accusation with an answer, he changed the subject instead. 'Speaking of my heir, where is Wyn? And what were you doing down on your knees, scrubbing the floor? I didn't think you knew how.'

'It is not Greek or higher mathematics. I've watched servants scrub floors all my life.' Caroline pushed a fallen lock of hair off her forehead. 'Wyn is with Albert, back at the inn. I was trying to get this room fit for us to sleep in tonight. It hasn't been easy, considering the place has not been cleaned in years. Now it's a worse mess than ever.'

Gazing down at the drenched floor, she shook her head and heaved a weary sigh. She looked so thoroughly discouraged Bennett could not suppress a secret pang of shame. 'I had no idea you would find the house in such a state. I thought there was still someone taking care of it.'

Caroline cast him a look that made it clear she did not believe his excuse any more than he believed she'd been a faithful wife. Did she think he had sent her to such a dirty, deserted old place on purpose? Not that it would harm her to do a bit of honest work and learn how ordinary folk lived. Still, after seven years of marriage, she should know he took his responsibility to provide for her seriously—even when she neglected her duty to be faithful.

'But why were *you* scrubbing the floor,' he persisted, 'while Albert plays nursemaid?'

'Because Albert is in no fit condition to do anything else at the moment.' Caroline told him how the footman had injured his ankle. 'Parker flatly refused to scrub floors and I didn't dare press her for fear she might leave on the next boat. She agreed to do the marketing and cooking, both of which take more skill than this.'

By the smells rising from the kitchen, Bennett had grave doubts about Parker's culinary abilities. 'Why did you not stay a few more days at the inn and engage some local women to set this place to rights?'

Caroline reached around to rub the small of her back. 'Most of the money I brought with me was spent on our journey. Since I didn't know when I might get more, I was obliged to be careful with what I had left. Keeping four people at an inn with meals can add up quickly, you know.'

Under other circumstances, it might have been amusing to hear his wife preach economy. Those inn charges of which she complained would not have equalled the cost of a single gown or an elaborate fan she'd have purchased on a whim last week.

Still, Bennett's conscience troubled him for ordering Caroline so far away without making certain she had sufficient funds to supply her needs. 'I am here now and I have brought plenty of money. You can stay at the inn until this place is fit to occupy. Before I leave, I will hire some local folk to serve you.'

If he provided his wife with plenty of servants to cater to her needs, perhaps he might feel less guilty for leaving her here—even if this was by far the best place for her, under the circumstances.

'How soon do you intend to leave?' Caroline's question carried an unspoken plea.

Bennett steeled himself to resist it. 'Tomorrow. The boat I chartered from Penzance is anchored in the cove. I must get back to Parliament.'

He'd had great hopes for Lord Liverpool after the earl spoke in favour of Abolition at the Congress of Vienna. But lately Liverpool's ministry seemed more inclined to deprive ordinary citizens of their freedoms than to free the enslaved.

'I suppose you will be very busy with your work when you return to London?'

'Of course.' What in blazes did Caroline care about his work?

'Then why not let Wyn stay here with me? You will have no time to spend with him, while I will have nothing else to do with mine. Besides, we just arrived last night after a long journey. It cannot be good for the child to make another again so soon.'

She expected him to *reward* her for going behind his back to spirit his son away? Next the woman would demand a medal for her adulterous affairs! 'Perhaps you should have thought of that when you dragged the boy away from his nursery under false pretences.'

'I didn't think you would come so soon to fetch him back.' Caroline's winsome pleading gave way to indignant anger. 'Why can you not give me a little more time with him if you are determined to part us for ever? Is it because you care more about punishing me and exercising ownership over your heir than you do about a small child's feelings?'

The charge infuriated Bennett. She made him sound like the most heartless slave master. 'When did you begin to care about the boy's feelings or anything else to do with him? I'm certain if this island had a pleasure garden or assembly hall to keep you amused, you'd be only too happy to be rid of him. I will not let you use my son for your plaything, then cast him aside when you grow bored. Motherhood is not a game!'

Carolyn reeled as if he'd boxed her ears. However vigorously she might deny the charge, it was clear his accusation had struck a nerve.

She wasted no time striking back. 'How dare you question the sincerity of my feelings for Wyn? I have never seen you show him the least sign of affection.'

'I care for my son!' Bennett raised his voice to drown out the traitorous whisper of doubt in his thoughts. He knew he loved his son, but did Wyn know it? 'All his life I have watched over him and made certain he had everything he needed to be safe and well and content. I dropped everything and travelled all this way to fetch him home. Actions like those speak far louder than your lavish, hollow gestures.'

Caroline flinched. 'If I have been more effusive in showing my affections towards him, it was not for my own amusement, but to make up for your coldness. I know I have not been as constant and attentive a mother as I should. That is why I brought Wyn with me—so I might have an opportunity to make it up to him. Please, let me keep him here a while longer.'

'Why should I? So you can make him so deeply attached to you that he will be devastated by our divorce?' Striving to keep the sparks of hostility between them from blazing into something far more dangerous, Bennett encased himself in a crust of frosty disdain that had served him well in the past.

But even that stout armour was not impervious to Caroline's next strike. 'Devastated? Was that how you felt when your father divorced your mother?'

How much did she know about his family? Bennett struggled to regain control of his vocal organs. Not all the sordid details, obviously. But her guess about his feelings was far too close to the truth for his liking.

'Who told you about my parents' marriage?' He forced out the words in a headlong rush.

'What does it matter?' Caroline countered. 'Don't you think I should have heard it from you long before this?'

Talk to her about such an intimate and painful subject? He'd never even considered it, least of all after their marriage had begun to go as disastrously wrong as his parents'. 'What would have been the point of telling you? It was ancient history and not any business of yours.'

'I think it is very much my business when you intend to tear Wyn away from me just as you were torn away from your mother when your father divorced her.'

Her words dealt a sharp blow to an old wound that had never healed properly. 'I was *not* torn away from my mother! She abandoned me for her paramour, in spite of all her protestations of maternal devotion. So you must excuse me for looking upon yours with a jaundiced eye.'

His revelation clearly struck a blow to Caroline's hopes. She reeled, as if buffeted by a violent gust of wind that stole her breath away.

Had it been a mistake not to tell her what his mother had done? If nothing else, his shameful family history might have provided a cautionary tale about the consequences of a woman breaking her marriage vows.

Bennett had not intended to utter another word on the subject of his past. But now that the stopper had been pulled from the jug, he found it hard to contain what came pouring out.

Bennett's mother had deserted her son to run off with another man? A confused cascade of thoughts rushed through Caroline's mind. Almost as many and conflicting as the emotions that scoured her heart. She found herself torn between sympathy for what her husband must have suffered as a child and indignation that he believed her guilty of repeating his mother's mistakes.

How could a woman abandon her child and bring such shame upon him? Unhappy as her marriage had been in recent years, she'd never seriously considered taking a lover, let alone running away with one. There was only one man she'd ever loved, one man with whom she'd been happy, however briefly. She had lost his affection, if indeed she'd ever inspired more than physical desire.

Bennett's sudden arrival had thrown her into confusion. When she'd glanced back to find him standing in the doorway, Caroline felt as if she were seeing someone she barely recognised. He had grown into his height since the days when he'd visited her girlhood home to confer with her father. Where he'd once been lanky and a bit awkward, he was now broad-shouldered and imposing. There was a becoming maturity about his crisp patrician features as well. The full black brows that had given his younger face an almost comical severity now suited him all too well.

The dark eyes beneath those brows had not changed, though. They still radiated fierce intelligence that shielded their enigmatic depths. In all their years together, Caroline had never succeeded in divining her husband's feelings by gazing into those well-guarded eyes.

Today, however, she was not obliged to guess. For once, Bennett was more than willing to speak his mind. 'For your information, my father did *not* divorce my mother. No doubt she'd hoped he would, so she could salvage some shred of her reputation by marrying the scoundrel she'd run off with.

Father refused. He believed she deserved to suffer the full consequences of her folly. You do not seem to appreciate the service I would do you by seeking a divorce.'

'You expect me to be *grateful* to you for ruining my life over one foolish mistake?' Caroline's pity for the young Bennett was seared away by a blast of rage at the man he'd become. 'Tell me, have you never made a mistake that you would give anything to undo? But of course you have. Marrying me was your great mistake, wasn't it? One you've regretted and wanted to undo for years. Now I have given you your chance.'

Five years of pent-up longing and frustration demanded release. Wrenching the wedding ring off her finger, she flung it at him with all her might. 'Go ahead, then! Divorce me, steal my son, drive me out of society! It cannot be any worse than being married to a man like you!'

Part of her relished the look of horror that gripped his dark, handsome features. It gave her an unaccustomed sense of power to make him feel *something.* Yet all the anger, hurt and guilt their quarrel had stirred up raged within her, demanding another outlet. If she stayed there a moment longer she feared she would break down in tears. She could not bear to betray that kind of weakness in front of Bennett.

Taking advantage of his momentary daze, she dodged past him and fled the room. But when she reached the hallway, Caroline found herself confronted by a sight that stunned and horrified *her.*

Her son's small face peeped up just above the head of the stairs. His eyes were open so wide, they looked twice their normal size, while his mouth had fallen slack. He looked as if he'd seen a ghost or witnessed some other terrifying sight.

How much of their vicious row had the poor child over-heard?

'Wyn…' She wanted to assure him it was all right, but that obvious falsehood stuck in her throat.

Before she could think of anything better to say, the child spun around and disappeared from view.

'Wyn!' she cried, running after him. 'Come back, dearest! You needn't be frightened!'

Her words brought Bennett thundering down the stairs after her. 'I thought you said he was back at the inn with Albert.'

His words seethed with accusation. Did he think she'd lied about that, risking Wyn overhearing them? Was there any conduct so vile he would not believe her capable of it?

'He was at the inn!' she insisted. 'Albert must have brought him back here. I don't know why.'

From the parlour, the hinges of the front door shrieked as it was wrenched open. Caroline and Bennett raced toward it, jostling one another in their haste. When they reached the en-trance, the door hung open, swinging back and forth as the wind blew in gusts of hard, cold rain.

When had this storm started? She'd been too deeply im-mersed in her quarrel with Bennett to notice. Could this be why Albert had brought Wyn from the inn—to get here ahead of the rain?

How her son had come to be there did not matter, now. Caroline and Bennett ran outside, peering frantically around for some sign of the child, calling his name at the top of their lungs to carry over the gathering fury of the storm.

The rain lashed down in sheets out of a dark, angry sky. It soaked Caroline to the skin before she had taken half-a-dozen steps. Though it chilled her to the bone, it was nothing compared to the icy fear that clutched her heart at the thought of her son wandering out in this deluge.

'Wyn! Come back, dearest! Come to Mama!' Where could he have gone? Surely he could not have got far in such a short time. Had he ducked behind the house perhaps, seeking shelter from the wind and rain?

She groped her way around the house, continuing to call out for the child as she went. But the howling wind seemed to catch her voice and steal it away. Would Wyn be able to hear her? And if he did, would he be willing to come to her after the scene he'd witnessed between her and his father? Caroline struggled to subdue her alarm, but it seemed to feed on the power of the storm and grow stronger.

As she rounded the corner to the back of the house, she saw Bennett moving towards her from the opposite direction.

'Get back inside!' he bellowed. 'I'll look for Wyn!'

'No!' Caroline pushed a hank of sodden hair off her face. She was not going to be Bennett's wife for much longer, so what was the use of obeying his wishes now? 'I *have* to look for him! Don't you understand? It's my fault he's out here! If any harm comes to him...'

Fearing Bennett might try to stop her, she turned and ran blindly. To her relief, he did not follow. He must realise it was no use wasting time they desperately needed to search for their son.

'Where are you, Wyn?' she cried, though the question was more to herself than to him.

Calling his name again and again, she staggered forwards. Her dress and shoes were so thoroughly soaked they weighed her down almost as much as her guilt. She was the one who had taken Wyn from his safe, familiar nursery and brought him to this stormy island with its turmoil and danger.

If any harm befell her son, it would be a judgement upon her for putting her needs ahead of his well-being. Perhaps that was what Bennett had meant when he'd accused her of not knowing what love was. All these years, she had thought of love in terms of endearments and gestures of affection, when in truth it might be something simpler and far more substantial.

Would she ever get the opportunity to learn to love her son that way?

'If any harm comes to him…' As Caroline ran off into the rain, her last unfinished sentence echoed ominously in Bennett's mind.

It conjured up terrifying visions of the dangers their son might encounter if he strayed any distance from the house. The sea-swept cliffs. The ancient tin pits that pocked the hills above Dolphin Town. The restless, hungry ocean that gnawed at the edges of the island. By force of will, Bennett wrenched himself back from the perilous downward spiral of such thoughts.

Caroline's barely contained panic was contagious. One glance at her and his heart had raced even faster, his stomach lurched and he had trouble catching his breath. He knew he could not allow such potent emotions to overcome him. His son's life might depend upon him keeping a cool head.

Since Caroline had struck out towards the interior of the island, he would search along the coast, where the greatest danger lay.

'Wyn!' he bellowed as his gaze ranged desperately. 'Where are you? Come to me, son!'

Yet while he walked and called out and scanned the area, he could not banish his last glimpse of Caroline from his mind. Her porcelain skin had the bluish pallor of whey. Her eyes had been opened too wide and moved restlessly. Not even the legendary Mrs Siddons could have put on such a convincing performance of distress. Much as Bennett longed to doubt her, he could not. She'd looked so vulnerable, so worried, so guilt-ridden, it stirred a sense of protectiveness he had not felt towards her in a very long time. He struggled to subdue it, but the two of them were bound tightly together by something far more important than their many differences.

He could no longer deny that Caroline loved their son. She might not have been the most attentive mother, but perhaps he had not been the most affectionate father. Faced with the dark dread of losing his child for ever, Bennett began to understand the desperation that had driven her to keep Wyn with her at all costs.

As more and more time passed with no sign of his son, Bennett found it harder to contain his mounting anxiety. Wyn was the only person in a very long time he'd permitted himself to love. There were others he might respect or admire, but none for whom he felt this consuming mixture of pride, protectiveness, fondness.

If Caroline was right, he had not done nearly enough to show the child how he felt. It grieved Bennett that Wyn might regard him in the way he had his own cold, distant father. Worse yet, what if he never got the chance to let his son know how much he cared?

That dread brought back wrenching memories of his mother's

abrupt disappearance and the grim silence that had met his anxious inquiries. After years spent protecting his heart from ever suffering that kind of ordeal again, he'd been powerless to keep from loving his son.

Now he feared he might experience that same torment again. Only this time it would be real. And it would never end.

'Bennett!' Caroline's voice, faint and hoarse, called him back from the edge of the bottomless abyss into which he'd been staring.

His gaze flew towards the sound of it and he saw her standing near the house clutching Wyn.

In a daze of joy and relief more profound than any he'd ever experienced, Bennett ran towards them and caught up with Caroline as she reached the kitchen door.

She looked like a half-drowned angel with her golden hair hanging drenched around her shoulders and her eyes sparkling with unshed tears. Yet, never in all the years he'd known her had she looked so beautiful. Not swathed in the finest silk and decked with sapphires, nor gloriously naked in the throes of newlywed desire. For now she held their son in her arms, safe from dangers Bennett could not bear to contemplate.

He longed to wrap his arms around them both and clutch them tight to his heart. But if he did, he feared he might lose control of his tightly bound emotions. Instead he channelled his overwhelming relief and concern into practical action.

Throwing open the door, he ushered Caroline into the kitchen. The disagreeable smells he'd noticed upon first entering the house overwhelmed him, but he had more important things to worry about.

'We need to get you both into dry clothes. Are there any

here?' He addressed the question to Parker, who swooped toward her mistress the moment they entered.

In answer to his abrupt question, Caroline's maid bobbed a nod. 'That fellow with the cart fetched them from the inn when he brought Albert and the young master.'

'Good. Then attend your mistress while I see to my son.' Turning to Caroline, Bennett opened his arms. 'I can take Wyn now.'

But the child tightened his hold around Caroline's neck and hid his face against her shoulder. 'Papa will be angry with me for running away, like he was with you, Mama!'

Wyn began to shiver. Was it from the cold, Bennett wondered with a pang, or was the child trembling with fear?

'No, son.' He tried to pitch his voice in a way that would reassure the child, but he was not certain he'd succeeded. 'I'm not angry. I was worried about you, that's all.'

'We both were very worried, dearest.' Caroline nuzzled the crown of Wyn's head with her cheek. 'But it's all right, now. Go to your papa. He'll take good care of you.'

Did she mean that? After the insults and accusations they had hurled at one another such a short time ago, Bennett had his doubts. Yet when he scrutinised her tone for any barb of derision, he detected none.

'Your mama is right, Wyn. You need not be afraid of me.'

Their efforts to transfer the child from Caroline's arms to his brought them into unsettlingly close contact. The back of his hand rubbed over the bosom of her sodden dress. The soft flesh beneath yielded to his touch. His leg brushed against hers. Her lips issued a silent but insistent call to his. It took little to rouse his gnawing hunger.

Was that what Caroline wanted—to make him captive to

his desires and slave to her whims? The mistrust Bennett had put aside came roaring back. Now that his wife had got a bitter foretaste of the life that awaited her outside the gilded bubble of their marriage, he would not put it past her to employ any means necessary to regain her position of privilege.

That included seducing the husband she despised.

Chapter Four

How long would it be until Bennett got over his relief at finding Wyn and recalled that their son would never have been in danger if not for her?

That thought plagued Caroline as her husband took charge to make her and Wyn as comfortable as possible after their ordeal. His reaction to the child's sudden flight into the storm had proven that he cared more for Wyn than she'd ever suspected—far more than he had been able to show.

She knew that should make her happy for Wyn's sake. She wanted her son to have a father who loved him, even if he had trouble expressing it. But the more Bennett cared about their son, the less likely he would be to consider letting the child stay with her on Tresco. Especially now that he knew how dangerous it could be.

'We'll get you dried out yet.' Bennett tucked a blanket around her and Wyn as they huddled together on the sofa, which he had pulled up closer to the parlour hearth. 'It looks as though we may be obliged to spend the night here since the storm shows no sign of easing up.'

Vexed as she was with Bennett for the hurt he'd caused her

in the past and the worse harm he intended to inflict, Caroline appreciated his calm resourcefulness in a crisis.

'What about you?' She wrapped her arms around their son and pulled him closer. The child had not stopped shivering in spite of dry clothes, a blanket and the warmth of the fire. 'You look half-drowned.'

And yet it did not make him a whit less attractive... unfortunately. His close-cropped dark hair was only a little damp now and he had removed his sodden coat and waistcoat. But the driving rain had penetrated all the way to his shirt, which clung to his broad shoulders and well-proportioned chest in a way that made Caroline feel altogether too warm. It also made her self-conscious of what a fright she must look with her hair hanging lank and damp.

'Half-drowned?' Bennett glanced down at his clothes. 'More than half, I should think. Perhaps I can borrow some dry clothes from Albert, for mine are still on the ship.'

Parker bustled in then with cups of hot tea for them all.

When Caroline took a sip of hers, her stomach squealed, as if demanding something more substantial.

She cringed with embarrassment until Wyn gave a little chuckle—a sound so sweet it made her laugh along with him. 'Are you hungry, Mama?'

'I believe I am. All that housework must have given me an appetite.'

'Dare I ask what you've prepared for supper, Parker?' Bennett cast a dubious glance in the direction of the kitchen.

'A mess, I'm afraid, my lord.' The maid cowered. 'At least that's what Albert says, the useless lump. I tried to make a fish stew, but I'm a lady's maid, not a cook. It got all thick like paste and it burnt to the bottom of the pot and...'

Parker gulped and sniffled.

'Never mind that.' Though Bennett's gruff tone expressed horror at the prospect of female tears, it also carried a note of reluctant sympathy. 'Is there any other food you didn't cook?'

'Some of the potatoes, sir. And eggs and a flitch of bacon for breakfast. Why?'

Bennett squared his shoulders. 'I mean to prepare a supper that might conceivably be edible.'

'You can cook?' Caroline would have been less surprised if he'd declared his intention to walk back to Cornwall on the water. How many other things about her husband had she never suspected because he'd never let her close enough to find out? 'When did you learn how?'

Bennett shrugged, as if to say it was not such a remarkable accomplishment. 'I hung about the kitchen on my school holidays. I've always thought it a great disadvantage for a man not to be able to get himself a bite to eat in a pinch.'

Now she understood. He had learned to cook so he would not be altogether dependent on others for nourishment.

Without another word, Bennett strode from the parlour. Soon the hearty aroma of frying bacon wafted from the kitchen, overpowering the sickening stench of Parker's burnt fish stew.

Caroline cradled Wyn in her arms and tried to still his shivering. Deep in her heart, she quailed, too. During those terrible moments when she'd feared for Wyn's safety, she began to understand how her husband must have felt when he'd returned to Sterling House to find their son gone. Soon Bennett would remember, too. No doubt he would also realise it was her fault Wyn had run away. If he had been determined to take their son back to London before, there would now be no hope whatsoever of him permitting Wyn to stay with her.

A while later, the five of them sat around the table, masters and servants equally ill at ease dining together. Only Wyn seemed unperturbed by the situation.

'Don't forget grace,' he reminded the adults, bowing his head and folding his small hands.

Glancing down at her son, Caroline smiled with a mixture of amusement and doting pride. It gave her features a winsome glow that caught Bennett off guard.

'Will you say it, Papa?' the boy asked.

'Er...of course.' Bennett muttered something vague about giving thanks for the food before them. 'Now, tuck in.'

Caroline took a reluctant bite, perhaps wondering what harm this fry-up of bacon, eggs and potatoes would do to her delicate digestion. Her wary look soon melted into one of wholehearted pleasure. She cleaned her plate as if she were starving.

'That may be the most delicious meal I have ever eaten,' she declared when she had finished. 'Thank you.'

Her eyes had glowed with sincere appreciation.

So his wife was capable of showing gratitude, after all. The revelation came as an awkward surprise to Bennett.

'I'm...pleased my efforts met with your approval.' His reply came out stiff and self-conscious. Uncomfortable being the centre of attention, he turned his upon their son. 'I fear Wyn does not share your enthusiasm for my cookery.'

Caroline glanced at the plate Wyn had scarcely touched. 'You should try to eat, dearest. It tastes very good and hot food will help warm you up.'

Albert chimed in, 'Try breaking open your eggs and dipping the tatties in the yolk. They taste even better that way.'

Wyn pushed a chip of fried potato around his plate. 'I'm not hungry.'

Bennett was tempted to insist their son finish his supper, but Caroline forestalled him, indulgent as always. 'You're probably too tired to eat, poor darling. We must get you to bed.'

Unaccustomed though he was to agree with his wife about anything, Bennett had to admit it was not a bad idea. The sooner Wyn got a good night's sleep, the sooner he could begin to put the day's distressing events behind him.

Together they took the child upstairs, helped him change into his nightclothes and tucked him into bed.

'What's that smell?' Wyn wrinkled his nose.

'Cedar shavings, dearest.' Caroline pressed a kiss to the child's forehead. 'All the linens were packed up with them to keep moths away. I hung the sheets out to air this morning, but I think they need more.'

Bennett could not have imagined his wife hanging out bedding if he hadn't seen her on her knees scrubbing the floor. She might not have managed *well* under such conditions, but at least she'd made an effort. That earned her something he did not give easily—a measure of his respect.

'Now, son,' said Bennett, 'there is something very important I must ask you to promise me.'

'Yes, Papa?' Wyn lowered his gaze and clung to his mother's hand.

'I told you I am not angry with you.' Bennett strove to moderate his tone so he would not intimidate the child, while still impressing upon him the seriousness of the situation. 'I must have your word that you will never run away like that again.'

'Your papa is right, dearest,' Caroline added her support, somewhat to Bennett's surprise. 'We were very worried about you. You could easily have come to much worse harm out there today.'

Wyn gave a contrite nod. 'I promise. The rain was cold and I was afraid the wind would blow me into the sea.'

'Why did you go?' The question seemed to slip out before Caroline could prevent it.

'I heard you and Papa shouting at each other. You said something about me and I thought it must be my fault you were quarrelling.'

'No!' Bennett and Caroline cried in unison.

Bennett cast his wife a look that urged her to reassure the child. Though he had been acclaimed as one of the finest orators in the House of Lords, he was not certain he could explain such a volatile, complicated situation to a young child. He hoped Caroline would be able to find the right words, which eluded him.

Inhaling a deep breath, she smoothed back a tumbled, brown curl from Wyn's forehead. 'Your papa and I were not quarreling *because* of you, dearest. In fact, the one thing we completely agree upon is what a fine boy you are and how much we both love you. Isn't that true, my lord?'

'Quite true,' Bennett replied after a brief hesitation. It made him vastly uneasy, being forced to admit his feelings. But he must prove to her that he was capable of it. 'We both…care for you more than anything.'

Wyn's small brow furrowed. 'Then why were you shouting at each other in that angry way?'

'Well…' Caroline struggled to put the complex state of their marriage into simple words. 'Our love for you is one important thing we share. But apart from that, we are quite different in many ways. We like different things…want different things. Sometimes those differences make us get angry with one another.'

Did Wyn understand what she was trying to say? No doubt the boy was clever enough to recognise some of the more obvious differences between his parents.

But he still did not seem entirely satisfied with her explanation. 'I never heard you shout at each other before.'

'That is…true.' Though her words were for the child's benefit, Bennett found himself curious to hear what Caroline would say. 'But often when people are very angry, perhaps because their feelings have been hurt, they don't talk to each other at all. They may think it will only make things worse. Or they may be too proud to admit anything is wrong. Or they may be afraid their feelings will get out of control. But if they never talk, nothing ever gets settled because one may not know the other *is* angry. Or they may not understand why.'

Where was all that coming from? Bennett wondered. He had never thought about their marriage in that way before. And yet, more than a little of what his wife said rang true. He had never really tried talking to her about the widening gulf between them because he'd been certain it would do no good… and because he had not wanted to provoke a row like the one they'd had this afternoon. Yet now that it was over, he had to admit the festering bitterness within him had eased.

Wyn pondered his mother's explanation and seemed to grasp enough of it to be persuaded he was not the cause of their hostility. With that worry relieved, the child relaxed and yielded to his exhaustion.

He gave a wide yawn, then asked in a drowsy murmur, 'Wouldn't it be better if you *did* talk but without shouting?'

The words had scarcely left his mouth before his eyelids drooped and closed.

Caroline caressed the child's cheek. 'I suppose it would.' She did not seem fully aware that she was speaking aloud. 'But I'm afraid it isn't always so easy.'

That was certainly true, Bennett acknowledged privately. There was so much about himself and his past that he'd never told her. He'd convinced himself she would not be interested. Yet some of the comments she'd made today suggested otherwise. Not only had she wanted to know him better, she seemed to resent his secrecy about his past. Could that be why she had turned to other men without a qualm—because they were no more strangers to her than her own husband?

It no longer mattered *why* she'd been unfaithful, reason insisted, even if his behaviour had contributed to it. After that scandalous scene at Almack's, Caroline had given him no choice but to divorce her.

Wouldn't it be better if they talked without shouting? Her young son's innocent but wise advice echoed in Caroline's mind as she and Bennett worked to prepare the other two bedrooms to be occupied that night. As they went about their tasks in pensive, guarded silence, the storm continued to rage outside. Were they both afraid to open their mouths in case they unleashed another angry tempest that had been brewing inside them for years?

A familiar flicker of resentment had flared within her when Bennett had made her explain to their son why they'd been arguing so heatedly. She'd been about to shoot him a hostile glare when she sensed an air about him unlike any she'd noticed before. It was as if the stout shield behind which he usually hid had slipped for a moment, allowing her to glimpse the kind of feelings he usually took care to hide. Those emotions—guilt, regret and a certain helplessness—were an almost perfect mirror of their son's.

It made her wonder if Bennett hadn't intended to foist that difficult task upon her as punishment. What if, for the first time in their marriage, he'd been seeking her help, trusting that she would be able to find the right words to reach their son?

If that were true, then Bennett had more confidence in her abilities than she. To her astonishment, that confidence had not been misplaced. The words that poured out of her seemed to come from some other source, yet intuition assured her they were true. Both she and Bennett had their faults, but neither was nearly as bad as the other had come to believe.

Those thoughts ran through Caroline's mind as she swept her bedroom floor, when suddenly Bennett appeared. 'Could I trouble you for some help making my bed? I'm having a devil of a time squeezing in the side against the wall.'

'Of course.' She strove to ignore the treacherous skip her heart gave when he spoke to her.

They spread and tucked the bottom sheet in silence.

Then, as they draped the top sheet, Bennett spoke. 'I wanted to…thank you for finding Wyn this afternoon. I was very anxious about him.'

He refused to meet her gaze, keeping his stubbornly fixed on the task at hand.

'I had to find him,' she muttered fiercely. 'It was my fault he was lost out there in that cold, driving rain. Shrieking like a mad woman—no wonder the poor child was frightened out of his wits.'

'That hardly makes it *all* your fault,' Bennett protested gruffly. 'It takes two to quarrel and I may have said some things that were better left unsaid.'

Until a few minutes ago, Bennett had been quick to think the worst of her and blame her for things she'd never done. Now, when she'd freely admitted her responsibility for something so serious, he refused to condemn her as she'd expected and deserved. Did he not realise their argument was only part of her wrongdoing?

'I'm not sure those things *were* better left unsaid,' Caroline mused. 'We were open and truthful with one another about how we feel. Perhaps if we'd done that sooner...'

As they unfolded a blanket, his hand brushed against hers. The brief contact sent a jolt of disturbing energy crackling between them.

Caroline's fingers still tingled from it hours later as she tossed and turned, unable to sleep.

Partly it was the storm that kept her awake. Rain pounded against the windows like the fists of an angry giant, determined to shatter the thick panes of glass. The wind sounded like the creature's shrieks and howls of frustration at being denied entrance. Any minute she feared it might rip the roof off!

Yet the storm did not alarm her as much as the prospect of Bennett sailing off with their son tomorrow, leaving her on this remote island with nothing but her regrets to keep her company...

The final thing that plagued her was the vexing awareness of Bennett sleeping so nearby. Though his bedchamber at Sterling House was only a few doors down from hers, it had seemed like a vast distance. Here, he felt so much closer. During the past several hours, they had talked more than in the whole previous month at least.

'Greggy? Greggy!' Wyn's terrified cries pierced the storm's tumult.

Caroline sprang from her bed. A shiver quaked through her when her bare feet made contact with the cold floor. The night air chilled her to the bone. She longed to burrow back under the bedclothes, but she could not resist the urgent summons of her son's cries, even if her name was not the one that sprang to his lips.

Wrenching open her door, she stumbled out into the pitch-dark hallway and directly into her husband. The unexpected contact made her gasp and jump back. Even through their nightclothes, his flesh felt so hot she wondered if it would sear her skin where they touched. She had a desperate urge to plaster herself against him, simply to soak up his warmth.

Wyn called out again. 'Mama? Papa?'

Their son's cry propelled them down the hall, jostling against one another in the darkness. Caroline reached for the latch of Wyn's door, only to feel Bennett's large, powerful hand close over hers. Immediately he wrenched it back again. When the narrow door swung open, they both rushed forwards, mashing their bodies together as they squeezed into the room.

Her husband's nearness waged an assault on Caroline's senses. The swift rasp of his breath seemed to drown out every other sound. His hot, vital scent invaded her nostrils, plunging deep into her lungs. The unyielding pressure of his lean-muscled frame against her made the blood race through her veins.

'What's wrong, son? Did you fall out of bed and hurt yourself?' Bennett's question made Caroline feel sick with shame for letting those sensations distract her from her child.

Groping towards the bed, she sank on to it and reached for Wyn.

'I dreamt a giant was chasing me!' Her son nestled into her embrace. 'When I woke up I could still hear it roaring.'

'That was only a dream,' said Bennett. 'And nothing that happens in dreams can hurt you.'

'They can frighten you, though.' Caroline ran her hand over Wyn's hair. Much as she relished this opportunity to cuddle and comfort him, a stab of guilt pierced her to think how often he might have taken refuge in his nurse's arms while she was off at one of her social engagements. 'I thought the storm sounded like a giant, too.'

'You did?' Wyn sniffled. 'Were you frightened?'

'A little,' she admitted. 'Would you like me to lie down with you until you get back to sleep? Perhaps I could tell you a story to take our minds off the storm.'

Wyn's soft cheek and silky hair brushed against her upper arm as he nodded. 'Yes, please, Mama.'

Caroline was only too glad to slip under the covers.

She almost forgot Bennett was still in the room until he spoke. 'If you're not hurt, then, Wyn, I will return to my bed. Goodnight.'

A fierce gust of wind rattled the window sashes.

The child gave a terrified yelp and clung to Caroline. 'Please, Papa, can you lie down with us too?'

'It is only the wind,' Bennett tried to reassure the child.

'It sounds louder because this house is so much smaller than you're used to.'

Caroline sensed his reluctance to get in bed with her, even with their son between them. Though she did not relish the prospect any more than he, she wished he would make an effort to understand how storms and nightmares might frighten a small child, even if they posed no real danger. Had he never been afraid of anything when he was a little boy? It was difficult to imagine her husband as anything but the strong, self-reliant man she'd always known.

'Please?' Wyn repeated. 'Mama and I won't feel so frightened if you're with us, will we, Mama?'

Though she had good reason to fear Bennett's wrath, Caroline forced herself to say, 'No, indeed. Even a storm giant would be very foolish to take on your papa. Here, I'll move to the other side of the bed to make room for him.'

Bennett gave in to their combined entreaties. 'Just for a little while. There truly is nothing to fear. This house has withstood the pounding of storms for many years.'

As he slid on to the bed, Caroline moved as close to the edge on her side as she dared to avoid having her bare leg brush against his.

'Is that better, dearest?' she asked Wyn.

'Yes, Mama.' The child snuggled against her. 'Why do they call these islands *silly?* I haven't seen anything comical here at all.'

Was that the sort of place to which he thought she'd been bringing him? Caroline wondered. An island of harlequins, performing monkeys and endless Punch-and-Judy shows? Storm-swept Tresco must have come as a great disappointment.

Before she could answer her son's question, Bennett's voice rose out of the darkness, just loud enough to carry over the furor of the storm. 'Scilly is the name of the islands, but it does not mean comical. The word may come from the old Cornish tongue or a lost language even more ancient. There are those who believe these islands are all that is left of the drowned kingdom of Lyonesse.'

'How can a whole kingdom drown?' asked Wyn.

'By a great flood, I suppose.' No sooner had Bennett spoken than another powerful gust rattled the house.

'Like the one in Noah's Ark?' Wyn's voice squeaked with terror. 'Greggy told me that story. Do you think this storm will make a great flood and wash us away?'

Recalling how tiny these islands were, out in the vast Atlantic, Caroline wondered the same thing.

'Not a bit of it.' Bennett's voice rang with steadfast certainty that banished her fear. Then it softened in a way she'd never heard him speak before. 'You needn't fret, Wyn. I am here and I will not let any harm come to you.'

Was it the storm from which Bennett was anxious to protect their son? Caroline wondered. Or was it her?

In the past few hours, she'd begun to realise that he cared for Wyn as more than just his necessary heir. For some reason, he was unable to show those feelings except in tangible, practical ways such as cooking a meal or protecting their son from harm. Worthy and important as those things were, she still believed the child needed more from him.

Bennett had told his son there was no danger of the storm engulfing them in a great flood. Yet, as he squeezed into his old bed with Caroline and Wyn, Bennett felt as if he'd been swept out to sea.

He was not accustomed to sharing a bed. Even in the early days of their marriage, he'd been reluctant to linger with Caroline after they'd taken their pleasure. He always felt so deucedly self-conscious after having been carried away in the throes of passion. Besides, he'd sensed there was something more his bride wanted from him that he'd been unable to provide.

Her earlier accusations still echoed in his thoughts. He might not feel comfortable lavishing their son with the caresses and shallow endearments she bestowed so easily, but he could express his devotion in practical ways. Comforting his son's fears fell into an awkward middle ground where he did not particularly care to tread, but knew he must.

Who could understand better than he how Wyn must be feeling? When a tempest of scandal had engulfed his family, he'd been cast adrift into a disturbing new world. If he wanted Wyn to be able to turn to him in the difficult days ahead, Bennett knew he must begin laying the groundwork tonight.

'I've seen far worse storms than this on Tresco.' The words stuck in his throat, for he never liked to speak of his early years. Especially not the happy times he'd spent on this island with his mother. For they had been swept away as completely as lost Lyonesse, until only a few scattered, lonely peaks remained.

'You have?' Wyn asked in a doubtful tone. 'When?'

'When I was your age. I used to come here on holiday. This was once my bed.'

'Oh.' Wyn sounded as if he could scarcely believe his father had once been child like him. 'Did you come with her and your papa?'

That innocent question hurtled out of the darkness at him, an ambush he should have foreseen, but hadn't. Bennett told himself it was a perfectly natural enquiry and there was no reason why he should not be able to answer. 'Only my mother. We came every autumn for several years and this one time—'

'What was your mama like?'

Perhaps it was being back in this house again after so many years, but suddenly Bennett could recall his mother far more vividly than he'd been able to in a great while. Though part of him cherished this clearer memory, another part shrank from it.

'We'll talk about her some other time. Now I want to tell you about that storm. Besides the wind and the rain there was lightning and thunder so loud it sounded as if the heavens were cracking open.'

Bennett paused, hoping Wyn would not raise the subject of his mother again. But it seemed his story had provided an effective diversion. Or perhaps the child grasped his reluctance to talk about it.

'Were you very frightened?'

Uncertain what answer Wyn was hoping for, Bennett fell back on the truth. 'Very frightened indeed.'

His mother had held him, crooning endearments, running her hand over his hair. In the middle of violent chaos, she had made him feel secure in her love. Reluctant as Bennett was to admit it, that memory reinforced some things Caroline had said about their son's needs.

'But after a while the storm let up and a huge, brilliant rainbow appeared in the sky.' He continued to talk quietly to the child, telling him about some of the points of interest on the island. The castles that stood guard over the northwest coast. Piper's Hole, a vast underground cavern that was said to connect with one of the other islands. The smaller islands off shore that were home to great colonies of birds.

One instant Bennett had been telling Wyn about the old abbey ruins and the next he found himself waking in the rosy light of morning with one arm flung protectively over his wife and son. When he tried to shift it, the stubborn limb resisted his efforts, as if it was quite content in that position.

With her delicate features in repose, framed by soft golden curls, Caroline looked so young and vulnerable, part of him felt compelled to protect her. Experience reminded him that a woman like her would find plenty of gullible men willing to offer her *protection*. He should be more concerned with guarding his son and his reputation. In both cases, she constituted the greatest threat.

That thought gave him the spur he needed to move his obstinate arm and shift his gaze away from the tender sight of mother and son snuggled together.

Chapter Five

When she woke the next morning, Caroline basked in welcome tranquillity after the storm. Rain no longer hammered against the windows. The wind had stopped moaning in the eaves and battering the house with violent gusts. Off in the distance, she heard waves breaking upon the shore in a muted bass harmony. Last night's violent tempest had passed over the island, leaving the sun to rise on a new day and the birds to sing as if nothing had happened.

Then she recalled the tempest of scandal that had ravaged her life, threatening to leave nothing but desolation in its wake. Her eyes flew open.

She barely managed to stifle a gasp of astonishment at the sight of Bennett lying on his side facing her, with their son cradled between them. All that prevented her from tumbling backwards off the bed was Bennett's arm, draped over her and Wyn in a protective embrace.

After the first shock wore off, the soft, rhythmic drone of their breathing lulled her to gaze at her husband's face as she'd never seen it before. Sleep had softened the fierce angles of his nose, brow and cheekbones, giving him a much stronger resemblance to their son than she'd ever noticed before. The past twenty-four hours had shown her many facets of her husband that she'd never suspected. It had been a strange experience, drifting to sleep with the sound of his voice in her ears, so gentle and soothing she could scarcely believe it belonged to him.

That thought fled from her mind when Bennett suddenly stirred.

Fearing his reaction if he woke to find her watching him, Caroline quickly shut her eyes and pretended to sleep. After a few tense moments, she felt Bennett carefully withdraw his arm from her shoulder. Then she heard him slip out of the bed and steal from of the room.

Once he had gone, she opened her eyes again to drink in the bittersweet sight of her sleeping child. Her yearning gaze lingered over his features, as she strove to commit his dear little face to memory…in case today might be the last she ever saw of him.

Wyn's eyelids fluttered open. 'I'm cold, Mama. Still so cold.'

Though the child was covered up to his chin with several blankets, Caroline could feel him begin to shiver again. Her hand flew to his forehead, only to find it fiery hot.

Wyn thrashed about, giving a soft moan.

'I think you may be ill, dearest.' She strove to conceal her alarm from him. 'Lie quietly like a good boy and I'll fetch your papa. He'll know what to do.'

She rushed into the hallway, calling Bennett's name.

Finding her husband's bedchamber empty, she was about to start down the stairs when he came flying up them. 'What's wrong, Caro?'

He hadn't called her by that diminutive in years. His use of it now, together with the look of concern that furrowed his brow, stirred something inside her that she did not want stirred.

'It's Wyn. He's running a fever. Quite a bad one by the feel of his forehead. He must have picked up a chill yesterday, out in that cold rain. We must summon a doctor for him.'

'This isn't London, where you have scores of fashionable physicians within easy call. There *might* be one doctor on St Mary's to tend to the townsfolk, but on the off-islands...' Bennett shook his head.

'There must be someone we can call.' Caroline chided herself for not considering this when she'd made her impulsive decision to bring her son to these isolated islands. 'What do the people here do when they fall ill or get injured?'

'They send for one of the Aunts,' Bennett replied after a moment's thought. 'Healer women who brew them a tea or fix a poultice. My mother used to consult them often when we came here. She said the Scilly Aunts did her more good than any physician or apothecary back on the mainland. Can you tend Wyn, while I go find one?'

'I'll try.' Caroline caught her lip between her teeth. 'I've never looked after a sick child before. What should I do?'

'You'll be fine,' he insisted gruffly. 'Bathe his forehead with cool water. I'll have Parker fetch you a basin and cloth. I won't be gone long.'

She was surprised Bennett hadn't proposed that Parker take charge of the feverish child, Caroline reflected as he hurried away and she returned to sit with their son. She was tempted to suggest it herself when her maid appeared a few minutes later with a brimming basin. Not because she didn't want to help Wyn feel better, but because she felt so inadequate to the task.

What if he began to cry and wouldn't stop? What if he had a fit? She had heard a very high fever could cause them.

'I'm so c-cold, Mama,' the child whimpered. 'I feel like I've got a toothache in all my bones.'

Her son needed *her* to comfort him. That conviction helped ease Caroline's paralysing self-doubt. After all, bathing his forehead was not so very different from a loving caress.

'You're running a fever, dearest.' She took the basin from Parker and dipped the cloth into the cool water. Then she pressed it to Wyn's brow. 'Papa has gone to fetch someone who may be able to make you feel better.'

'I wish Greggy was here,' Wyn murmured plaintively.

'So do I, dearest.' Much as it grieved her to hear her son yearn for his nurse, she could not blame him. Until now, Mrs McGregor had always been the one to take care of him when he was ill. She'd been particularly insistent on keeping his mother away from the nursery at those times.

Now Caroline bitterly regretted that she had not done whatever was necessary to be with her child when he needed her most. 'Why don't I tell you a story about Mrs McGregor?'

The child nodded. 'You tell good stories. So does Papa. I hope he'll take me to visit some of those places on the island he told us about last night.'

Caroline doubted that would happen. Now more than ever, Bennett would surely want to whisk Wyn back to the safety and comfort of London the moment he was well enough to travel.

'Once upon a time,' she murmured, moving the cloth down

from Wyn's brow to cool his blazing cheeks, 'Mrs McGregor set out from Sterling House for a holiday in Scotland.'

Caroline spun out the story for as long as she could, hoping it would distract Wyn from how miserable he felt. When at last she heard a door open and close, followed by Bennett's brisk, purposeful footsteps on the stairs, she heaved a sigh of relief.

An instant later, he strode into the sick room, his striking features set in an anxious look. 'How is Wyn doing? Any improvement?'

'I don't think so.' Caroline leaned down and cupped her son's cheek. It alarmed her how hot he still felt in spite of her best efforts. 'He says he's cold and he aches all over, but he has been quiet for the past little while.'

A small, solid woman hobbled into the room behind Bennett. 'It looks as though you got him to sleep, ma'am. Whatever ails your boy, that's one of the best remedies.'

The woman had deep-set eyes and plain, broad features. Tufts of grey hair protruded from beneath her cap. She had an air of calm capability that reassured Caroline without intimidating her.

Bennett lowered his voice. 'My dear, this is Mrs Hicks. I'm told she is the most knowledgeable and experienced healer on the island.'

'Thank you for coming at such an early hour, Mrs Hicks.' Caroline rose from the edge of Wyn's bed. 'I hope you will be able to help our son.'

The woman chuckled. 'I get called out at all hours, ma'am. And nobody on Tresco calls me Mrs Hicks. It's always Aunt Sadie.'

She drew closer to the bed, looking Wyn over carefully. 'Your husband tells me the lad was caught out in the rain yesterday.'

'That's right. We got him dried off as soon as we could, but he seemed chilled and he didn't have much appetite for his supper.'

The healer asked several more questions. When Wyn woke up, she examined him, looking in his mouth, checking his skin for pockmarks, feeling his belly and behind his ears. All the while she spoke to him in a quiet, soothing tone. Mrs Hicks might not have trained at any fine college of medicine, but already Caroline trusted her.

'Is there anything you can do?' she asked the healer in an anxious whisper.

Mrs Hicks nodded. 'I'll make him up a brew of yarrow tea. That often eases a fever. You keep bathing his face and get him to drink and sleep as much as he will.

'One more thing,' she added when they began to thank her, 'do all you can to keep the boy from getting agitated, or this could turn into brain fever. Bad business, that.'

A bone-deep chill swept through Caroline. She glanced down to find herself holding tight to Bennett's hand. Flustered, she tried to pull her fingers away, but he clung to them and would not let go.

The next evening, Bennett's hand still ached faintly from Caroline's bruising grip. The physical proof of her fear for their son had further persuaded him that she loved Wyn as much as he did. That love and fear had kept them awake ever since, sitting vigil by the child's sickbed.

Mrs Hicks had come back to check on him and bring

more of her yarrow tea. Her brew had seemed to ease the fever, allowing Wyn to sleep more comfortably. But later he would wake, achy and fretful, quaking with chills as the fever returned.

Then his parents had sprung into action, his mother bathing his face while his father coaxed him to drink the yarrow tea. Later, when the healer's brew had begun to work, Caroline told stories to divert him until he fell back to sleep. In spite of his concern for Wyn, Bennett had found it strangely satisfying, working together for the good of their child.

Once Wyn had slipped into a deep doze, they collapsed back on to their chairs, watching for any change in his condition.

'Go ahead,' Caroline demanded during one such respite, 'say it.'

Bennett cast her a wary glance. 'What is it you expect me to say?'

'That you think it's my fault Wyn is ill.' Her delicate features looked drawn and…haunted. 'He wouldn't be lying there burning with fever if I hadn't brought him to Tresco in the first place.'

'I cannot pretend the thought never crossed my mind. But it also occurred to me that you would not have brought him here if I hadn't ordered you away with so little warning.' He swung around to face her. 'Blaming each other is not going to make Wyn well again…and neither is blaming ourselves. Quite the contrary, I suspect. So let us try to put it from our minds and concentrate on what we *can* do for him now.'

She stared intently into his eyes for longer than he found comfortable, perhaps trying to decide whether his offer was sincere. At last she gave a brief nod.

'Good.' Bennett rubbed his whisker-stubbled jaw. 'Then

why don't you go get some sleep? I'll call you if he wakes or there's any change.'

'I can watch him while you sleep,' Caroline replied in a weary murmur. 'Or do you not trust me to do something so simple?'

Fatigue smothered any spark of irritation her remark might have provoked. Lately Bennett had begun to wonder if her lack of attentiveness to their son over the years sprang from something other than indifference to his welfare. 'I was only trying to show you a little consideration. I realise it is not something you're accustomed to.'

He expected a bitter quip in return, but instead she replied, 'Thank you, but I'd rather stay with Wyn. I owe it to him for all the times I wasn't there when he needed me.'

It was clear she recognised her shortcomings as a mother and was trying to atone. How could he disapprove of that?

'I will let you see him sometimes, if you want to,' he said, referring to what would happen after their divorce.

'Of course I *want* to.' Her words wafted out in a wistful sigh. 'Though I wonder whether it might be better for him if I didn't.'

'How could that be better for him?' Bennett rubbed his aching temples. 'I would have given anything to see my mother after she left—even to know what had become of her. One day she was there and the next she...wasn't. No one would tell me where she'd gone or why. I thought she must have been abducted or worse.'

Those words slipped out past the guard he usually kept on his tongue to prevent such lapses.

'How awful!' Caroline started to reach for him, then seemed to realise what she was doing and pulled her hand back. 'It was hard enough when my mother died. But at least I wasn't left to wonder and worry. And I was young enough that I didn't really understand our parting would be for ever.'

This was the first time she'd talked about her mother and it came as an unsettling revelation to Bennett. Though he'd been aware that her father was a widower when they'd first met, he'd never stopped to consider that she, too, had suffered the loss of a beloved mother.

'What about your father?' Caroline asked. 'Wouldn't he tell you anything?'

An arid, rasping chuckle broke from Bennett's lips. 'If you'd ever met my father, you would know how absurd that notion is. The servants warned me never to mention my mother to him. Everyone acted as if she'd never existed. I was punished for asking about her. On my father's orders, for all I know.'

He really must wake that lazy guard and put a stop to all this talk of his past, but he could not exert himself. Besides, it wasn't as painful to speak of as he'd feared.

'If your father was that cruel, is it any wonder your mother fled from him?' Caroline's question succeeded in rousing his slumbering defences at last.

'Her going was what made Father that way!' he insisted in an emphatic whisper, even as his conscience questioned the truth of his denial.

Was Caroline trying to excuse his mother's actions because she'd justified her own dalliances on the basis of *his* short-comings? Perhaps he hadn't been an ideal husband, but he'd tried to give her everything she could want, while getting far less than he'd expected in return.

Leaning back in his chair, Bennett crossed his arms over his chest. 'I see no point in talking about any of this now. It is all long past and nothing we say or do can change what happened.'

'Perhaps not,' Caroline replied. 'But don't you think the past might influence our present decisions and actions? Would you have been so quick to brand me an adulteress if your mother had not run away?'

Would he? That question made Bennett even more uncomfortable than sitting for hours on end in this hard chair. 'I told you, I don't want to talk about it.'

'Your father didn't want to talk about what had become of your mother,' she countered. 'But that does not mean it was the right thing to do. How did you finally learn what had happened?'

His chair had become a torturer's rack with Caroline as his personal inquisitor. Bennett had no intention of revealing anything further, but the truth was like a mouthful of poison. He must spit it out or choke on it.

'Fitz Astley told me!' he hissed. 'Every sordid detail while two of his cronies held me down so he could thrash me bloody during my first week at school!'

'The scoundrel!' Caroline cried as Bennett shot to his feet. 'But I don't understand. How did *he* know what happened when you didn't?'

'He knew,' Bennett growled, 'because his father was the scoundrel my mother ran away with. Now, if you'll excuse me, I believe I will try to get some sleep, after all.'

As he strode towards the door, Wyn stirred and whimpered. Bennett recalled the healer's warning about not upsetting their son. Could the boy hear them, even through the haze of sleep, their angry tones disturbing his rest?

Freezing in mid-step, Bennett returned to his chair and sat back down.

'Who am I trying to fool?' he muttered. 'I'd never get a wink of sleep anyway.'

No wonder Bennett had forbidden her to have anything to do with Fitz Astley. His revelation shook Caroline to the core, like a sudden glimpse into the murky depths of her husband's past. If only she'd guessed what hidden dangers lurked there…

She wished he had told her about his mother's betrayal long before this. If she'd known, perhaps she could have made allowances for things he'd said and done during their marriage, rather than letting her grievances drive an even deeper wedge between them.

As they continued to sit with their son, Caroline watched her husband out of the corner of her eye. After what he'd told her about the collapse of his parents' marriage, she could better understand why he'd been so quick to believe she had betrayed him.

'There's something else that puzzles me.' Though she knew it was something Bennett did not want to talk about, she could not bear to remain in ignorance. 'Why did Astley give *you* a beating over something *his* father did?'

She knew better than to blame all the troubles of her marriage on Bennett's past, especially the enmity between him and Astley. But she sensed it was part of the reason he refused to believe her and why he could never forgive her. Surely she deserved to understand.

'Astley blamed my father for driving *them* into exile in Ireland. If he'd divorced my mother, she could have remarried and become semi-respectable again. As it was, they were total outcasts, living in sin.'

'But none of that was your fault.' Caroline's keen sense of injustice was roused. She could picture a gang of older boys picking on Wyn that way for something over which he'd had no control. It made her wish she could relive that night at Almack's long enough to give Astley a taste of what he deserved!

Bennett scowled. 'Astley never cared who had to pay for whatever was done to vex him, as long as someone suffered. He would exploit any weakness to make certain he got what he wanted.'

This time the weakness Astley exploited had been hers. Caroline's gorge rose and her skin crawled with shame. Because of what she'd done, not only had Bennett suffered, her son would, too. So would the Abolition Movement for which her father and husband had worked so hard.

'I wish you'd told me *why* you wanted me to stay away from…*that creature,* rather than just forbidding me to speak to him again.' Though she doubted Bennett would believe her, Caroline still felt compelled to speak. 'If I'd had any idea what he did to you, I never would have…encouraged him.'

Had it been Astley's plan all along, to manoeuvre her into a compromising situation, then expose her indiscretion in a way that would do the most damage to Bennett's family and his cause? That did not diminish her responsibility, for she had made it all far too easy for him. The scoundrel had used *her* to strike Bennett a humiliating blow, just as he'd used his friends at school all those years ago. Now Bennett must despise her, as he'd despised those boys.

She did not expect her husband to answer. But after several minutes of tense silence, he did. 'Perhaps I *should* have told you the whole story. But I feared it might have quite the opposite effect.'

Though he spoke in a tone of quiet resignation, his words stung. How could he believe she would behave with such malicious defiance? She had no right to be indignant, Caroline reminded herself. After all, she had defied her husband's wishes and done him great harm. Why *should* he believe that knowing about his past would have made any difference in her behaviour?

'I didn't expect him to kiss me that night.' Why was she bothering to repeat things Bennett would never believe? 'And I didn't want him to.'

Her husband shot her a look that seemed to ask what was the use in lying now—to herself especially.

Perhaps she shouldn't be talking about any of this, with her guard down and her emotions so dangerously close to the surface. She now understood it would be impossible to persuade Bennett of her innocence. He was determined to be free of her and nothing short of her infidelity would provide the escape he sought. So he would cling to the false certainty that she'd betrayed him with the same stubborn tenacity that had fuelled his fight for the abolition of slavery.

But after so many years of corrosive silence, she could no longer hold her tongue. 'I admit I went too far flirting with Astley. But only because it had been such a long time since *you* wanted anything from me in that way. I suppose I needed reassurance that I was not entirely undesirable.'

A harsh, dry chuckle burst from Bennett's lips. 'You must be joking! Haven't you noticed the way men look at you, the way they behave around you?'

What did other men matter? Their attention might raise her

confidence a little, for a while. But afterwards she would go home to a husband who could scarcely bear to be in the same room with her, let alone the bedchamber. 'That is nothing but a silly game.'

'To you perhaps.' Bennett rubbed his eyes. 'But some games can have serious consequences.'

Caroline glanced down at her son, whose sleep was growing more restless again.

'I know that now.' She had learned it in the hardest way possible. 'I hope you got back at Astley for that beating he gave you.'

'Indeed I did.' Bennett sounded as if he savoured the memory. 'I soon learned to stand up for myself and for other boys who were being bullied. It was good training for my Abolition work.'

She had always thought of Bennett as so powerful and in control. This glimpse into his past made Caroline see him in a whole new light. 'Is that why you became an Abolitionist?'

'In part.' Bennett's lips settled into a pensive frown. 'I also read a book by a former slave. It described how families were torn apart—children taken from their mothers, never to see them again.'

His sympathy with those slave children must have risen from his own experience, Caroline realised. All these years, she'd thought his commitment to Abolition sprang from abstract principles about rights and humanity. Now she understood it was a passionately personal crusade.

She admired the way Bennett had channelled the pain of his past to do something good for others. However, it put her life of trivial pleasure into harsh perspective.

Caroline could not deny there were things about that life

she would miss. Not the gowns and jewels and opulent amusements, but the admiration of society. She had been hailed a *toast* and a *diamond of the first water.* Ladies had copied her little innovations in fashion. Gentlemen had vied to dance and flirt with her. They were not very substantial accomplishments, perhaps, but they were all she had to compensate for the failures in far more important areas of her life. She might not be an adulteress, as Bennett was so determined to believe, but she still fell far short of the kind of wife a man like him needed.

She wished she could tell Bennett how sincerely she regretted the damage her indiscretion had done to his pride and his cause. But he would never believe her, any more than he would believe her protestations of fidelity.

The deeper Caroline reflected on all that, the deeper she sank into her own thoughts.

Some time later, she was distantly aware of being borne securely in Bennett's strong arms. Her head lolled against his chest as she inhaled breath after slow, deep breath of his scent. All her hurt, anger and guilt had been lulled to sleep and did not stir.

She felt herself being laid gently upon a bed. Warm ripples of sensation fluttered through her in response to Bennett's touch. She yearned to raise her arms and pull him closer, but the bonds of sleep were too heavy to cast off.

Besides, a quiver of fear warned her that he might despise her overture, even if he was too tired to resist it.

Chapter Six

Did Caroline truly not recognise what a desirable woman she was? Bennett pondered that preposterous notion as he lowered his sleeping wife on to the bed in her darkened room.

It was like being unaware the sun was as golden as her hair or parts of the sea as blue-green as her eyes. Ever since he'd returned to Tresco, he'd been taunted and tempted by her allure. He found her far more appealing in a simple dress, her hair tumbled and her face aglow with motherly affection. The fashionable London socialite, perfectly gowned, coiffed and bejewelled, had left him cold.

He found it difficult to believe that elegant façade had concealed deep doubts and insecurities. But why should that confound him so? He knew all about maintaining a strong, confident image. Sometimes that involved keeping secrets.

These past two nights he'd told Caroline far more about his past than he'd ever intended to—far more than he might have under any other circumstances. It had come out piece by painful piece, like drawing rotten teeth. Yet, once they were out, he had felt a strange sort of relief from the constant dull ache he'd trained himself to ignore all these years. Who'd have guessed Caroline would prove such a sympathetic listener? Not he, that was certain.

Having settled his wife on the bed, Bennett hovered over her, savouring her beguiling scent and the warmth that radiated from her body. He finally managed to wrench himself away only because he feared losing control if he lingered. But when he rose to go, a wave of dizziness knocked him back to perch on the edge of the bed.

The only light in the room came from the distant glow of candles in Wyn's bedchamber and the faint, silvery glitter of moonbeams filtering in the window. They cast everything in deep, gracious shadows, masking all the imperfections that might have been exposed by the unforgiving glare of daylight.

Carolyn looked so soft and vulnerable, lying on her bed in that dim light. Even as his body roused from the recent sensation of her in his arms, Bennett felt himself responding to her in a different way than he ever had before. In the shadowy depths of night, hovering dangerously near the brink of sleep, he gave that bewildering new feeling a wary welcome.

She had made mistakes in their marriage, but now he was forced to acknowledge that he had, too. Was it possible he had driven his wife to seek companionship elsewhere when she could not get it from him? Had she believed he was signalling his indifference to her taking a lover? Such arrangements were common enough in their circles, especially after the wife had done her dynastic duty by providing her husband with a healthy male heir.

Rising slowly to his feet, Bennett was relieved when his head did not spin this time. Reluctant as he was to leave Caroline, he knew he must get back to their son.

As he unfolded a blanket from the foot of the bed and spread it over her with gentle care, he reflected on the peculiar irony of their situation. After seven years of wedlock, he and Caroline were finally beginning to understand one another just as their marriage was falling apart.

Tired though she must have been, Caroline did not sleep long. The next time Wyn woke, she heard his voice and responded at once.

'Please, dearest, drink a little more of the tea.' Supporting their son's shoulders, she held the cup to his lips. 'I know you don't like the taste, but it always makes you feel better after you take it.'

The child turned his head away, whining, 'I don't want any.'

'Wyndham Wilberforce Maitland.' Staring down at his son from the foot of the bed, Bennett spoke his son's impressive full name in a tone that brooked no defiance. 'You must do as your mother says.'

The child's bottom lip quivered, making his father feel like the vilest ogre. But he turned his head back towards Caroline and took a long sip from the cup.

'That's my good, brave boy,' she crooned, pressing a kiss to his moist brow.

When she glanced towards Bennett, he expected her to shoot him an indignant glare for speaking so severely to their ailing child. Instead her eyes glowed with such warm gratitude she hardly needed to mouth the words *Thank you.*

Bennett sensed something else in her gaze as well—a plea of sorts. To his surprise, he thought he understood.

'Well done, son.' He smiled down at the child, hoping Wyn might understand why he'd spoken sharply before. 'All we want is for you to get better soon.'

'Yes, Papa.' The boy took another drink of the yarrow tea, grimacing after he swallowed it.

They managed to coax the rest of the brew into him, as well as some broth. Then Bennett helped the child up to use the chamber pot, after which Caroline changed him into a clean nightshirt.

'Shall I tell you another story?' she asked when he was tucked back into bed.

'I'd like a story from Papa,' Wyn replied, 'about when he used to come here with *his* mama.'

The look on Bennett's face must have betrayed his reluctance, for Caroline tried to intervene. 'Your papa is very tired, dearest. He should try to get some sleep. Perhaps he can tell you a story later.'

'It's all right.' Bennett moved to take his wife's place beside their son. Though grateful to her for trying to spare him, he knew he must seize this opportunity to forge a closer relationship with Wyn. 'I believe I can recall enough about those days to make a story. But you must promise to give me a nudge if I start to snore.'

'I will.' Wyn sounded a bit more like his old cheerful self. The yarrow tea must be working. Bennett only hoped this time the cursed fever would not return.

Taking advantage of his slumbering defences, Bennett began to tell Wyn everything he could recall about his childhood holidays on Tresco. To his relief, the effort brought back only warm memories that he had buried away. He found it impossible to reconcile the doting mother of those happy times with the wanton adulteress who had abandoned him. At the moment, his wits were too addled to try.

He was in the middle of a story about *Tekla Theis,* the island harvest festival, when he felt Caroline's hand upon his arm and her breath caress his ear as she whispered, 'Wyn's gone to sleep again and so should you.'

'I'll sit with him.' Bennett staggered as he tried to shift from the bed to his chair.

'Please be sensible.' Caroline grabbed hold of his arm to keep him from falling. 'That usually isn't difficult for you. If you fall asleep sitting up, I won't be able to carry *you* off to bed, as you did with me. So come now, while you can still move under your own power. If you do, I promise I will sleep the next time Wyn does. We won't be any good to him if we exhaust ourselves.'

'That does make sense.' His words slurred as if he'd had too much to drink. 'Will you steer me in the proper direction so I don't fall down the stairs?'

A few days ago, he wouldn't have put it past her to give him a push down those stairs. Now their shared concern for their son overshadowed their differences.

'Of course.' Caroline gave a low, melodious chuckle, almost as if she sensed his thoughts. 'Let's go.'

They managed to reach his room without mishap. Through the gable window, the eastern horizon was streaked with the opal gleam of dawn. Bathed in that blushing light, Caroline had never looked lovelier. With a pang, Bennett wondered what quiet delights he might have missed by not lingering more often in his wife's bed until morning.

'I know we both need sleep,' he acknowledged in a drowsy murmur as he lay down. Catching hold of Caroline's hand, he gave her fingers a brief squeeze. 'But I will miss the chance to talk. Perhaps if we'd talked like that sooner…'

* * *

*Perhaps if they'd talked like that sooner…*what?

Bennett was too exhausted to finish his thought. He paused as if searching for the right words to continue. But before he could find them, his hand fell slack from around hers and his breath settled into the slow, easy rhythm of sleep.

With great difficulty, Caroline stifled the urge to linger there watching him, as well as even more daring inclinations. She reminded herself this unlikely intimacy between them was only a sleep-starved dream. A few reluctant confidences exchanged in the middle of the night would not save their marriage.

Once Wyn recovered and Bennett caught up on his sleep, everything would go back to the way it had been before. The only thing to change would be her understanding of *why* their marriage had failed—why it might have been doomed from the beginning.

She wanted to allow Bennett a good long sleep, but that proved impossible. Barely two hours passed before Wyn woke again. His forehead felt hotter than ever this time. What frightened Caroline even more, her son did not seem to recognise her or know where he was. He kept calling her *Greggy,* begging her to stop his parents from shouting at each other. Could this be the brain fever Mrs Hicks had warned them about?

'Parker, please call his lordship!' Caroline ordered the maid, who had just arrived with more water. 'Then send Albert to fetch Mrs Hicks. And bring me another cup of her tea for Master Wyn.'

'At once, my lady.' Perhaps alarmed by the edge of panic in Caroline's voice, the maid hurried away.

A moment later, Bennett rushed into the room. 'Is Wyn worse? I knew I should have stayed with him.'

'There was nothing you could have done.' Caroline's hand trembled as she tried to hold the damp cloth to her son's fevered brow, but he resisted her clumsy ministrations, tossing his head from side to side on the pillow. 'He was sleeping quietly until a little while ago. But when he woke…he didn't seem to know me.'

Would her son have called her by another woman's name, her conscience whispered, if she had not abdicated so many of her motherly responsibilities to a hired servant?

Before Bennett could reply, the child grew more agitated and began to whimper. 'Stop, Greggy! I already had my bath. Is Mama coming to say goodnight before she goes out?'

Caroline glanced back at her husband, seeking reassurance that this was not as troubling a development as it seemed to her. But when their eyes met, she glimpsed fear in his that mirrored her own.

'Have you sent for Mrs Hicks?' Bennett strode to their son's bedside and knelt next to Caroline, who nodded in response to his question.

'Your mama is here, Wyn, and so am I.' He grasped the child's hand and spoke in the most soothing tone Caroline had ever heard him use. 'You must try to lie still.'

'Papa?' Wyn shrank from him. 'Please don't be angry with me and don't shout at Mama.'

The more Bennett tried to calm the child and reason with him, the more upset he grew and the more frightened Caroline became.

By the time Mrs Hicks arrived, Caroline was at her wits' end. The healer's worried look drove her over the edge. 'This *is* my fault! I should…never have brought him here. What if he…?'

She could not bear to put her deepest dread into words.

Bennett and the healer exchanged a look. The next thing Caroline knew, her husband rose from his knees and pulled her away from their son's sickbed with a firm but tender hold.

'Hush, Caro. All will be well.' He spoke as he had to Wyn, all the while drawing her towards the door. 'Come, we must let Mrs Hicks do what she can for him.'

Though she allowed Bennett to lead her away, Caroline could not contain her tears. It was as if a dam had burst inside her, releasing all her pent-up fear and guilt and longing for things she could never have because she did not deserve them. Her little son was going to die because of her selfish actions and she would have to live with that burden. She would willingly surrender him to Bennett in a divorce a hundred times rather than this!

Though her feet moved, she had no idea where she was going until Bennett eased her on to the edge of her bed and sank down beside her. Adjusting his embrace, he drew her towards him until her forehead rested against his broad shoulder. He raised his other hand to pat her back with awkward tenderness.

'Hush, now, or you'll make yourself ill.' He sounded uncomfortable with such an outburst of emotion, yet sincerely concerned about her. 'I'm certain it isn't as bad as you fear. You're just exhausted and overwhelmed by all this.'

Taking his hand from her back, he produced a handkerchief and began to wipe her face with a soft, hesitant touch. The warmth of his concern wrapped around Caroline, sustaining her and helping her gain control of her runaway emotions.

'There.' The mellow murmur of Bennett's voice went straight to her heart in that vulnerable moment. 'That's better.'

Pressing the sodden wad of linen into her hand, he raised his to her cheek in a featherlight caress. Then an irresistible magnetism seemed to draw their lips towards one another.

The first warm, tremulous contact after such a long absence made Caroline's senses crackle with suppressed desire suddenly reignited. It flared and spread swiftly until it felt like wildfire raged through her veins.

The blaze swept through Bennett, too. His embrace tightened, as if to claim her. His kiss grew deeper and more demanding, while she ached to give him everything he wanted and more. Her lips parted to invite the hungry thrust of his tongue.

Old desires fused with strange new emotions to make this kiss sweeter and more satisfying than any they had shared before. Caroline savoured it like a serving of her favourite food after a long fast. She sought to hoard the feel and taste of it, knowing this would surely be the last time Bennett ever kissed her. While his lips moved over hers with such thrilling fervour, she could pretend that he cared for her in the way she'd once longed for.

'My lord! My lady!' Parker's urgent call from the hallway shattered the fragile delight of their stolen kiss. 'Mrs Hicks says to come quick!'

Caroline and Bennett flew apart with an abrupt, guilty start, as if they were a pair of adulterous lovers caught in an illicit embrace rather than a married couple exchanging a kiss in the privacy of the bedchamber.

Wyn! A cold wave of shame doused the blaze of Caroline's

passion. How could she have forgotten her sick little son for even a moment in the selfish pursuit of her own pleasure?

Bennett's compelling features clenched in a dark scowl. His inscrutable gaze darted furtively, refusing to meet hers. It was clear he also regretted succumbing to the reckless impulse of desire. Perhaps he even blamed her for tempting him to it.

What had just happened here? Bennett wondered as Parker's urgent summons ripped him from the sweet, sultry depths of Caroline's kiss.

Part of him wanted to rail at the maid for so rudely interrupting the most exquisite moment of pleasure he'd enjoyed in a very long time. Reason and paternal instinct reminded him that Wyn's well-being mattered far more than his carnal desires.

Yet another part of him was desperately grateful for the interruption. Who knew where that imprudent kiss might have led otherwise? His loss of control unnerved him. It would be easy enough to blame his impulsive actions on the perilous combination of exhaustion and desire. But deep down he knew it might be the work of something even more dangerous.

Those contradictory inclinations battled within him as he and Caroline sprang from the bed and rushed to Wyn's room. Though he moved swiftly to answer the healer's summons, part of him longed to hang back, dreading what might await them in that chamber.

Bracing himself to find his son lying cold and still, he could scarcely believe his eyes when the child held out his arms to Caroline. 'Mama, I'm hungry. Can I have some porridge?'

Caroline hesitated for an instant, making Bennett wonder if she might frighten the child by breaking into fresh sobs of relief. He could hardly blame her, for a great choking lump rose in his throat. But somehow she marshalled her composure, venting her emotions in a burst of frenzied laughter instead.

'Of course, dearest! Porridge or whatever else you wish.' She glanced towards the healer. 'As long as Mrs Hicks says you may.'

The woman nodded, her plain, kind face beaming with satisfaction. 'Not too much to begin with, and nothing too rich. But now that his fever's broke, the lad needs to eat well to gain his strength back.'

Bennett exhaled a deep breath of relief at hearing his son was out of danger. But with that worry eased, the matter of *the kiss* returned to plague him. He told himself it was only the strain of the past few days looking for an outlet. Just as it made Caroline break down in tears, it had unleashed his tightly bound desire.

Was that also what had made her return his kiss so passionately? he wondered as he watched her fuss over Wyn. Or had she hoped to exploit his passing weakness to prevent him from divorcing her? Not long ago, he'd have had no difficulty believing she might try to manipulate him that way. Now, he was far less certain.

Whatever their reasons for kissing one another, he could see that living under the same small roof as his estranged wife would be far more complicated as a result.

Now that Wyn's fever had broken, the healer packed up her basket of home remedies, preparing to leave.

Bennett nodded towards the hallway. 'Might I have a word before you go?'

The woman gave an obliging nod.

Before they could get more than two steps, Caroline bounded up from Wyn's bedside. Clasping the healer's gnarled hand, she pressed a kiss upon it. 'I cannot thank you enough for all you've done for our son!'

Mrs Hicks appeared surprised but pleased by such an ardent expression of gratitude. 'I only helped him get well on his own, dearie, and I was happy to do that.'

'The people of Tresco are very fortunate to have your services,' Caroline replied, 'and I shall be for ever in your debt.'

Wyn called out for his mother's attention and she was obliged to return to him as Bennett and the healer stepped out into the hallway.

'How soon do you think my son will be sufficiently recovered to sail back to the mainland?' he asked.

The prospect of spending much more time in close quarters with Caroline troubled him, though not for the same reason it had before.

Mrs Hicks pondered his question for a moment, perhaps wondering what answer he was looking for. 'It may take no more than a week, my lord, if he's fed well, gets plenty of sleep and nothing upsets him. Children can come around quick after an illness. But the longer you stay, the stronger he'll get. I reckon you and your wife will know when he's ready to travel.'

A week? Bennett could not decide whether that represented an eternity or a far-too-brief instant. He'd already been absent from Parliament for nearly a fortnight and it would take at least another week to get back to London once Wyn was well enough to travel. Duty obliged him to return as soon as possible. Caution warned him it could be dangerous to stay. But concern for his son's well-being urged him to remain on

the island longer, as did other motives he was reluctant to acknowledge.

'We will see how he gets on, then.' Bennett insisted the
healer accept a generous fee for her services. 'If it is not too
much trouble, I hope you will look in on him in a few days to
see how he is recovering.'

'Of course.' Mrs Hicks wagged her forefinger at him. 'And
now that the lad's fever has broken, there's no need of you and
your wife sitting up with him night and day. If you must have
somebody watch him, let that Parker lass earn her wages. You
both need your sleep or you'll fall ill next.'

Bennett promised to follow her orders and make certain
Caroline did, too.

Once he'd seen Mrs Hicks on her way, Bennett returned
to his son's room, wary of facing his wife again without the
welcome buffer and distraction of the healer's presence.

Fortunately Wyn was still awake, telling his mother all he
could recall of his strange fever dreams. Not trusting himself
to get too close to Caroline, Bennett stood at the foot of the
bed, listening to their son. He made every effort to avoid her
gaze, though now and then he could not resist slanting a swift
glance at her.

It seemed she must be as unsettled as he by their kiss. If
that were the case, then perhaps she would prefer to join him
in pretending it had never happened.

Wyn's conversation had just begun to lag when Parker appeared with a steaming bowl of porridge for him.

The child eyed the dish and his mother's maid. 'Did you
cook that?'

Parker seemed torn between indignation and amusement.

'You needn't fret about that, Master Wyn. Your father hired a proper cook.'

The child grinned and sniffed the air. 'It smells good.'

'Shall I feed it to him, my lady?' Parker asked.

Caroline shook her head. 'I can manage, thank you.'

'I can feed myself,' Wyn insisted. 'I'm not a baby.'

'Of course you're not, dearest.' Caroline took the bowl from Parker, scooped up a spoonful of porridge and blew to cool it. 'But you have been very ill and it's not easy to eat in bed without spilling.'

When the child kept his mouth stubbornly closed, Bennett was about to order him to behave.

But Caroline managed to secure his cooperation by coaxing. 'Humour your mama, like a good boy. I never had many chances to feed you when you were a baby.'

Did he detect a catch in her voice, Bennett wondered, or was it merely his fancy?

He watched while she fed the child. When the little fellow drifted back to sleep quite soon afterwards, he reached for the empty bowl. 'I will take this down to the kitchen and tell Parker to come sit with Wyn. Then you and I need to sit down to a proper meal.'

Caroline shook her head. 'I'm not very hungry. I'd rather stay here in case Wyn needs me.'

Was it that? Or was she reluctant to dine with him and make stilted table talk? He did not relish the prospect either, but he knew better than to ignore the healer's warning.

'You don't need to prove anything to me, you know.' In spite of her past actions, he'd finally come to accept that she cared deeply for Wyn, though her manner of expressing that feeling was far different than his.

'I need to prove something to *him,* and to myself.' Caroline tilted her chin. 'Besides, I can sleep as much as I like when he's gone.'

'We won't be going for a while yet. You don't want to exhaust yourself in the meantime.'

She handed him the porridge bowl. 'Is that what you were talking about in the hallway with Mrs Hicks—how soon Wyn will be well enough to travel?'

Bennett nodded.

'What did she say?'

'That it could be as little as a week.'

'Surely not.' Caroline glanced down at the sleeping child. 'See how thin and peaky he looks. The crossing to Cornwall is so rough. Then you will have more days of travel over bad roads in draughty coaches—every night sleeping in a different inn, some of them none too clean. I can't help wondering if the journey here was what made him come down with that awful fever.'

'What's done is done. Fretting about it now will not change anything.' Was he talking about her bringing Wyn to Tresco, or about the mistakes they'd made in their marriage? Nothing that had happened these past few days could alter the past.

Then why, Bennett wondered, did he feel as if something deep and vital *had* changed between them?

Chapter Seven

One week.

The moment Bennett told her what Mrs Hicks had said about how soon Wyn might be fit to travel, Caroline knew what she had to do with that time. She must prove to Bennett that she had changed, was now capable of being the kind of mother Wyn needed. If she accomplished that task to his satisfaction, perhaps he would agree to let their son remain on the island with her until he was fully recovered.

Caroline knew she had her work cut out for her. With each passing day it became clearer that Bennett could hardly wait to get away from Tresco…and her. The reason was not difficult to guess. It was all because of that kiss!

When she recalled the stirring, sensual sensation of his lips upon hers, her heart began to race and ripples of fire and ice swept through her. Yet she still had no idea why Bennett had kissed her. Nor was she certain what had made her respond so passionately.

Was it only a desperate plea for comfort that had got out of hand? Or had her exhaustion let loose an urgent hunger she usually kept under tight control? Perhaps she'd only wanted to make certain Fitz Astley's kiss was not the last one she would ever taste.

She hoped it was one of those reasons and nothing more dangerous to her bruised, starving heart. For Bennett's manner afterwards had made it clear he regretted that impulsive embrace and was determined to pretend it had never happened.

If that was what he wanted, she could pretend, too.

'Mama!' Wyn's voice summoned Caroline back from her woolgathering. 'What happens next? You stopped right in the middle of the story.'

'Oh, dear, I did, didn't I?' Thank goodness Bennett was not on hand to catch her in this latest slip. It was now the fourth day of her precious week and her plan to show Bennett what a good mother she could be was not going well. 'Where was I?'

'The old woman just met an ox.'

'Yes, of course.' Caroline strove to keep her thoughts from straying this time. 'The old woman said, "Ox, ox drink water. Water won't quench fire. Fire won't burn stick. Stick won't beat dog. Dog won't bite pig. Piggy won't jump over the stile and I shan't get home tonight."'

'But the ox would not,' Wyn chimed in. By now he was so familiar with the story he probably could have recited the whole thing to her.

'Tiresome creatures, oxen.' Caroline smothered a yawn as she tried to recall the next bit of the story.

Though she and Bennett no longer had to sit up with Wyn through the nights, fatigue still sapped her strength and muddled her thoughts. Now that the child had begun to recover, he was impatient to be up and about. It took all her energy and resources to keep him entertained and in good humour.

Simply coaxing him to eat and take his nap were feats that seemed to grow more arduous with each passing day. Caroline had begun to understand why Mrs McGregor often seemed out of temper.

Still, she knew she must not complain, least of all to Bennett. She did not want to give him any excuse to whisk Wyn away to London as soon as the week was up.

These past few days he'd seemed to watch her more carefully than ever, silently critical of everything she did with their son. No matter how hard she tried to be a better mother to Wyn, Bennett's oppressive scrutiny reminded her that once again her best effort was not good enough. Though she told herself his disapproval no longer mattered, deep down she feared it still did and always would.

'Then the pig jumped over the stile—' Caroline strove to turn her mind away from such troubling thoughts as she concluded the story '—and the old woman got home that night, after all.'

No sooner had the last word left her mouth than Wyn begged, 'Tell me another story, Mama. Please!'

The child's wide, dimpled smile made all her difficulties and worries pale into insignificance. It buoyed her spirits to realise how much Wyn enjoyed her stories and games. Now that he was old enough to take an interest in such things, she felt better equipped to make him happy.

She lifted his hand and pressed a kiss upon it. 'If I tell you just one more, will you go to sleep?'

'I'll try.'

Three stories later, he seemed no closer to nodding off, while Caroline's throat felt raw.

Just then Bennett looked in. Meticulously clean shaven and

wearing fresh clothes, his appearance made Caroline acutely self-conscious of hers. That was ridiculous, she reminded herself. She did not care in the least whether her looks pleased her husband. It might only provoke another awkward incident like that disastrous kiss.

'I thought I heard voices. Is it not long past time for his nap?' The implied censure in Bennett's look and tone rasped upon her frayed nerves.

She sighed. 'I've been trying.'

'I don't want a nap,' Wyn protested. 'I want to go outside and see all those places on the island you told me about. The castles and the beaches and that *Gimble* place.'

Bennett listened with a grave frown. 'You will not be able to go anywhere until you have recovered your strength. For that you need to rest and eat, neither of which you appear to be doing as much as you should.'

The child shot his father a look that was part reproachful and part sulky. Caroline could tell Bennett's rebuke had stung.

'Your mama is going to leave now so *she* can get some rest,' Bennett announced in a tone that brooked no opposition from her or their son. 'Perhaps with the room quiet and nothing to excite your attention, you may be able to sleep for a while.'

What was he trying to say—that her stories prevented Wyn from sleeping and thus from recovering as quickly as he might otherwise? Did Bennett imagine it was a deliberate scheme of hers to keep them both on the island longer? Considering the other offences of which he'd judged her guilty, she would not be surprised.

During the worst of Wyn's illness it had felt as if some of the barriers between them were beginning to crumble. But now that their son was out of danger, Bennett seemed eager to build those barricades up again, thicker than ever and bristling with defences. How could she have been so daft as to suppose the grim antagonism of years could melt away in a matter of days?

Clearly Bennett did not want to believe she was capable of being a more attentive mother. As long as he judged her an unfit parent, he would feel justified in taking her son—just as believing she was an adulteress gave him a pretext for divorcing her. Was it futile trying to change his mind when he seemed so determined to always think the worst of her?

Their son's illness had brought him and Caroline together, Bennett reflected as he beckoned his wife away from Wyn's bedside. But the child's recovery seemed to be pulling them apart again, throwing their many differences into sharp relief. He tried to tell himself that was all to the good, considering what the future held. But his brief taste of domestic harmony made him regret losing it.

The past few days had made Bennett question a few of his cherished assumptions—something that did not sit well with him. For most of their son's life, he had prided himself on being the more constant, devoted parent. But lately, in the absence of Mrs McGregor's capable management, it was Caroline who had demonstrated far more patience with Wyn's complaints and caprices.

More than once lately, she'd seemed to be near her wits' end. Yet somehow she had managed to hold her temper and soldier on. Bennett had never guessed his wife possessed such tenacity. It made him wonder if perhaps he had misjudged her in other ways, too. He needed to get back to London before he started to question *everything* about his marriage and his life.

Ushering her through Wyn's bedroom door, he pulled it partly closed behind them and lowered his voice for Caroline's ears alone. 'You aren't obliged to give him everything he asks for, you know.'

Bennett meant the advice kindly. He did not want her to wear herself out catering to their son's every whim.

Caroline pushed back a lock of hair that had fallen over her brow. She looked thoroughly harried, yet still far too attractive. 'I'm only trying to make him as comfortable and happy as possible under the circumstances. It is the least I can do to make up for bringing him here.'

As they descended the stairs together, Bennett recalled their last headlong rush down those narrow steps. He'd almost trampled over her to get to their son. 'You must understand, it isn't good for children to have their own way all the time. They need firm limits and a stable routine they can depend upon. It helps them feel safe.'

Caroline sniffed. 'The Gospel According to Saint McGregor, I presume?'

Her quip made his lips arch in a reluctant smile. 'The woman knows her job. And you must admit she has done well raising our son. I know he's become a bit of a handful now that he's getting better, but he is a fine little fellow.'

They paused in the parlour, which looked like an entirely different room than the one Bennett had first entered upon his return to Tresco. While Caroline had been busy tending Wyn these past few days, he had hired a crew of local women to come in and clean the house. He could not help but contrast their experience and efficiency with Caroline's awkward attempt to wash the floor. Still, she had made the effort, for Wyn's sake. That counted for a great deal in Bennett's opinion.

He owed it to Caroline to put the house in good order for her—well cleaned, provisioned and staffed. Then perhaps he would not feel so guilty about leaving her here when the time came for him and Wyn to return to London.

In response to his comment about Mrs McGregor, Caroline gave a grudging nod. 'How did you become such an expert on child-rearing, pray?'

'I don't claim to be an expert. But I was a child myself, once, hard as that may be for you to imagine. I remember what it was like. The orderly, predictable routine of nursery and school gave me something to hold on to after the rest of my world turned upside down.' He wanted his son to have that, too.

'But did you have to be so harsh with Wyn just now? I'm afraid he'll think you're angry with him.'

'Harsh? Nonsense. I simply enforced a perfectly reasonable request. It's about time someone did.' He wished he'd put down his foot with Caroline long ago about her endless social engagements, before the situation got so badly out of hand. He was not about to make the same mistake with their son, overindulging the boy just because he'd been ill.

'You don't have to lash out with your hand or your voice to hurt him.' Caroline rubbed her temples. 'Your cold, disapproving silence is quite enough.'

The charge hit Bennett like an iron fist in a kid glove. 'Wyn knows I care about him. There is more to life than doing whatever you fancy regardless of the consequences.

The sooner he learns that, the less trouble he will have in the years ahead.'

He braced for their exchange to spiral into yet another argument that would go round and round, striking sparks of hostility without leading anywhere.

Before Caroline could reply, he raised his hand. 'There is no use trying to talk about this, is there? You have your opinion and I have mine. Like everything else about us, they are as opposite as they can be.'

The gathering antagonism he'd sensed building between them seemed to diffuse a little. He beckoned her towards the kitchen, 'Now, come have a cup of tea and something to eat while you have the chance.'

She followed. 'I don't want Wyn growing up spoiled and selfish either. I know you care about him. I only wish I could be certain he knows it, too. I hate to think of him growing up feeling he can never meet your expectations…never be good enough to secure your affection.'

Her words slipped past Bennett's defences to strike deep. He sensed Caroline wasn't only talking about their son.

The appetising aromas of fresh-baked bread and mutton stew enveloped them as they entered the kitchen. The cook was stirring batter in a bowl while Parker attended to some sewing and Albert buffed a pair of Bennett's boots.

Caroline sank on to the nearest chair. 'Tea, if you please, Mrs Jenkins, and a slice of that bread. It smells wonderful.'

The cook set down her bowl and lifted the kettle off the hob. She glanced towards Bennett. 'For you as well, my lord?'

'No…thank you.' He couldn't stay there and try to make banal conversation in front of the servants. Not with all the unsettling thoughts their private exchange had sparked swirling in his mind. 'I've been cooped up inside too long. I need to get some fresh air.'

Hardly breaking stride, he marched to the kitchen door and let himself out.

'I want to go and see more of the island.' Wyn thrust out his lower lip in a mutinous scowl. 'I'm not ill any more. I'm tired of staying in bed day after day!'

The child hadn't gone to sleep, in spite of his father's stern warning. Now he was more fractious than ever.

Reminding herself, yet again, that she had brought him here and she was trying to be a better mother, Caroline inhaled a deep breath and summoned up as much patience as she could muster. Unfortunately, it had never been one of her most abundant virtues.

'But, dearest, even if you were quite well, it is cool and windy out today. Mrs Hicks says you need at least another day's rest before you're strong enough to be up and about.'

'I don't like her!' The sharp pitch of Wyn's voice reminded Caroline too much of his endless infant squalls. 'She made that awful tea I had to drink. Now she won't let me go out and play. Papa went out. Where did he go?'

'I don't know,' Caroline admitted. 'He didn't say.'

She'd been so relieved to see Bennett go, she hadn't asked where he was headed. Now that their son was out of danger, the differences they'd temporarily put aside had come crowding back between them, stronger than ever.

It did not help matters that she was more aware than ever of her husband's intense, commanding presence. In these confined quarters, they often brushed past one another in the narrow corridors. At the table, their hands grazed briefly when reaching for the salt. Every fleeting touch stirred her in ways she did not want to be stirred by him.

'Can I go out somewhere tomorrow?' Wyn's petulant demand set his mother's teeth on edge.

Tempted as she was to appease him with such an assurance, she did not want to make promises she couldn't keep. 'It will depend on the weather and how you are feeling. I have no control over either of those.'

She seemed to have far too little control over anything any more, least of all her own feelings. If Wyn had to stay in bed another day, she would be shut in with him, trying to keep him entertained with stories and games that were rapidly losing their charm. But if the child was well enough to be up and about, Bennett might decide their son was sufficiently recovered to travel.

'Would you like me to tell you another story?' she asked in a tone of forced brightness.

'I'm tired of stories.' The child heaved a great sigh and flopped about in the bed. 'I can see the Blockhouse from my window. I wish I could go there.'

Caroline strove to tamp down her mounting frustration. 'What about a game instead?'

Wyn shook his head. 'Can I have something to eat? Not all that broth and jelly and porridge, but proper food. Cake!'

The child's behaviour was making Caroline understand Bennett's point about not catering to his every whim. It seemed as if the harder she tried to please him, the more demanding he became. On the other hand, when she tried to impose some limits, Wyn grew cross and fretful. She did not want him upset with her during the last few days they might spend together.

As usual, she could not seem to do anything right. 'What about "Henny Penny"?'

'That's a baby story!'

Caroline threw up her hands. 'Then what *do* you want to do?'

'Eat cake! I know Cook made some. I can smell it.'

Caroline's heart fell. She had certainly walked into that hole. 'Wyn, you know Papa would not want you spoiling your appetite for supper.'

'I don't care!' The child thumped his mattress. 'Papa isn't here. He's off having fun and he didn't take me!'

'Wyn, please…' This whole day had brought back wretched memories of when her son was an infant and nothing she could do would make him stop crying. Just like today, everything she'd tried only seemed to make it worse.

The child began kicking his feet under the covers. 'I don't like it here! I miss Greggy. I want to go home!'

Some barrier inside Caroline gave way. 'You'll go home soon enough. Though if you behave like this I doubt your precious Mrs McGregor will want you back!'

'You don't care about me and neither does Papa!' Wyn burst into tears. 'I want Greggy!'

Before Caroline could say anything more, Wyn pulled the covers over his head, wailing as if his small heart would break.

The tears she'd been fighting back all day began to fall as the frustration and failure of a lifetime overwhelmed her. What had made her think that just because Wyn was older she could redeem her past mistakes and be a proper mother to him at last?

Once again her efforts had ended in disaster. In the years to come, whenever Wyn thought of her it would be of a selfish monster who had dragged him away from his safe, comfortable nursery and made him miserable. By then, he would also know she had mired the family in scandal with her reckless indiscretion. No doubt he would believe she had betrayed his father with other men.

Scraping the heels of her hands up her cheeks, Caroline tried to push the tears back into her eyes, but they would not go. Instead, more poured out, hot and salty, stinging her eyes and leaking through her fingers. Some ran down into her nose and the back of her throat, choking her.

She turned and ran from the room…straight into Bennett's arms. Part of her longed to subside into the strength of his embrace, but she knew she would find no comfort there because she did not deserve it. She had fallen far short of everything he wanted in a wife.

'What's happened?' Her husband's question sounded harsh and accusing.

Caroline struggled even harder to stifle her flood of tears and gusting sobs. She might as well have tried to hold back an Atlantic gale. 'Wyn…h-hates me! He thinks I do not l-love him. I n-never should…have brought him here. G-go ahead and take him away. H-he is better off…without me!'

'Calm down, now. You don't mean that.'

'I d-do mean it! And you know it's t-true.' She struggled to escape Bennett's surprisingly gentle hold. If she yielded to it, who could tell where it might lead? 'You t-told me what Mrs Hicks said about not upsetting him. What if he comes d-down with brain fever?'

'He'll be fine, I'm certain.' In spite of his reassuring words, her husband didn't sound certain. He sounded worried, as he had every reason to be.

'I've f-failed!' she cried. 'As a wife and a daughter and a m-mother!'

Her outburst succeeded in loosening his grip more than all her squirming. Caroline seized her chance to spin away from Bennett and bolt through the door to her bedchamber. Closing it firmly behind her, she pressed her back against it. Though she knew her slender weight could not keep her husband out if he was determined to force his way in, pride demanded she put up at least a token resistance if he did.

But he did not even try to follow her. After a long silence, she heard his footsteps move toward their son's room, then the muted murmur of voices.

Her legs gave way beneath her and she sank to the floor in a heap of wretched misery.

Chapter Eight

His wife's distraught outburst stirred up the stew of conflicting thoughts and feelings already seething inside Bennett.

Cool reason and practicality assured him it might be for the best if he took Caroline at her word and whisked Wyn back to London the moment he was able to travel. That way he would not have to worry about her making a scene when it came time for them to leave. And it was less likely the child would pine for her, as he'd begun to fear might happen.

But his sense of justice resisted. During the past several days, he had watched his wife trying to be the best possible mother to their son. It did not seem right that such a brave attempt should end like this.

As Caroline's door slammed shut between them, he was tempted to go after her, but he did not want to risk being alone with her again when emotions were running high. Ignoring one kiss had been awkward enough. Ignoring a second would be impossible.

Besides, Wyn might need him more right now, though he was far from certain of his ability to comfort and reassure his young son.

'Wyn?' He peered into the child's room. 'Your mother is very upset about something. Can you tell me what happened?'

For an instant, he saw no sign of the boy. Then he caught the sound of a faint sniffle coming from a lump beneath the bedclothes.

Bennett forced himself towards the bed and sank on to the edge of it. 'Son, I'm not angry with you, but I need to know.'

'I'm sorry, Papa.' Wyn's muffled voice emerged from under the covers. 'I was naughty. I shouted at Mama. I said I didn't like it here and I want to go home to Greggy.'

Surely that could not have upset Caroline so much. 'Was there anything else?'

Wyn's head slowly emerged from his cocoon. He responded to his father's question with a guilty whisper. 'I said she didn't love me because she wouldn't let me eat cake or go outside.'

'There now...' Gingerly, Bennett reached out and ran his hand over his son's head. It felt rather warm, perhaps from being buried under the covers.

Would the gesture help Wyn realise his father loved him, though he might not approve his behaviour? 'That wasn't a very kind thing to say to your mama, was it? Especially after she's tried so hard to keep you amused these past few days. I'm afraid you hurt her feelings'

'I'm sorry,' the child squeaked.

Stroking his son's hair seemed to help, so Bennett continued in spite of how self-conscious it made him feel. 'Luckily for you, your mother loves you no matter what you say or do. Though I still believe you owe her an apology.'

Wyn gave a silent nod.

Bennett seized upon something practical he could do for

his son. 'First let me fetch you something to eat. Not cake, but it might make you feel better all the same.'

After he had settled Wyn for the night, Bennett made another trip to the kitchen and returned upstairs bearing a bowl of Mrs Jenkins's mutton stew.

He tapped softly on Caroline's door, not wanting to wake her if she'd managed to fall asleep. She needed rest even more than food.

But a muted answer to his knock emerged from the room. 'Go away and let me be.'

Balancing the bowl in one hand, Bennett opened the door with the other and entered. The room was swathed in shadows, the only sounds intermittent drops of rain splattering against the window and the constant low murmur of the sea. 'You need to eat...and sleep. I don't believe you've done enough of either lately. It's no wonder you're worn out and easily upset.'

'I told you to go away.' Caroline rolled over in bed, turning her back on him. 'Haven't I done you enough harm? I'll have all the opportunity in the world to eat and sleep after you're gone.'

Bennett did not want to think about the harm she'd done him for fear it would reignite his anger. Instead, he found himself wondering what harm he might have done her. 'How am I supposed to persuade Wyn to eat if you won't? Come now, try a little of Mrs Jenkins's stew. The local mutton has a rather sweet flavour.'

'I'm not hungry! Why do you suddenly care whether I eat or not?'

What could he tell her when he did not know the answer to that question himself? 'Wyn doesn't seem to be falling ill again, though he is sorry for what he said to you. He wanted to come and apologize, but I thought that might not be the best thing for either of you tonight.'

When he received no reply, Bennett continued, 'He didn't mean it, you know. He's just frustrated at being shut in when there is so much he wants to see and do on the island.'

Caroline heaved a sigh and turned back towards him. 'I'm not angry at Wyn. I'm disgusted with myself for losing patience and not knowing how to handle him. Just like when he was a baby, everything I do is wrong. I was a fool to think I could be a good mother just because I want to.'

'What do you mean, *when Wyn was a baby?*' Bennett eased himself down on the edge of her bed.

'You don't remember?' A convulsive sound burst from her, something between a bitter chuckle and a sob of despair. 'I only wish I could forget. But what is the use in dredging all that up again? There is nothing I can do to change it now. It will only make me feel worse to dwell on it.'

Had he ever truly taken the time to listen to her or get to know her in more than a superficial way? Bennett's conscience demanded an accounting. What would he have found out if he had? Something that might have prevented that humiliating scene at Almack's, perhaps? Something that might have kept their marriage from crumbling?

Perhaps the smell of the stew tempted Caroline, after all. Or perhaps she'd decided the only way to get rid of him was to eat. Whichever was the case, she sat up and reached for the bowl of it.

When their hands touched, Bennett felt something stir inside him. It was a different sensation from the sparks of physical desire that had flared between them constantly since they'd been pushed into such intimate contact with one another.

The touch provoked a reaction from her as well. Not a pleasant one, judging by the way she wrenched the bowl away from him. 'If I promise to eat, will you go away?'

Her bargain tempted him, but deep down he knew he must not accept it. 'I haven't forgotten what a difficult time you had after Wyn was born. But everything got straightened out in the end.'

He felt almost as helpless now as he had then, flailing about for some solution to a problem beyond his understanding and experience. A problem that none of his practical actions would remedy.

Caroline heaved a ragged sigh. 'It got straightened out by taking my baby away and handing him over to someone who could care for him properly. That is what you need to do again.'

The bleak, hopeless pain in her voice compelled Bennett to defend his past actions. 'I thought you would be relieved to have someone else tend to the baby. His crying upset you so.'

'Of course it upset me! When he tried to suckle, it hurt so much I could hardly stand it. Then he would bawl until his little face turned purple. None of the doctors could tell why he cried so much except that it was my fault. I wasn't handling him properly. He wasn't getting enough milk. I was afraid he would *die* because I was such a wretched failure as a mother. I was relieved when he thrived with the wet nurse, but miserable, too, because it proved I *was* to blame.'

Bennett feared such bitter memories might make her weep again, but Caroline remained in control somehow. Or perhaps this hurt ran too deep for tears to ever wash away. And he had been responsible for inflicting that hurt upon her, shattering her already precarious confidence in her ability as a mother.

'I'm sorry, Caro.' In all their years together, had he ever once said that to her before? 'I didn't know what else to do. I felt so blasted helpless. The doctors kept saying the child needed nourishment and you needed rest. I thought you'd *want* someone else to look after the baby so motherhood wouldn't interfere with your social life.'

Caroline inhaled sharply, as if he'd struck her. 'I'm afraid you have it the wrong way around. I cultivated a busy social life as a diversion so I wouldn't miss my baby so much. When I was out in society, being flattered and fêted, I didn't feel quite so useless as I did at home.'

Cold nausea gripped Bennett deep in the belly. He'd had no idea she felt that way. Of course, he'd never bothered to ask, had he? Instead he'd privately blamed her for being a less-than-devoted mother. It had never occurred to him that a woman of her beauty and allure might doubt herself and seek from strangers the kind of fulfilment that eluded her in their marriage.

He could not deny her claim that their marriage had been a mistake. They were as ill suited a couple as he had ever met—complete opposites in so many ways. He was cautious where she was impulsive. He was steady and practical where she was an adventurous dreamer. He was serious and intense where she loved to tease and laugh…at least she once had.

Caroline was right about one other thing as well. Their marriage was *his* mistake. He'd been besotted with her almost from the moment they met. He'd wanted her, pursued her and gone to great lengths to win her. Too late, he'd learned the meaning of the old saying, *Marry in haste, repent at leisure.*

Could it be that he had tried to punish his wife not only for her mistakes, but for his as well? 'None of what happened was your fault, Caro. You'd had such a hard time bearing the baby and no experience nursing one. Surely it cannot be the sort of thing every woman is born knowing. You made mistakes. That is not failure.'

Bennett was not certain where his words of reassurance were coming from, or whether they would help. 'Failure is when you give up altogether. When you stop trying and stop caring. You never did that.'

Was it a good sign or a bad one that Caroline did not reply? At least she had not disagreed or bade him leave again. That gave him hope he was getting through to her somehow— saying things she needed to hear, even if they were five years too late in coming. 'You know how many setbacks the Abolition Movement has had over the years, how many mistakes have been made, opportunities lost. And yet we muddle on somehow and try not to lose sight of our goal. As long as we keep striving for it, I believe we will succeed in the end.'

Fine sentiments, his conscience protested. But how was Caroline supposed to keep trying to be the kind of mother she wanted to be when he was about to take her child away from her again?

When Caroline woke the next morning to find golden spring sunshine streaming through her bedroom window, her heart gave a hopeful bound. Then memories from the previous day washed over her, sinking her spirits again.

Wyn would soon be leaving Tresco and she had begged

Bennett to take him away. Now her son's last memory of her would be a terrible one. Would it reinforce his belief that she did not care about him? Or might he think she no longer wanted to be his mother because he had misbehaved? Much as her heart rebelled at that thought, she could not help wondering if Bennett had secretly blamed himself for his mother's desertion.

As she dragged herself out of bed to face the day, she thought back on her husband's late-night visit. Had it truly happened or had she only dreamed it? In some ways it seemed as improbable as any dream—her cool, guarded husband fetching her supper and urging her to talk about the most painful time in their marriage.

Reliving those wretched days and nights following Wyn's birth had been worse than any nightmare. Yet, somehow, confessing her frustration and inadequacy had brought an unexpected sense of release. Hearing Bennett admit to being almost as overwhelmed by events as she somehow lightened the burden of guilt she'd carried for so long. It gave her a certain belated comfort to know he had engaged the wet nurse and Mrs McGregor only because he could not think what else to do.

What surprised her most were the things Bennett had said about failure and not giving up. When his voice reached out of the darkness to enfold her in its deep, mellow cadence, she'd sensed that he judged her more mercifully than she judged herself. But his reference to the Abolition Movement reminded her of the damage she'd done to the cause.

When she'd finally dressed and rallied her composure to face the day, Caroline emerged from her bedchamber. Once out in the hallway she lingered there, not certain where to go or what to do. She heard the low murmur of voices from Wyn's room, but in spite of Bennett's assurances, she was still not convinced her son would want to see her again.

'Caro?' her husband called. 'Are you out there? Can you come in here for a moment, please?'

Wary of Wyn's reaction, she peeped in hesitantly.

'Mama!' the child cried when he caught sight of her, stretching his arms out in an unmistakable invitation to an embrace.

Though Bennett had told her Wyn was sorry for the way he'd behaved yesterday, Caroline still found it difficult to believe her young son harboured no resentment towards her. But here was proof she could not deny.

'Dearest boy!' Rushing to his bed, she scooped him into a fierce embrace.

When she glanced up briefly, she spied Bennett standing back watching them with an expression she could not identify. Satisfaction, perhaps...with an edge of longing?

'I'm sorry I hurt your feelings, Mama.' Wyn burrowed deeper into her arms, as if he feared she might try to push him away. 'I miss being home with Greggy, but I do like being here with you and Papa. I just wish I could go out.'

'I'm sorry, too, dearest, for losing patience with you.' Caroline pressed a kiss to the crown of her son's head.

'That's all right.' He sounded more like his cheerful self. 'Greggy scolds me when I'm naughty, too. Papa told me you would always love me no matter what I do or say. Is that true?'

She nodded. 'I'll tell you something else. Your papa will always love you that way, too.' She cast Bennett a challenging look. 'Won't you, my dear?'

He might not be comfortable expressing his feelings, but

he would have to start if he was going to have sole charge of their son.

'That's right.' The gruff assurance of his tone was tempered with genuine warmth.

Wyn finally seemed convinced of his mother's forgiveness enough to pull back from her embrace with an eager grin. 'Papa said I can go down to the parlour for a while, if you agree. He says we can have a picnic in front of the fire and he will teach me to play draughts. May I, Mama? Please!'

Why must it all depend on her consent? Caroline wondered. Was this Bennett's way of making certain their son would be grateful to her, after what had happened yesterday? 'It sounds like a fine idea to me.'

While Wyn cheered, she glanced over his head at her husband and mouthed the words, *Thank you.*

He acknowledged her gratitude with a self-conscious nod.

'There is one condition,' he informed Wyn. 'If your mother and I feel you are over-exerting yourself, you must promise to come back to bed without a lot of complaining.'

The child agreed readily. Caroline sensed he would have promised anything to be allowed out of bed for a while.

Perhaps because the previous day had been so fraught with tension, they all seemed to make a special effort to be agreeable to one another. The result was one of the most pleasant afternoons Caroline had enjoyed in a great while. How could an elaborately staged opera at the Haymarket compare with a lively round of charades that made Wyn fall about in fits of giggles? Even her solemn, high-minded husband managed to relax sufficiently to enter into the nonsensical spirit of the game. What was even more surprising, he appeared to enjoy himself.

The mild exertion seemed to stimulate Wyn's appetite. Or perhaps it was being permitted to eat something more tempting than bland invalid food. Whatever the reason, Caroline was relieved to see him eagerly consuming their indoor picnic lunch. Afterwards Bennett taught him to play draughts, as promised, while Caroline acted as her son's adviser, pointing out jumps he could make to capture his father's pieces.

Much as Wyn had enjoyed being out of bed and pleasurably occupied, it had tired him out. By evening, he could scarcely keep his eyes open long enough to get tucked in by his parents.

'Sweet dreams, dearest.' Caroline kissed him on each cheek, then wrapped him in a warm embrace.

It was a precious opportunity she'd feared she would never get again. She was so grateful to Bennett for making it possible that she could not summon even a flick of exasperation when he bid their son goodnight with only a brief pat on the head.

'I want to thank you for today,' she murmured as they crept out of Wyn's room. 'It felt like a gift I scarcely deserved.'

Bennett replied with a vaguely dismissive grunt as if to say it was nothing. Perhaps it had been nothing to him, but it meant so much to her.

'Would you mind coming back down to the parlour?' he asked. 'There is something I'd like to discuss with you that I did not wish to bring up in front of Wyn.'

'Yes, of course.'

His grave tone and brooding look made Caroline fear the

matter he wanted to discuss was something she would not care to hear. Was that why he had made such an effort to be agreeable today—to soften the blow?

Was he making the right decision? Bennett asked himself as he and Caroline returned to the parlour and took their places on opposite ends of the sofa. Without their son sitting between them, it seemed horribly awkward. It still wasn't too late to change his mind and return to his original plan. Once he informed Caroline, he would feel honour bound to go ahead in spite of his reservations.

'I hope you got a decent rest last night,' he blurted out the remark abruptly when the tense silence between them grew unbearable.

'Better than I had any right to expect,' she replied. 'Now please don't keep me in suspense. You're going to take Wyn back home tomorrow, aren't you?'

Caroline's question shattered his indecision as her wistful air called forth his protective instincts. Unlikely as it might seem, this beautiful, much-admired woman was a slave to her self-doubt and feelings of failure. She had made valiant efforts to escape, but they were cruel masters, always drawing her back into their thrall.

And he had helped place her in their power.

'Quite the contrary. I have decided he should stay longer. It is clear Wyn needs more time to recover before he is strong enough to undertake the journey back to London. Besides, if I take him away so soon after what happened yesterday, I fear he might think he was being punished, that you did not want him here any more because he misbehaved.' Bennett knew how the boy might feel because that was how he'd felt when his mother abandoned him all those years ago.

Caroline's painful wince told him she had experienced the private torment of such feelings, too.

'You're right.' She sounded surprised to find herself agreeing with him about anything. Or was she astonished to find him so sensitive to their young son's feelings? 'I cannot bear to have him think he is to blame for any of this. But aren't you needed back in Parliament?'

It was on the tip of his tongue to remind her that his allies in the Abolition Movement might be better off without him until the stench of scandal grew a little less pungent. But he refrained. He sensed she was sincerely sorry for whatever harm her behaviour might have done to her father's great cause. Perhaps that was what she meant when she'd claimed to have failed as a daughter.

'Heaven knows what mischief Sidmouth and Castlereagh will get up to in my absence.' Bennett strove to make light of it. 'But I am not quite so arrogant as to suppose the House of Lords cannot carry on its business without me for a few weeks.'

Caroline seemed astonished to hear him admit such a thing, even in jest.

'There is one more reason I want to postpone our return to London.' Bennett turned serious again. 'I believe you deserve another opportunity to be the kind of mother you want to be to Wyn.'

Caroline inhaled sharply, then opened her mouth, no doubt to remind him of what she considered her recent failure.

Before she could speak, he hastened to answer her objections. 'You won't be all on your own this time with no one to turn to, like you were when he was an infant. I promise to help you out and pass along any wise advice on child-rearing that I have picked up from Mrs McGregor over the years.'

Caroline caught her lower lip between her teeth. He sensed she was tempted by his offer, but afraid she would still make mistakes even with all the assistance and support he could provide. Somehow, he needed to shore up her badly shaken confidence.

'In return, I must ask for your help. You've made me realise I may not have been the kind of father Wyn deserves. I see now that he needs more open affection, though I am not convinced I have it in me to give in the way he requires. You make it look so effortless, but whenever I try, it feels forced and awkward.'

It had been easier when Wyn was ill. Exhaustion had weakened his defences and the child did not seem aware of his actions. Now that his son was on the mend, self-conscious reserve had frozen him again. If anyone could thaw him out, it was Caroline.

Staring into her beguiling blue-green eyes, Bennett felt a faint but persistent echo of the fascination that had gripped him the first time their gazes had locked over her father's dinner table.

But that was madness. They had been married for seven years, and both miserably discontented for most of that time. He knew that marrying her had been a mistake. The differences between them had widened to an unbridgeable gap. When he discovered her in Fitz Astley's arms, his humiliation and sense of betrayal had been accompanied by a secret whisper of relief that he finally had an honourable excuse to be rid of her.

But coming to this blasted island had changed all that. He'd glimpsed a side of his errant wife that he'd never seen before nor guessed she might possess. Against his will, it intrigued him. What was worse, he'd caught an unsettling glimpse of himself through her eyes. It challenged everything he'd long believed about himself.

Having mulled over his proposition, Caroline asked, 'So you think we can help each other become better parents?'

Bennett shrugged. 'That remains to be seen. But I believe we owe it to our son to try, don't you?'

'That is the least of what we owe him. How much longer do you plan to stay?'

'I thought perhaps…a month.' It came out sounding more like a question.

His wife made no effort to conceal her happiness at the prospect of another four weeks in the company of her child. But how did she feel about spending all that time in such close contact with her estranged husband? Bennett could not be certain.

A month away from Parliament seemed like a very long time, but it was far too short to repair a marriage that had taken seven years to destroy.

Chapter Nine

A whole month with her son and a fresh opportunity to make things right with him—how could she refuse such a generous offer? Yet Caroline feared she would still make mistakes, even with all the assistance and support Bennett could provide.

It puzzled her why he had proposed such a plan after what had happened yesterday. She sensed there was something more behind his decision than the sensible, practical reasons he'd given her, but she could not fathom what it might be.

Whatever his true motive, there was one thing they must discuss first. 'If we are going to share this little house for that long, we need to come to some understanding.'

Bennett raised one dark eyebrow. 'What sort of *understanding?*'

'Wyn ran away after he heard us arguing,' Caroline reminded him...and herself. 'Then when he had the fever, he talked about us not shouting at each other. If the past few days have taught us anything, it's that we both made our share of mistakes over the years.'

Staring off into the fire, Bennett gave a vague grunt that might have been agreement or chagrin.

'When Wyn first fell ill,' she continued, 'you said that blaming each other and ourselves for it would not make him better. You said we must concentrate instead on what we could do for him. I believe the best thing we can do for Wyn during the next month is to make every effort to get along with one another.'

Bennett glanced towards her suddenly, his look almost accusing. 'I was so done in, I hardly recall anything I said the whole time. I'm amazed you can.'

Her first impulse was to resent his tone and deliver a stinging reply, but that contradicted the very point she was trying to make.

Though it was not easy to put aside the habits of many years and give a soft answer, Caroline knew she must try. 'I remember, because what you said made me feel better and helped me do what Wyn needed.'

Her reply appeared to catch Bennett off guard, as if he'd drawn his pistol only to discover it had no ammunition. 'Well…that's good. Do you propose we stop blaming each other for all the…*mistakes* we made in our marriage? Spend the whole month pretending they never happened?'

It was clear he doubted they could do it, perhaps questioned the wisdom of even trying. After all, focusing upon each other's failings had long made it easier for them to justify their own less-than-admirable behaviour.

'Do you have a better idea?' Caroline strove to keep any bite of sarcasm from her words, offering only a sincere question and willingness to listen if he proposed an alternative. 'In the end I suppose it comes down to whether we love our son more than we hate each other.'

Not that she *hated* her husband, Caroline conceded privately.

Her marriage and her life might have been easier if she could have felt that way about him. Then he would not have had so much power to hurt her—the kind of power she was determined never to give him again.

Bennett considered her proposition. His handsome face might have been a wax mask for all the feeling it betrayed. His inscrutable dark eyes had never guarded the secrets of his heart more resolutely.

Finally he extended one large, powerful hand towards her. 'You have a bargain. This coming month, for our son's sake, we will put on a performance of marital harmony worthy of Edmund Kean and Sarah Siddons!'

Caroline hesitated for an instant before grasping his hand, steeling herself against the tingling sensation she knew his touch would provoke. Though she was pleased Bennett had agreed to her plan, she must remember that any attention he paid her during the next month would be an act and nothing more.

This was all meant to be an act, Bennett reminded himself during the next two days, as their son was allowed out of bed but remained housebound. He had long been skilled at disguising his true feelings—appearing calm when he was seething with anger, indifferent when he was grieving, aloof when he was passionately attracted. It was a different matter altogether to display emotion of any kind, let alone emotion he did not feel. Yet, as he watched Caroline make such a determined effort to be a better mother to their son, he found it perilously easy to act as if he cared about his errant wife.

The first real test of their temporary alliance came three days later. Wyn had been content at first with simply being allowed out of bed and permitted to eat the same meals as his parents. But before long he began to chafe at the restriction of being kept indoors, insisting he was recovered enough to go on an outing. Bennett and Caroline finally agreed to take him on one the following day, only to have the weather suddenly turn foul.

'I want to go out!' Wyn cried when he was told they would have to postpone their excursion.

'But it's raining, dearest.' Caroline strove to pacify the child. 'Remember how ill it made you the last time you went out in the rain.'

'But you promised.' Wyn pressed his nose against the parlour window. 'Can't we go to the Blockhouse? It's just over there. We wouldn't get very wet going only that little way.'

Bennett sensed his wife was beginning to waver. It seemed she could not bear to have their son vexed with her. Did it remind her of those long, lonely, exhausting nights when Wyn was an infant screaming in her arms, resisting her efforts to nurse him? Bennett acknowledged that he had not given her the support she'd needed then. It was an omission for which he now felt compelled to atone, while he had the chance.

'Perhaps we can go there tomorrow…' Caroline wrapped her arm around the child's shoulders '…if the weather improves.'

Wyn refused to be consoled. 'You said we could go today. It's not fair!'

A look of annoyance mixed with chagrin twisted Caroline's comely features at hearing her own frequent complaint hurled back at her by her fractious little son. She cast Bennett a pleading glance.

Not long ago, he would have taken a certain vindictive satisfaction in seeing her get a taste of her own medicine. But Wyn's illness and its aftermath had shown him a side of parenting he'd never experienced before. If he had to put up with much more of Wyn's bad temper, he might seek any possible excuse to escape the house. He could only imagine a squalling infant must have been a hundred times worse.

Now Caroline was appealing to him for help and he could not let her down as he had in the past.

'If you insist on going out today,' he addressed their son in a firm tone that he hoped was not too severe, 'I suppose your mother and I cannot stand in your way.'

Caroline's eyes widened in a look of dismay as she silently mouthed the word, *No!*

Bennett met her anxious gaze with one that begged her to trust him.

'But remember,' he warned Wyn, 'if you catch another chill and fall ill again, you will have to stay in bed a great many more days, drinking a great many more cups of yarrow tea.'

His son's small face creased in a frown of deep concentration as he weighed the possible consequences. Clearly deciding it was not worth the risk, he heaved a pathetic sigh. 'I'm never going to get to see the island.'

'Of course you are,' Bennett replied, proud of his son for making the prudent choice. 'And you need to be prepared.'

'Prepared how?' The child sounded dubious.

'Well...I was planning to take you up on the heath to fly a kite—there's always a good stiff breeze blowing. But first we will need to make a kite for us to fly. Would you like to help me?'

'A kite?' Wyn brightened. 'Oh, yes, Papa!'

* * *

The cook offered to let Wyn help her bake while his parents scoured the house for kite-making materials.

As they headed up to the attic, Caroline said, 'That was quite a risk you took telling Wyn we wouldn't stop him going out. What would you have done if he'd called your bluff?'

'I don't know,' Bennett admitted with a shrug. 'Appealed to you to rescue me, perhaps. I'm relieved it didn't come to that. Consider it a lesson in setting limits without seeming like a tyrant: Give him choices when you can. But either make one choice much more attractive or give him a choice between two things, either of which you can tolerate.'

'I like that.' Caroline gave a nod of approval. 'Though there is a certain deviousness about it that I would not have expected from you.'

Her voice carried a teasing note, which he might once have resented. Today it only made him grin. 'An unfortunate consequence of my frequent dealings with politicians.'

Caroline laughed as she opened a large brass-bound trunk and began rifling through it. Bennett had not heard her laughter in quite some time. He'd forgotten how sweet and melodious it sounded. Having succeeded in coaxing it from her brought him a curious sense of satisfaction.

In a corner of the attic, behind a rolled-up rug, Bennett found several pieces of thin wooden strapping. He held them up in triumph. 'These should do nicely for the kite frame. Now it is your turn to provide me with a lesson about how I can show Wyn more affection.'

She dug deeper into the trunk. Was it a deliberate effort to hide her face from him? 'I have a feeling you know what to do, if only you wouldn't stop yourself from doing it when the opportunity arises.'

'That is not terribly helpful.'

'You want rules and procedures for showing love?' Caroline peeped out at him from behind the trunk lid. 'Very well, then. Rule one—scowl less and smile more. Is *that* helpful?'

'Very much.' His wry grin blossomed into a full-blown smile. 'Have you any more nuggets of wisdom to impart?'

'I would not want to overwhelm you with too many lessons at once,' Caroline answered with feigned solemnity. 'Let us see how you get on practising this one before we move on to more advanced skills such as holding hands.'

Though he chuckled at the quip, Bennett could not deny the eagerness that reared in him at the prospect of practising that particular skill with her.

'Look here,' she cried, holding up a large scrap of golden-yellow cloth. 'Fine silk. There isn't enough to make anything else, but plenty for a kite. And what's this?'

The question drew Bennett to her side. That, and an unaccountable hankering to be near her.

From the bottom of the trunk, Caroline lifted out a small wooden casket with the image of a rose cleverly carved into the lid. She opened it to reveal some old coins and fragments of jewellery. Though Bennett could tell that none was of any particular value, they still gave the illusion of a small treasure hoard.

'None of this will be any good for your kite.' Caroline let a tarnished silver chain trickle through her fingers back into the box. 'If we had a daughter, I think she would have been happy to stay indoors for days on end, dressing up in some of these old clothes and playing make believe.'

A whisper of yearning in her voice made Bennett ask, 'Did you ever wish we'd had a daughter instead of a son?'

'I would not trade Wyn for a hundred daughters.' With a hard snap Caroline shut the casket. 'But I did once think that if we'd had a daughter first, we would have been obliged to keep on trying for an heir.'

Her reluctant admission reminded Bennett of other references she'd made to their son being his heir. The implication provoked a response from him before he had time to censor it. 'You thought the reason I didn't get you with child again was because I was satisfied at having bred an heir?'

'Of course.' Caroline replaced the wooden casket at the bottom of the trunk. 'Why else?' She didn't sound angry about it. Only resigned...and rather saddened.

This was not the time to air such contentious issues, Bennett reminded himself. They had agreed to forget any problems between them and pretend all was well. But wasn't that what they'd been trying to do throughout their marriage, without success? By contrast, he recalled recent times when they'd lowered their guard and confided in one another. He had never felt closer to Caroline, not even in the deepest throes of passion.

'Because...' it was too late for him to back out now '...I didn't want to put you...and me...through that whole ordeal again. At least not right away. Then later I didn't think you wanted any more children.'

Slowly Caroline closed up the old trunk. 'Which you concluded because I wasn't paying enough attention to the child we already had.'

Bennett gave a halting nod. He wasn't proud of the harsh misjudgements he'd made about her over the years. 'I would have quite liked a little daughter. I might have found it easier to show *her* affection.'

'Perhaps.' A subtle inflection in Caroline's voice betrayed her grave doubts. 'As long as a son was born soon afterwards. Otherwise....'

Her words trailed off as she rose and brushed the dust off her skirts.

'Otherwise what? Do you think I am so hardhearted that I would have held the child to blame for being a girl?'

'Not to *blame*...exactly...' Caroline's hand moved over the folded piece of silk she held in a restless caress. 'But you would have been disappointed. And that disappointment would have influenced your feelings.'

Would it? Bennett wanted to protest otherwise with the utmost vigour. But when he recalled how he had let the experiences of his past affect his feelings towards *her,* he found it harder to defend himself.

Why had Bennett brought up that wretched subject? Caroline strove to push their conversation from her thoughts while the two of them helped Wyn construct his kite, but the memories stalked the edges of her mind, waiting for any lapse in concentration to pounce.

Somehow she and Bennett contrived to keep their son amused through that long rainy day. As soon as they'd tucked him in for the night, she quickly slipped away to her bedroom before Bennett asked any more questions she could not bear to answer. But with no one and nothing to distract her, she could not keep from going over and over their earlier conversation.

Talking about fathers and daughters had revived unwelcome

memories of her girlhood. It also saddened her to realise that her failure to be a good mother to Wyn had convinced Bennett she would not want any more children. When she questioned the effect another baby might have had upon their family, she was torn between hope and fear. Hope, that she might have learned from her mistakes and been able to be a better mother the second time. Fear, that she would have failed again, compounding her guilt and making their present situation even worse.

In hindsight, Caroline recognised one consolation she'd scarcely noticed at the time for which she was now deeply grateful. It was the knowledge that Bennett had *not* abandoned her bed because he was satisfied to have bred a healthy heir on a wife he no longer desired. Instead, her husband had denied himself the pleasure of her favours because he did not want to put her through the ordeal of bearing more children.

If only she'd known his true motives at the time, would it have made a difference? Might they have been able to salvage their marriage before it was irreparably broken?

Tantalising glimpses of what might have been had flitted in and out of her dreams that night, yet somehow Caroline still woke feeling rested and renewed. Perhaps it was the return of the sunshine that lifted her spirits, she mused as she rose from her bed that morning and glanced out her window.

Just as Bennett had predicted, a fine breeze was blowing. There should be nothing to keep Wyn housebound today. They would be able to take him out kite flying, keeping him happily occupied with far less effort than it had required in recent days.

* * *

'How soon can we go out, Mama?' the child demanded when she went to get him dressed for the day.

'We'll need to eat breakfast first.' She helped him out of his nightshirt and into his white skeleton suit and blue jacket. 'After that we'll see what your papa says.'

'But I'm not hungry,' Wyn protested. 'I want to go now before the wind dies down or it starts to rain again.'

Caroline sympathised with her son's fear that something might come along to spoil his fun yet again. But she could not let him go on his first outing since his illness with an empty stomach. She feared they were in for another upsetting argument. Then she recalled the advice Bennett had given her about choices.

Surely it was worth a try. 'Would you rather have porridge for your breakfast or a boiled egg and toast?'

Just then she glimpsed Bennett peeping into the room. He gave an approving nod to the choice she'd offered Wyn.

The child hesitated for a moment, then answered in a rather put-upon tone, 'Egg and toast.'

'That sounds like a fine breakfast for kite-fliers,' said Bennett as he stepped into the room. 'I believe I shall have the same.'

When Wyn spun around to greet his father, Caroline prompted her husband with an exaggerated grin. He took her cue, arching the corners of his mouth upwards in a smile that looked quite sincere.

Together they headed for the kitchen. Wyn's feet hardly touched the stairs as he raced down them. When Mrs Jenkins served breakfast, the child bolted his portion in his eagerness to be off. His parents ate theirs more slowly, but did not dawdle over their tea in deference to his impatience.

A few minutes later they followed their son as he scrambled up the rise behind the house, clutching his colourful kite.

'You did a fine job,' Bennett praised Caroline, 'putting my lesson about choices into practice with Wyn.'

His tone of respect heartened her, though she did not feel the desperate craving for his approval she had once had. In her own heart, she knew she'd done well and that nurtured a precious feeling of capability. So did the realisation that there were lessons she could teach him—lessons that would benefit their son. 'So did you with your smile.'

'Do you think I am ready to move on to more advanced skills?' Before she knew what was happening, Bennett reached out and took her hand in his. 'I reckon myself a quick study.'

Her start of surprise made him smile. Caroline's insides fluttered as breathlessly as the very first time he'd smiled at her.

'I meant our son's hand.' She nodded towards Wyn, but made no effort to extract her fingers from her husband's firm, warm grasp.

Bennett shrugged. 'I thought it might be better to practise on you first. That way you can evaluate my technique and offer suggestions for improvement.'

'It is quite good, actually.' She concentrated on the sensation of his touch but strove to suppress the intense reaction it kindled in her. 'Not too tight, but not too tentative either.'

'So I'd receive a passing grade, would I?'

She nodded. 'On your smile, too. The light of it has travelled up to your eyes.'

'Fancy that?' Bennett chuckled. 'I made no deliberate effort. It happened of its own accord.'

Had she coaxed that eye-shining smile from him? The possibility brought Caroline a sweet sense of accomplishment. Caution tried to warn her that Bennett was only doing this for their son's sake and that their marriage would soon be over. Guilt tried to remind her of the unforgivable harm she had done to his pride and his cause. But the power of his grasp anchored her firmly in the present moment.

'If you give a gentle squeeze now and then,' she demonstrated, 'it is like a private message of affection.'

As soon as she'd done it, Caroline worried Bennett might take the squeeze as an indication of her feelings for him, but his reaction assured her otherwise.

'I believe I can manage that.' When he returned her hand squeeze, he seemed to concentrate on duplicating the precise force and duration of hers. 'The more private the better. It is open declarations of affection that give me the most trouble.'

'Were you always that way, even as a child?' Caroline tried to picture him as a little boy before his mother disappeared from his life so abruptly. The innkeeper's wife had claimed the countess doted on her son. Surely that must have meant kisses and cuddles and sweet maternal endearments.

Bennett kept his eyes fixed on *their* son, now standing on top of the low hill, clutching his kite against the greedy tug of the wind. Was he picturing himself in this familiar spot all those years ago?

At last he spoke, as if dredging up memories that had lain buried for a long time. 'My mother was very…generous with her affections. Far too generous, apparently. After I learned what she had done, it made me doubt the sincerity of all her petting and sweet words.'

Not only his mother's, Caroline sensed, but all displays of affection. It still troubled her that he had questioned the sincerity of her feelings for Wyn. But since she understood the source of his doubts, they no longer stung so much.

She gave his hand another light squeeze, this time not as a demonstration.

Chapter Ten

They spent a whole glorious morning launching Wyn's kite in a stiff Scillonian breeze, then watching it glide and swoop through the sky.

Bennett was beginning to wonder if Wyn had had enough excitement for one day when a sudden powerful gust of wind jerked the kite, making the string snap.

'Oh, no!' Wyn's eyes filled with tears as he watched his plaything lofted high in the air and blown off towards the neighbouring island of St Martin's.

'Don't fret. We can always make you another kite.' Bennett strove to cheer his son as he wound the remaining string back around the spool.

His brisk reassurance did not seem to comfort the child.

Caroline dropped to her knees in front of Wyn and gathered him into her arms. 'There, now. It is sad to lose something that has given you so much fun. I wonder where your kite will come down? In Cornwall, perhaps, or do you suppose it might fly all the way to Wales? Some boy or girl there might find it caught in a tree and wonder where it came from. They might patch up its tears and tie on a new string.'

By now Wyn seemed less upset about his lost kite and more absorbed in his mother's story. Bennett could not help but admire her skill at offering healing sympathy while providing an amusing diversion. To think he had spent so many years blind to her unique talents.

'When the kite has had its spell of fun in Wales—' Caroline rose to her feet and took Wyn by the hand '—it may break free again and fly away to...'

'France,' Wyn suggested. 'Papa once showed me where it is in the atlas. I want to visit there some day.'

'To France it is.' Caroline caught Bennett's eye, then darted a pointed glance toward Wyn's free hand, signalling that the time had come to practise his latest lesson in affectionate fathering. 'And as it swoops and soars through the sky over England on its way there, people will look up and wonder if it is a small piece of the sun that broke off and fell to earth.'

As she continued to spin her tale of the kite that flew around the world, Bennett offered Wyn his hand. The child grinned up at him and seized it eagerly. Then the three of them headed back down the hill together. The sweet sense of family harmony persisted until they reached the house and Bennett told Wyn he should take a nap.

'But I'm not tired.' The child's petulant tone assured his father of quite the opposite. 'Please, Mama, can't you take me down to the beach instead?'

Though she looked reluctant to disappoint the boy, Caroline surprised Bennett by supporting his decision. 'Papa is right, Wyn. You need plenty of rest so you don't fall ill again. Perhaps we can go down to the beach after you wake up.'

Faced with his parents' united front, Wyn gave in grudgingly, but fell asleep within minutes of lying down.

* * *

He woke later in a much better humour, so they took him down to the beach be0tween the Old Blockhouse and Rushy Point. Something about the murmur of the surf caressing the sand seemed to reach inside Bennett and loosen his tightly clenched defences, making him forget all the disappointments and frustrations of the past few years. In this moment, there was only his little family, together in a way they had never been before.

The next several hours passed every bit as enjoyably as their morning of kite flying. As they built an elaborate sandcastle, Caroline laughed and larked about in a way Bennett had not heard in a very long time. It was not the artificial high spirits she displayed at assemblies and pleasure gardens, but a natural exuberance that appealed to him too much for his peace of mind.

Only when they headed home for supper did she glance down at her skirts and notice the ruin she'd made of them. 'Parker is sure to complain, but I don't care. It would be worth a hundred gowns to hear Wyn chatting away so happily and...'

'And?' Bennett prompted her.

'And...to play like a child again myself,' she replied after a brief hesitation that told him she'd meant to say something else instead. 'My parents used to take me to the seaside when I was very young. I remember games and stories and laughter. After my mother died, Father hired a succession of strict, solemn governesses to care for me. They possessed a finely honed talent for taking all the joy out of life.'

Had she been trying ever since to recapture that joy, Bennett wondered—at the theatre, pleasure gardens and assemblies? Had she sought to give their son a taste of what she had so desperately missed?

Caroline seemed to realise she'd said more than she meant to for she hastened to change the subject. 'The waves are so much closer than they were when we started building our castle. I suppose it will not be long until they wash it away altogether.'

The wistful note in her voice made Bennett wish he could offer her some comfort, but he did not share her singular skill. Even if he had, how could he deny the truth? By this time tomorrow there would be nothing left to show that their castle had ever been.

'If it's something lasting you want,' he suggested, 'I have an idea. But it will have to wait until our next outing.'

'Next outing?' Those words brought Wyn running over from where he'd been making patterns with his footprints in the sand. 'Where are you going to take us, Papa?'

'Do you remember me telling you about Gimble Porth?' Bennett pointed towards the high ground behind the house where they'd flown Wyn's kite. 'It is a cove on the other side of that ridge. Lots of seashells wash up there, and at low tide you can see the outlines of enclosed fields and buildings that were lost beneath the sea.'

The child's eyes grew big and round. 'I'd like to visit that Gimble place. Doesn't it sound good, Mama?'

'It does indeed.' She pulled their son close and gave his hair an affectionate ruffle that stirred a faint pang of envy in Bennett.

As they made their way back to the house, hand in hand

again, Wyn heaved a sigh of surpassing contentment. 'This has been the *best* day—all three of us having fun together.'

Over their son's head, Bennett's gaze sought, met and held Caroline's. Some deep, wordless communication seemed to pass between them about how a difficult task could yield unexpected rewards.

It gave Caroline a foolish pang of regret to think how the incoming tide must have washed away their lovely sandcastle.

The next day, as she, Bennett and Wyn headed back up the ridge behind the house, she could not help comparing that sandcastle with the home they were making here on the island. Time and events would soon demolish it, too. But while it lasted, she was determined to hoard up happy memories to sustain her in the years ahead.

When they reached the crest, the three of them paused for a moment to look down on the horseshoe-shaped bay, sheltered by steep dunes. It had a wide strip of white sandy beach at the centre, but the shore on either side was thickly strewn with rocks.

'What are all those places?' Wyn gazed out towards the many large rocks and small islands jutting out of the sea.

'That nearest island is Northwethel. Beyond it is St Helen's.' Bennett pointed to each in turn. 'Over that way is Tean. Farther in the distance is St Martin's.'

'Can we visit them all?'

'Some day, perhaps,' Bennett replied. 'For now, we have Gimble Porth to explore. Let's go find out what seashells the tide has washed up.'

Together they collected many shells of every different shape and size.

'What is this one, Papa?' Wyn asked over and over as he added some new specimen to his collection.

'I am no naturalist.' Bennett examined the latest addition carefully. 'I must buy you a book on the subject. But look how this one is nearly the same shape as those other two, only wider at the base.'

As she watched her husband and son together, Caroline saw they shared more of a bond than she'd realised. Bennett was clearly committed to fulfilling his fatherly responsibilities with his accustomed diligence—teaching Wyn new things, encouraging him to question and explore. Now that he understood the development of their son's heart was as important as that of his mind, she sensed he would do everything possible to foster that, too…no matter how difficult.

When the child's interest in shells began to wane, Bennett suggested they pile some of the stones to make a cairn. 'It will be harder work to build than our sandcastle and the result not nearly so handsome. But the sea will not wash it away in a single night either.'

'Why are these stones all round?' asked Wyn.

Bennett rolled a large one over to make part of the base. 'Probably from the action of the waves washing over them, year in and year out. All this sand you see is made from the tiny specks of rock that have been worn away.'

'Fancy that.' Caroline marvelled at the results subtle, patient action could accomplish given enough time. 'What can I do to help with your construction?'

As he hefted another stone into place, Bennett nodded towards the water. 'You could fetch some wet sand to act as mortar.'

He was right about this being harder work than building a

sandcastle, she reflected as the tower of stones slowly took shape. But the result was not without its own rugged, enduring appeal. Was it really too late for them to rebuild a strong, lasting marriage on the site of the fragile illusion that had been washed away?

By the time they had finished, their cairn stood almost as tall as Wyn, who seemed very proud of what they'd built together.

'The tide is at its lowest ebb,' said Bennett. 'If we climb up to the top of the rise again, we should be able to see those submerged fields and buildings I told you about.'

The promise of such sights sent Wyn scrambling up the bank at once.

Caroline dusted the dried sand off her hands, surprised to find how soft and smooth it left them.

'Was that your way of getting our son halfway back to the house without a battle?' she asked Bennett with a teasing chuckle.

'It worked well, didn't it?' He looked vastly pleased with himself. 'That was a trick I picked up from Mrs McGregor.'

He extended his hand to help her up the bank. She took it, bracing herself for the unsettling rush of sensation that swept up her arm.

A few moments later, as they looked down on the waters of the bay, she marvelled at all the different shades of blue. 'Could that be part of an enclosure?'

'I believe so.' Bennett hoisted Wyn on to his shoulders for a better view. 'See how that line of stones meets the other one so squarely? That is the work of man, not chance.'

Caroline gave a little shiver. 'It feels eerie and a little sad.

Think of all that work to build, only to be claimed by the sea. I wonder if it was one great flood or if the waters inched up year by year as gradually as the tide goes out or the stones get worn away.'

This drowned landscape reminded her of their marriage. The scandalous incident at Almack's had been the sudden flood that swept it away. But any bond of trust that might have saved it had been slowly eroded long before. If there could be any possibility of reclaiming what they'd lost, surely the first step must be trying to understand what had gone wrong between them.

She knew some of it…or thought she did. But Bennett's surprising disclosure of the true reason he'd abandoned her bed made her question how many of her long-held assumptions about her marriage were correct. Discovering the truth would require talking over a great many sensitive subjects with her husband. The prospect did not appeal to her—she feared it might spoil their pretence of harmony. She knew Bennett would like it even less, for he had often remarked how pointless it was to dwell on past events that were beyond their power to change.

But she was not seeking to alter the *past* by talking it over, Caroline reminded herself. Rather, it was the present and the future she hoped to set on a new course. As for their feigned felicity, surely it was worth risking for the chance to experience true happiness.

Bennett lifted Wyn down from his shoulders and set the child on his feet.

Wyn rubbed his belly. 'I'm so hungry.'

'Building and beachcombing will give you an appetite,' said Caroline. 'Not to mention the sea air. We should have brought a picnic lunch with us. Why don't you go on ahead and ask Mrs Jenkins for a biscuit to stay your stomach until dinner?'

The child evidently liked that idea, for he set off at once, moving much faster than his mother was comfortable walking on the uneven ground.

Bennett must have sensed her misgivings, for he offered her his arm. She was more than happy to accept, for a number of reasons. 'Thank you for another splendid outing. I enjoyed myself thoroughly. It reminded me of the day you took me boating on the Thames. Do you remember?'

'How could I forget?' He gave a rumble of gruff laughter. 'I blistered my hands raw on those beastly oars.'

'We were happy then, though, weren't we?' She slanted a glance towards him, anxiously watching for his reaction. 'When did we lose that?'

Bennett's features tensed, along with the muscles of his arm. Would he remind her that it had been *her* idea to put the past behind them?

To her surprise he answered in a murmur of wistful regret, 'I believe you're confusing happiness with pleasure.'

So she had *never* made him happy, not even during their brief, intense courtship or the early days of their marriage? Caroline bit down hard on her lip to stifle a whimper of pain.

Then some perverse misery-craving impulse urged her to speak. 'I thought it started when I didn't get with child right away. Every month that went by, the distance between us seemed to grow. Once I got pregnant our marriage seemed better...for a while.'

She'd hoped that once she fulfilled her prime duty as a wife, Bennett would care for her again. But the birth of their son had shattered that foolish, fragile dream.

'That had nothing to do with it!' The fierce denial broke from Bennett's lips. 'It wouldn't have made any difference if you'd fallen pregnant on our honeymoon. We grew apart because we are so different from one another. We see the world differently, we want different things. It is no one's fault—not yours, certainly. That's just the way we are.'

It wasn't her fault. As welcome a thought as that should have been, it brought Caroline little comfort.

'Perhaps if I'd had more experience of such matters,' Bennett continued, 'or if I hadn't been so besotted, I might have seen that no good could come of a marriage between two such opposites.'

'No good?' She wrenched her hand from his arm with such force that it almost made her stumble. 'Our son came from this marriage and he is by far the best thing in my life!'

As she dashed the last few steps to the kitchen door, Caroline strove to calm and conceal her overwrought emotions so she would not cast a shadow over her son's happiness. She'd hoped that discovering what had gone wrong with her marriage might help her find a way to correct it. But it turned out the problem was not what she'd done but who she was. How could she possibly *fix* that? She could not change who she was and she certainly could not hope to change Bennett.

Or could she?

How could he have made such a colossal blunder, speaking as if their son did not matter when nothing could be further from the truth? Bennett added another black mark to the tally against him. It was growing far too long for his peace of mind.

Over and over during their marriage, he'd made Caroline

feel as if she'd failed him. When she did not conceive right away. When she had trouble nursing. When he'd stopped coming to her bed. Could those things have been the reasons she claimed to have failed him as a wife? He'd been certain she was referring to the scandal at Almack's.

As they ate dinner, he marvelled how Caroline could behave as if nothing had happened, while he could not get her earlier stricken look out of his mind. Caution urged him to take his cue from her and try to forget what had happened. They had made that bargain, after all, and he did not want to risk an angry confrontation like the one that might have cost them their son. But since then they had begun to find ways to talk about sensitive subjects without provoking hostility. They hadn't always succeeded in resolving problems—today, for instance. Yet afterwards he often felt as if he understood Caroline, or himself, a little better.

After they'd put Wyn to bed that night, Bennett asked, 'Would you like to have a cup of tea? We could play at cards... or talk.'

'Talk?' Caroline sounded as if he'd proposed using her for an archery target.

'Just talk.' He tried to make it sound unthreatening. 'Without the risk of certain small ears overhearing.'

She considered his request, then gave a tentative smile. 'Very well. Tea and talk.'

A short while later, they sat opposite one another at a small table in the corner of the parlour, sipping their tea in self-conscious silence.

'Was there something particular you wanted to talk *about?*' Caroline prompted him at last.

Bennett nodded. He'd found it a good deal easier to talk in brief snatches while their son was out of earshot. 'I want to apologise for my remark this afternoon. It was quite thoughtless and I never meant for it to come out the way it did. I wasn't thinking of Wyn when I said nothing good could come from a marriage of two such opposites. I was only trying to assure you that the troubles between us were not all your fault.'

She hadn't failed him by taking almost a year to conceive their son or having trouble nursing the baby after he was born. Even the scandal with Astley was not to blame, as bitter a blow as it had dealt his pride. Their marriage had floundered long before that night at Almack's.

Where was the rush of indignant anger he should be feeling? Bennett wondered as he recalled the wrenching moment that had delivered the death blow to their marriage. Where was the bitterness of betrayal and the sickening sense of humiliation? He strove to summon them, only to find his heart empty of everything but disappointment and regret.

'I understand.' Caroline took a sip of her tea. 'I should not have made such a fuss. I knew what you meant.'

Her answer seemed to lift a weight from his shoulders. 'That is my point precisely. Throughout our marriage our differences have led us to misjudge one another, to misinterpret everything the other says and does, always jumping to the worst conclusions.'

She gave a rueful nod. 'I have been guilty of that.'

'No more than I.'

The way she looked at him, Bennett sensed there was something else very important that she was *not saying,* leaving it for him to work out on his own. How could she expect that, after all the years he'd failed to understand her?

Just as he was beginning to get an inkling of what she might mean, Caroline deftly nudged the conversation in a less awkward direction. 'Thank heaven we are learning to be a better father and mother than we were husband and wife. What is my next lesson about managing Wyn?'

Bennett thought for a moment. 'I was going to stress the importance of maintaining a united front. But you seem to have picked that up on your own. Well done.'

It gratified him to see how that little scrap of praise made her smile and blush. He fought a sudden urge to take her hand, lean across the table and kiss her. Not a kiss of sometimes hostile desire that he'd often wanted in the past. But a kiss of...what?

Contrition? Encouragement? Camaraderie?

Perhaps Caroline sensed the feelings he could not fathom, for she lowered her gaze and fiddled with her tea cup, turning it this way and that on the saucer. 'I do want to learn. So tell me what lesson comes after that.'

Was she trying to distract him from his dangerous impulses? The least he could do was make the same effort. Rallying his willpower, Bennett turned his thoughts away from the lure of those sweet lips. 'You need to make it clear to Wyn what the consequences of his actions will be.'

'Like you did the day he wanted to go out in the rain?' She lifted her gaze again to regard him as if he were the cleverest man alive. 'That would be an excellent lesson for Wyn to learn. I wish someone had instilled it in me when I was younger, instead of simply forbidding me to do what I wanted. It only made me rebellious and determined to have my way in spite of them...no matter what the consequences.'

A look of remorse clouded her features and he knew they

were both thinking about Fitz Astley. She had not anticipated the consequences of her behaviour that night at Almack's and Bennett had goaded her into defiance by treating her with less respect than he would have shown a child.

His conscience added another black mark against him.

'What more do you have to teach *me?*' he asked. The tasks had not been too difficult so far, but he feared they would soon become harder.

'You've nearly mastered the art of smiling.' Her quip coaxed one from him with almost no effort at all. 'And your hand-holding is progressing quite well. Now you need to move on to other forms of touch—a pat on the shoulder, ruffling his hair, an embrace, a kiss. I know they're hard for you because they remind you of your mother.'

'It isn't just that.' Bennett made himself reply quickly before his defences could stifle his confession. Caroline might not realise it, but what he was about to say amounted to an offering of atonement. 'I've been giving the matter some thought and I believe it has to do with how little affection I received from my father. Also the way I was made to suppress feelings of fear and sadness and...longing after my mother went away.'

He glimpsed a flicker of insight in the blue-green depths of Caroline's eyes. 'But there's something I don't understand. You were never hesitant about...kissing and caressing me when we were first married.'

The reminder roused his barely curbed desire. 'That was different. Passion is a strong, vital feeling. In some ways it is more akin to anger than to soft sentiments like affection and tenderness.'

Caroline gave a slow, rueful nod that troubled him almost as much as the way his breath was racing and his pulse pounding. Part of him wanted her back even when reason decreed any hope of reconciliation was futile. Bennett recognised the fierce craving he'd felt the first time she had smiled at him across her father's tea table. But he could not fathom why it had returned to bedevil him at the worst possible time.

Was it because he could not bear to surrender *anything* to Fitz Astley? Was it because winning Caroline back represented an impossible challenge he could not resist? Was it the same cursed stubbornness that kept him tilting at the windmill of slavery?

Bennett mistrusted what he did not understand, particularly after it had cost him so dearly in the past.

Almost as much as it had cost Caroline.

Chapter Eleven

Was Bennett capable of caring for her in the way she needed, even if he could be persuaded to try?

That thought haunted Caroline for the next several days as Wyn grew stronger and they gradually ventured farther afield in their outings. After they put him to bed in the evenings, they would sometimes go for a walk or drink tea or play cards. During that time, it seemed as if they had talked more than in their whole marriage. At least they talked more about things that mattered.

Chief among those was their son. They shared more advice about how to give Wyn the attention and affection he needed without overindulging him. Caroline was delighted to discover how well some of Bennett's suggestions worked. Every day, Wyn seemed easier to handle, less apt to fuss when he didn't get his way, more patient to wait for what he wanted.

There was one outing, however, that he still seemed especially keen to undertake. Every evening at bedtime, he asked, 'Can we please go visit the castles tomorrow?'

And every evening his parents replied that they would see how he felt the next morning and if the weather was favourable for such an excursion.

* * *

At last the perfect day dawned and Wyn could hardly suppress his excitement. After breakfast Mrs Jenkins packed them a basket of Cornish pasties, cheese and other good things. Then they set out along the road that led through Dolphin Town to the other side of the island. Just past the inn they turned north.

'I still find it hard to believe such a tiny island can boast one castle, let alone two,' said Caroline as they picked their way over the stony path.

'They are more forts than castles,' Bennett explained. 'From the time of the Civil War. These islands saw a good deal of fighting for their size. They were the last foothold of the Royalists.'

'Look, Mama.' Wyn tugged at her skirt. 'There's another island just across that little bit of water.'

Caroline raised one hand to shield her eyes from the sun. 'It's very close, isn't it? Do you suppose a man with a strong arm could hurl a stone across and hit it?'

Wyn nodded. 'I reckon Papa could.'

'Your father is a very determined man,' Caroline agreed. 'I suspect he could accomplish most anything he set his mind to.'

Did that include forgetting his mother's betrayal and his bitter feud with Fitz Astley to finally believe that she had not committed adultery? Did it include forgiving the way she'd defied and humiliated him like a headstrong child determined to get her way at any cost? Did it include bearing with their many differences to focus on their one deep bond as parents? It was a great deal to ask and she knew it would be more than she would dare hope from most men. But Bennett Maitland was not *most men.*

The question remained, would he be willing to try?

'The water is wider than it looks from up here.' Her husband seemed uncomfortable with her praise. Did he question her sincerity or did he assume she was putting on an act for Wyn's sake? 'That other island is Bryher. Local people come and go between the two islands all the time. At low tide in the summer, it is easy enough to swim across.'

'Can we visit there some day?' asked Wyn.

'Goodness…' Caroline swung their joined hands in a wide arch '…we shall have to stay here a very long time to visit all the places you have a fancy to see.'

Not that she would object to a protracted stay—quite the contrary. Bennett had promised her a month, which was more than generous. But the days were passing far too quickly, like luminous beads slipping off the thread of a broken necklace.

'There are the castles you've been so anxious to see, Wyn.' Bennett pointed to a circular stone tower perched on the shore and the ruin of a larger fortress sprawling over the crown of the hill behind it. 'I'm afraid you may not find them as impressive as their names make them sound.'

He seemed worried that their son might be disappointed.

'I think they're marvellous!' Caroline declared. 'Imagine the stories they might have to tell.'

She glanced towards Bennett. 'Did you visit these castles when you came to Tresco as a boy?'

She could picture him walking along this path, holding his mother's hand just as Wyn clung to hers.

'Every year. My mother and I would pack a lunch and eat it up on top of Cromwell's Tower or among the ruins of the old castle. I always looked forward to our autumn holiday. Mother seemed so much more carefree than during the rest of the year.' He seemed to shake himself from his reverie. 'Now, which of the castles would you like to explore first?'

Wyn looked down to the shore, then up to the hilltop. 'Which do you think, Mama?'

'Whichever you choose will be fine with me, dearest.' Caroline smiled down at him. 'As long as I'm with you, I'll be happy.'

Now that she had learned she didn't always need to give him his way in a desperate bid to keep his love, she'd begun to relax and enjoy their time together in a way she never could before. It had not been an easy lesson by any means, and she owed it to Bennett for teaching her, even when she'd resisted learning.

'That one first.' Wyn pointed to the round tower perched precariously on a spit of land protruding into the narrowest part of the strait between Bryher and Tresco. 'Can we climb to the top?'

Indeed they could, and did, by a staircase that wound around inside the wall of the tower. Bennett refused to let Wyn venture into any of the lower chambers for the floor timbers were clearly rotten. The stone roof of the tower was still as sturdy as ever, though.

Bennett hoisted Wyn on to his shoulders so the boy could see over the parapet. 'This is where the cannon would have stood to fire on any enemy ships trying to sail through the Channel between the islands.'

As Caroline watched her husband and son, she was delighted to see how much more at ease Bennett had become with the child. Though physical contact still seemed to make him a little self-conscious, there could be no mistaking how much he enjoyed their new sense of closeness.

She and Wyn peppered Bennett with questions about the history of the castle and the conflicts in which it had played a part. He proved a font of fascinating information.

Later, they scrambled up the steep, rock-strewn hill to the ruin of the older castle. After they admired the fine view of Bryher, Wyn challenged his mother to a game of hide and seek among the tumbled stone walls.

'Join us.' Caroline beckoned her husband.

Bennett shook his head. 'I'd rather watch from a distance to make certain Wyn doesn't venture anywhere he might come to harm.'

'As you wish.' She began counting loudly to twenty.

Not long ago, she might have taken Bennett's remark as a criticism of her. Now she understood that each of them was expressing their love for Wyn in the way that came most naturally. But that did not mean they must keep to one role exclusively.

After she and Wyn had played for a while, Caroline approached her husband and gave him a playful nudge. 'Now you take a turn finding him. I'll warn you, he's clever at finding places to hide.'

When Bennett hesitated, she lowered her voice so their son would not overhear. 'I will keep watch to make certain he does not come to any harm. You can trust me to do that, can you not?'

It was something of a step forwards for her that she felt confident to watch over Wyn. Learning that Bennett did not blame her for what she'd considered some of her greatest failures made her view their marriage in a new light. The fact that he had sought her advice about showing their son more affection gave her a greater belief in her abilities. Every step she took towards being a better mother to Wyn and drawing closer to Bennett brought a rewarding sense of accomplishment. It proved a potent antidote to her self-doubt and fear of failure.

'Of course I can trust you.' Bennett replied with scarcely a beat of hesitation.

Considering his harsh experience of betrayal, Caroline felt encouraged by his faith in her.

This island had a great deal in common with her husband, she reflected as she watched him and Wyn hunt one another through the ruins of the old fortress. From what she'd seen of Tresco, it was a place of stark beauty with a rich, mysterious history. But it was also harsh, forbidding and bristling with defences. At its worst, it could be dangerous to the weak or unwary.

Was she a self-destructive fool to risk her hopes and her heart on a man like that? Especially after he had told her she could never be the kind of woman he wanted?

He trusted her? Bennett could scarcely believe he'd spoken those words, least of all to the woman who had conspired with his worst enemy to make him the laughing stock of London.

But these isolated islands seemed so far removed from all that, as if his family had sailed more than thirty miles out into the ocean, perhaps even back through time. True, he had carried a great deal of resentment, suspicion and regret here with him, like so much heavy ballast of questionable value. But bit by bit he had begun to discard those encumbrances. Though he felt rather vulnerable without them, he felt freer, too.

Free to acknowledge that when it came to their son's welfare he could depend upon Caroline to care as much as he did and do whatever circumstances required for Wyn's sake. Free to show his love for their son in more than controlled, structured ways, with a casual touch or a spontaneous smile. Even a game that had no point or purpose beyond enjoying their time together.

Exercising that unaccustomed freedom, Bennett abandoned decorum and threw himself into playing 'hide and seek'. After eating their picnic lunch with hearty appetites, they played a little longer before finally heading back home.

Wyn could scarcely keep his eyes open through dinner. That evening when his parents tucked him into bed, he did not put up even a token resistance.

'Sweet dreams, dearest.' Caroline strewed the child's brow with kisses, then swept him into an affectionate embrace.

Wyn yawned deeply. 'Goodnight, Mama.'

When she rose from the child's bedside, Caroline cast Bennett an encouraging look. He knew what she wanted him to do and he had been working up to it. Two nights ago he'd patted his son's shoulder. Last night he had ruffled Wyn's hair. What would he do tonight?

Perhaps because Wyn was half-asleep, Bennett felt less awkward about putting his arms around his son's shoulders and pressing a kiss to his forehead. 'Goodnight, son. Rest well.'

He tried to pull away and might have succeeded if Wyn had been fully awake. Instead, the child flung his small arms around Bennett's neck and squeezed tight.

'Night-night, Papa.' He planted a hearty kiss on his father's cheek.

Bennett was not certain how he should react, but he sensed Caroline would be disappointed if he ended the embrace too abruptly. So he held his son close, his tense muscles gradually relaxing until Wyn's grip slackened and his breath became a soft, slow drone. Then he eased the child back on to his pillow and tucked the bedclothes around him.

When he straightened up and glanced at Caroline, he found her beaming with approval. 'Well done. I knew you could do it.'

His deeply ingrained habit in such situations was to dismiss her praise with a dry quip, but Bennett fought the urge and conquered it. Gazing down at the sleeping child, he soaked in the deep contentment he now found in Caroline's nearness. 'I think your father would be proud of his young namesake.'

Though he wished his mentor had lived to see his grandson, Bennett was relieved Sir Wyndham had not witnessed the break-up of their marriage or the shocking blow Caroline had dealt the Abolition Movement.

No sooner had he spoken than he felt a change come over Caroline.

Her warm, brooding stillness grew tense and brittle. 'Of course Father would have been proud. Wyn is a boy, after all, capable of inheriting your title and fortune, carrying on your work. It wouldn't matter if he were dim-witted or bad-tempered or dishonourable, as long as he's male. A girl could never be good enough to please my father or any man of his class.'

The bitterness of her words stunned Bennett. Prudence warned him to hold his tongue. He did not want to be drawn into a quarrel just when relations between them were going so well. Yet he could not ignore the pain he sensed, raw and vulnerable beneath the tough crust of resentment. He knew that kind of corrupted wound all too well, though lately it felt as if his might be starting to heal.

'You always seemed so devoted to your father.' He tried not to sound judgemental or accusing, only curious and sympathetic.

Caroline gave a rasping chuckle. 'So I was, for all it mattered. I would have done anything to win his approval…his love. But nothing I did was ever good enough for him. I got more attention by misbehaving. Since that was a great deal more amusing, I tried it for a while.'

That must have been part of the reason Sir Wyndham had approved their engagement so heartily. He might have thought his daughter needed a steady husband to control her. Bennett regretted having let the old man down on that score. Might it also be why Caroline had taken lovers—trying to provoke him into paying more attention to her, as she had with her father?

A melancholy sigh escaped Caroline's lips. 'That was one of the reasons I accepted your proposal. I knew my father was dying and I thought it might be my last chance to make him care for me.'

'I wish I'd known,' Bennett whispered, more to himself than to her.

It was a motive he could not despise. If he'd realised she was trying to please the man they both idolised, he might have worked harder to make a success of their marriage. Perhaps he would have withheld judgement after Wyn's birth, so Caroline would not have felt such a desperate craving for approval.

He risked a glance at her, wanting to say he was sorry, but the words stuck in his throat like sharp little fish bones. She had betrayed him, after all, humiliated him and brought his career to the brink of ruin.

In answer to his earlier comment, she gave a weary shrug. 'It makes no difference now. As you've said so often, there is nothing we can do to change the past.'

Bennett knew that was true. But since returning to this island, he'd learned it was possible to change one's *perception* of the past. That could make a great difference in the present and for the future. 'Your father cared about you more than you might have realised. He was very anxious to see you settled and provided for after he was gone.'

Her lips arched slightly in a wistful smile. 'He may have felt sorry for me. Perhaps he could have loved me if I'd been the son he longed for.'

Now Bennett understood what she'd meant the day they talked about having a daughter. 'If your father wanted a son, it may have been so his estate would not fall into other hands and you would be taken care of. He once told me he regretted being unable to provide you with a brother.'

'Are you certain that's true?' Her gaze bored into his with desperate intensity.

Bennett feared she might see deeper into him than he cared to let her. 'Quite certain. Perhaps your father had as much trouble showing his affection for you as I do with Wyn. Only he had no one to teach him as you've taught me.'

He sensed she wanted to believe his explanation, but was half-afraid to.

She turned towards the door. 'Speaking of Wyn, we should

leave him to sleep and get some ourselves. We'll need our energy to take him on more outings.'

As they lingered in the hallway in front of their bedroom doors a few minutes later, Bennett wished they did not have to part for the night. There was a familiar element of desire in that wish as well as one or two others with which he was less well acquainted.

'Goodnight.' Caroline pushed her door open then glanced back over her shoulder at him. 'Thank you for what you said about my father. I'll never know for certain if that is how he felt about me. But it might do me good to persuade myself it was.'

As he watched her cross the threshold of her bedchamber, it was everything Bennett could do to keep from following her. Not only because his whole body ached with desire to touch and taste her once more.

Then her door swung shut between them reminding him that, as a husband, he had repeated far too many of her father's mistakes—denying her affection, making her feel she could never live up to his expectations. She'd admitted marrying him to please her father, but might there have been more to it than that? In her innocence, had Caroline mistaken his fierce infatuation for love, believing he could give her the affection and approval Sir Wyndham had withheld?

If so, was it any wonder she'd described marriage to him as a *torture* worse than being deprived of her glittering social life or even the loss of their son?

His hand slipped into his pocket to fondle the wedding ring Caroline had flung at him that day. His deeply ingrained sense of self-preservation warned him against the destructive folly of falling in love with his wife five years too late.

* * *

For a moment, when she glanced back at Bennett, Caroline had thought he might follow her into her bedchamber. And how she'd wished he would!

During the following days, a potent echo of that desire smouldered in Caroline's flesh whenever she thought back on it.

What kind of daft fool was she? her reason immediately demanded. The needs of his body might drive Bennett into her bed for one last passionate coupling. But afterwards it would only make things worse between them. It was far too great a risk to the fragile charade of a happy family they were acting out for their son's sake, not to mention the risk it posed to her heart.

Yet, as they headed off on their next major excursion, it was far too easy to forget they were not the happy family they appeared to be.

'Where are you taking us this time, Papa?' asked Wyn as they strolled toward the Blockhouse, then turned inland along a narrow lane.

'It is a part of the island I'd like you both to see.' Bennett strode along with a rather jaunty gait, carrying their lunch basket. 'It was my favourite spot to visit when my mother brought me here as a boy. I've always wanted to go there in the springtime.'

'Your favourite spot?' Wyn skipped off ahead of his parents. 'Even better than the castles?'

Caroline stared about in wonder at a landscape far different from any she'd yet seen on Tresco. Unlike the forbidding rock-strewn heath on the northern part of the island, the view from the lane was all gently rolling downland, rich with verdant greenery. There were plenty of other sumptuous colours as well. Some trees sported purple blossoms that put amethysts to shame, while others were abloom with cascades of pale-pink catkins.

Even the stone walls bordering the lane were softened with a covering of moss and ivy. Wildflowers seemed to sprout wherever she looked. Purple heads of dainty violets peeping bashfully up from among their leaves. Bright, yellow-gold corn marigolds, like miniature suns. Century flowers in such a glorious shade of pink, Caroline could imagine the sensation she would have made if she'd worn a silk ball gown of that hue to an assembly in London.

But those days were over for her now, and she had brought it on herself with her heedless behaviour. Half the *ton* had probably suspected her of being a secret adulteress, whispering behind her back while toasting her to her face. Astley's vile ambush had only given them an excuse to turn on her.

Since coming to the island, she'd been surprised to discover how little she missed the glittering social life that had once meant so much to her. Now she found far more true enjoyment in simple family outings like this one.

'It's like a giant garden!' cried Wyn. 'I hope we can come here every year, the way you used to, Papa. We've had such a fine time I hardly miss Greggy any more.'

Every other occasion when her son mentioned his nurse, it had brought Caroline a stab of jealousy and resentment that he should care more for a hired servant than for her. But lately she'd come to view the situation in a different light.

It was only natural Wyn should love the person who'd cared for him so devotedly and spent almost every waking moment in his company. She felt sorry for having dragged him away from Mrs McGregor with so little regard for his feelings. And she was grateful to know he would have someone familiar and beloved to take care of him when he returned to London with his father.

'Do not worry too much about the future,' Bennett replied, clearly reluctant to make a promise he could not keep. 'Concentrate on enjoying the present.'

Her husband's advice struck a chord with Caroline. Worrying too much about the future could spoil one's enjoyment of the present. So could brooding about the past. She had done too much of both in her time. While her husband and son were with her, she must concentrate on here and now, savouring every precious moment.

Just then, Wyn stopped and sniffed the air. 'What is that smell?'

'Mmm.' Caroline inhaled appreciatively. 'A very sweet, wholesome scent, indeed. It seems familiar, but I cannot place it.'

'Camomile,' said Bennett. 'It grows wild around Great Pool and Abbey Pond.'

'Of course.' Caroline savoured the aroma. 'Our first night here, at the inn, Mrs Pender gave me some camomile tea to help me sleep. Did you say *Abbey?* Don't tell me this tiny island has one of those, too, as well as a pair of castles?'

Bennett nodded. 'It did once, centuries ago. There is not much left of the old abbey now except part of a wall and a fine spot for a picnic.'

Catching up to Wyn, they paused in the shade of a small tree. The lane they'd been following ran along a crest of higher ground. Now Caroline gazed out over a shallow valley dominated by a small, narrow lake that appeared to span nearly the width of the island. In places plots of farmland came right up to the water's edge. On the opposite bank was a bit of woodland and a green meadow sprigged with white flowers. In the pond's shallows, tall rushes waved lazily in the breeze.

'It is hard to believe such a place could exist on this island,' Caroline murmured in a tone of wonder, 'after seeing that rocky, barren terrain around the castles.'

'This high ground shelters it from the harsh sea wind.' Bennett pointed from the spot where they stood around to a hill on the opposite side of the pond. 'I expect that is why the monks chose this place to build their abbey. It has so many natural advantages, as well as being so far removed from the bustle and temptations of the mainland.'

'Papa.' Wyn tugged at his father's coat sleeve. 'What is that bird called—the brown one with the speckled breast?'

Bennett took their son's hand and walked forwards slowly so as not to frighten away the bird that perched on top of a nearby stone wall. 'I believe that is a song thrush.'

As if to confirm its identity, the bird opened its beak and launched into lengthy complex song, with each different phrase repeated several times. Wyn seemed much impressed.

Caroline and Bennett spent a magical day with their son, poking about the abbey ruins and eating their lunch in the shelter of the vine-covered abbey wall. Later Wyn and Bennett sailed boats made of leaves and twigs on the pond while Caroline strolled around the enclosure where many Tresco families still laid their loved ones to rest. The still air was fragrant with lilies of the valley and wild roses that grew over the old tombstones.

Hearing Bennett's laughter in the distance, Caroline pondered how much her husband was like this isolated island of fascinating contrasts. Tresco's barren, heavily fortified coast protected a garden of unexpected beauty and peace at its heart. Only after several unhappy years had she finally glimpsed the heart Bennett strove so hard to protect. After all he had endured, was it any wonder he'd been reluctant to risk his heart on a woman who must have reminded him too much of his adulterous mother?

But she had changed since then, Caroline's blossoming confidence insisted. And so had Bennett.

Three short weeks ago, she would never have believed they could confide so much in each other, learn so much from one another, or cooperate so well to care for their son. Yet they had. Not easily or without misgivings, but sincerely trying to understand and respect one another. With one more precious week ahead of them, Caroline hoped Bennett might finally learn to trust her enough that he could believe she had been faithful to him.

Then perhaps they would have the chance to become the happy family they'd pretended to be.

Chapter Twelve

Bennett could scarcely recall when he had spent three such happy weeks. After much reflection, he was obliged to search his memory all the way back to his boyhood, when he'd come to Tresco with his mother. Since then he had experienced pleasure, passion and success in rewarding endeavours. None of those equalled the quiet elation that he found spending time with his family.

The smallest things, such as going for a walk or sharing a meal, took on a whole new depth of enjoyment when he indulged in forgotten delights of childhood playing with Wyn or when he coaxed a smile from Caroline. He'd gained a fresh appreciation for the island he had long sought to banish from his thoughts. It had become his private treasure chest from which he drew unexpected delights to share with his wife and son.

Only two things cast a pall over his newfound felicity. One was the speed with which their time together was passing. When he'd first proposed extending his stay on the island, a month had stretched before him. Now it was fast running out and every day he spent with Caroline made him less willing to leave. The other shadow was his growing awareness that the troubles in their marriage were far more his fault than hers.

He'd rushed her into marriage for all the wrong reasons. Once his infatuation had begun to wane, he'd neglected her shamefully, then misjudged her as a means of justifying his behaviour. Worst of all, he'd made her feel as if she had failed him when the truth was quite the opposite. No wonder Caroline had hurled her wedding ring at him. Perhaps she wished it had been a more deadly projectile.

'Papa?' Wyn's insistent tone wrenched him from the murky depths of his brooding. 'Do you think we can go out in the boat today?'

Bennett looked up from the breakfast he'd scarcely noticed he was eating. Several days ago, he had promised the child they would row out to visit some of the offshore islands around Tresco. He had arranged to hire a rowboat and enlisted Albert as an oarsman. Then they'd waited for the weather to cooperate.

'Perhaps so.' Bennett glanced out the kitchen window. 'It isn't raining and it doesn't look too windy. If the sea is calm as well, I think this is our day.'

As Wyn cheered, Caroline watched the child with a doting smile that betrayed a hint of wistfulness. Was she thinking how soon she would have to bid him farewell and wondering when she would see him again? Somehow it no longer seemed so farfetched to call it *unfair* that he should get to keep their son.

Abruptly he pushed away from the table. 'I will go check on the state of the water and get the boat ready if you will arrange for a lunch to take with us.'

He tried to sound more cheerful than he felt, reminding

himself not to let regrets from the past and worries of the future spoil his enjoyment of this day.

Yet Caroline seemed to sense something was not quite right, for her smile faltered a little. 'We can manage that, can't we, Wyn? Fortunately Mrs Jenkins bakes plenty of Cornish pasties to have on hand.'

Determined to keep his thoughts firmly in the present, Bennett headed off to the Old Grimsby wharf where he was pleased to find the water calm. Not only that, but the local man from whom he'd hired the boat had it cleaned up and ready to go.

He was on his way back to the house to summon his wife and son when a woman coming up the road from Dolphin Town called out to him. 'Begging your pardon, my lord, but there's a letter come for you from the mainland.'

A letter? Bennett thanked the woman, who introduced herself as the innkeeper's wife, and took the thick folded packet she handed to him. It must be from his friend George Marlow, to whom he'd written of Wyn's illness and his intention to remain on Tresco while his son recovered.

Sure enough, the handwriting and the wax seal belonged to Marlow, a Member of Parliament and staunch Abolitionist. Bennett's sense of duty urged him to read whatever his friend had to say before embarking on a pleasure excursion with his family.

Entering quietly through the front door, he stole up to his bedchamber. He wanted to avoid his son, who would not be happy to postpone their outing, even for a few minutes. Fortunately as he mounted the stairs Bennett could hear the child in the kitchen chatting excitedly with his mother and Mrs Jenkins.

Once he gained the privacy of his room, Bennett broke the seal and hastily unfolded Marlow's letter. As he did so, two smaller pieces of paper fell out and wafted to the floor. For the moment, he ignored them to concentrate on reading the letter. As he scanned the page, a stew of outrage and guilt began to seethe in his stomach.

'You must come home at once,' Marlow wrote. 'Certain agitations in the north have led the Government to ram a Bill through the Commons that will make it illegal to hold a gathering of more than fifty people. I am certain you can foresee the effect this law could have on the Abolition Movement if it is enacted.'

Indeed he did. Abolition rallies featuring speakers like Thomas Clarkson and William Wilberforce had long been a favoured means of stirring up popular support for their cause.

'Your vote, your voice and your leadership are needed in the Lords as never before,' the letter continued. 'I pray your son is sufficiently recovered that you may come as soon as possible. As for her ladyship, I hope she has not worked her wiles to prevent you from proceeding against Astley, who has grown more insufferable than ever in your absence. I fear the scandal will not be put to rest until you have rid yourself of her. I enclose a tiny sample of what has been circulating, so you will understand how vital it is that you act with resolution and dispatch.'

Bennett forced himself to stoop and retrieve the fallen papers, which turned out to be vicious caricatures clipped from scandal magazines. One portrayed him with cuckold's horns, being led about on a lead by Caroline, while a parrot representing Mr Wilberforce squawked about the need for moral reform. The other purported to show the scene at Almack's when Caroline had been discovered in Astley's arms.

As he stared at it, Bennett felt as if he were reliving that cursed night. Only this time he felt more than outrage, humiliation and betrayal. Overriding all of those was a crushing devastation he'd felt only once before, when he had learned that his beloved mother had abandoned him.

Something else about the picture nagged at him, though he could not work out exactly what. Shards of memory lanced through his mind. Astley looming over him, landing blows with his fists and his vile accusations. Astley smirking in triumph as yet another Abolition Bill went down to defeat. Astley with his arms around Caroline, his lips on hers and that blasted curtain pulled back at the most incriminating moment.

Precisely at the most incriminating moment. Could that have been a coincidence? Or had the whole scandal at Almack's been orchestrated by Astley to destroy his marriage and ruin his reputation? If so, he had blundered into his enemy's trap like a blind fool.

If he'd reacted differently—demanded Astley unhand his wife, challenged the scoundrel to a duel in defence of Caroline's honour—how differently matters would have fallen out. But with their marriage in tatters and seeing his wife in the arms of the one man he'd ordered her to avoid, it had made it all too easy to believe she was repeating the sins of his mother.

But it couldn't all be a fiction...could it? If Caroline had been faithful, surely she would have proclaimed her innocence at every opportunity. Unless...

He had made it brutally clear he would never believe her under any circumstances. Might she have feared that if she protested too vigorously, he would leave the island straight away and take Wyn with him?

Or could it be that Caroline wanted to escape their miserable marriage so much she was willing to seize this opportunity, in spite of what it would cost her?

'Bennett, are you there?' Caroline tapped on her husband's bedroom door though she scarcely expected an answer. 'Wyn is beside himself with impatience. If we don't leave soon, I'm afraid he may try to swim out to one of those rocks.'

At her son's urging, she'd already looked down towards the wharf. She had glimpsed a small boat tied up there but she could not see any sign of Bennett. Though she hadn't expected to find him here, she'd promised Wyn she would check the house. Where else could he be?

Might something have happened to him? Though reason assured her it was unlikely, irrational worry began to gnaw at her the way it had when Wyn had run away and all the time he was ill.

She received no answer to her knock, but as she started back downstairs Caroline thought she heard a faint voice from behind Bennett's door. Could he have been taken with an apoplectic fit?

Before she had time to realise how ridiculous that fear was, blind panic sent her hurtling through the door, certain she would find Bennett collapsed upon the bed. But when she found the room empty and heard her husband's voice from outdoors, it was Caroline who sank on to his bed, her heart racing and her insides clenched in knots.

What had come over her? In all the time she'd known Bennett, even when she fancied herself madly in love with him, she had never felt such overwhelming anxiety for his welfare. Now she was so overcome with relief that she scarcely heard the crackle of paper beneath her.

But when her composure began to return, Caroline realised she'd sat on something she should not have. Hoping it was nothing too important, she budged over and looked to see.

When she first glanced over the magazine clippings, her mind refused to recognise what they represented. But her denial was not strong enough to hold the truth at bay for long. That was the card room at Almack's as it must have appeared to onlookers that terrible night. No wonder everyone believed Astley's accusations against her...including her husband. Any shame she had felt previously over her actions was nothing compared to the deluge of cold filth that swamped her.

Caroline could not keep from reading the accompanying letter. Though she knew it was wrong to trespass on Bennett's private correspondence, it scarcely signified compared to the harm she'd already done him. These vile caricatures and who knew how many more like them would have been circulating for weeks, provoking pity and contempt for her proud husband. Yet when she read George Marlow's letter summoning Bennett back to London, she knew he could not refuse such an appeal, no matter what public ridicule awaited him upon his return.

'Mama, where are you?' Wyn's call was a plea she could not refuse, though she would rather have crawled into a deep hole and never come out. 'I found Papa! It's time to go in the boat.'

Drawing on a strength of will she hadn't realised she possessed, Caroline stilled her trembling legs and forced herself to rise and put one foot in front of the other. Composing her features, she struggled to subdue her bitter disappointment that she would not have one more week to salvage her marriage. Perhaps not even one more day.

Did it matter, though? The past weeks on Tresco were nothing but a dream. Those obscene prints had made her face the true enormity of her indiscretion. It was beyond her power to atone for and beyond Bennett's to forgive.

'There she is.' Bennett gave his son's hand a squeeze as Caroline emerged from the house. 'You see, we were not playing hide and seek, after all.'

Since it seemed likely this would be their final outing together, he was determined to keep up the appearance of a united, happy family, in spite of the doubts that gnawed at him. Though Caroline would not be aware how quickly their time was running out, he knew he could rely on her to act her part for Wyn's sake.

The child's lips twitched. 'You're teasing, aren't you, Papa?'

'Surely not!' Caroline cried in mock horror before Bennett could reply. 'Your papa is always in earnest. He cannot abide teasing.'

That was quite true...at least it had been until recently. Now Bennett thought he could tolerate a jest or two at his expense, provided they brought a glint of merriment to Caroline's beguiling eyes. 'I'm not quite as thin-skinned as I used to be when a certain impertinent young lady made me an object of fun.'

Wyn looked up at his mother. 'Does he mean you, Mama?'

Caroline gave a rueful nod. 'I couldn't help myself. He was far too severe for a man so young and handsome. I had to do something to make him smile.'

Memories of those early days assailed Bennett as the three of them headed down to the quay. He'd been pursued by enough simpering débutantes that he found the surprising combination of Caroline Beresford's impudent wit and stunning beauty quite irresistible. Too late, he'd realised they were not enough to sustain a marriage. If only he'd taken the trouble to discover how much more there was to his wife, what misery would it have spared them all?

'Do you know what she said once when your grandfather could not find a poker to stir up the fire?' Bennett raised the pitch of his voice in an exaggerated imitation of Caroline's. '"I believe Lord Sterling must have sat on it and jammed it straight up his backside."'

Wyn laughed as if he'd never heard anything so funny in his life. 'I must go tell Albert.'

Before they could stop him, he dashed off after the footman.

'I was a heartless little beast, wasn't I, to torment you like that?' Beneath Caroline's jesting, Bennett sensed remorse far deeper than a bit of long ago mockery warranted. 'I must confess, when Father first invited you around to our house after singing your praises so incessantly, I was a bit jealous. You seemed to be the son he'd always longed for.'

That certainly rang true in light of what Caroline had told him about her difficult relationship with her father. Bennett wished he'd understood, at the time.

'We're quite a lot alike, your father and I. Perhaps too much, in some ways. Looking back, I suspect one of the reasons he took me under his wing was because he viewed me as a suitable husband for you.'

Caroline gave a rueful sigh. 'Which goes to show Father wasn't as clever as he was reputed to be.'

Bennett steeled himself to keep from wincing. Wyndham Beresford had been badly mistaken. The last kind of husband his daughter had needed was one too much like him, no matter how sensible, wealthy and titled. Caroline had needed a man capable of appreciating, understanding and cherishing her. A man capable of seeing behind her mask of rebellious banter to the girl who longed for love and acceptance. A man who would have had the sense and trust to take *her* word over that of his worst enemy.

By now, they'd reached the quay where a small rowboat bobbed in the gentle waves, awaiting their party. Albert had already climbed aboard the boat and lifted Wyn in after him.

Bennett helped Caroline into the boat, briefly savouring the warmth of her hand in his. As he watched her settle in the bow of the craft and take Wyn on to her lap, he was struck by how much she'd matured in the short time they'd been on the island. Was that because events had tested her character? Or had she always possessed the potential, if only he'd made the effort to foster it?

Untying the boat from the quay, Bennett scrambled aboard and took his seat beside Albert. Each of them grabbed an oar and began to pull.

'It's been a good many years since I rowed a boat, sir.' Albert's face was already growing red.

'That makes two of us.' Bennett thought back to that day on the Thames with Caroline and his blistered hands. 'Fortunately we aren't going far and the water is a good deal calmer than usual.'

Wyn pointed towards the nearest scrap of land protruding from the sea. 'Why is it called Little Cheese Rock, Papa?'

'Dashed if I know.' The exertion of rowing made Bennett's breath come quicker. 'Most of the smallest offshore islands are called ledges—Diamond Ledge, Paper Ledge, Tree Ledge.'

'Does Diamond Ledge have diamonds on it?'

Bennett chuckled. 'I'm sure the people of Tresco wish it did.'

Overhead the gulls wheeled in the vast blue sky, adding their haunting calls to the rhythmic dirge of the waves lapping against the shore.

Once they had reached the tiny islet, Wyn scrambled over the rocks, proud that he could quickly walk around the whole perimeter. He found an interesting seashell and fragments of an egg from some bird that must have nested there. He treated his finds as if they were the most priceless treasures.

After that they rowed out to two more of the uninhabited islands that clustered along Tresco's east coast.

When Wyn pleaded to visit just one more, Bennett shook his head. 'We need to get back. The wind is starting to pick up.'

Caroline sought to divert the child. 'May I have a look at your seashells, dearest?'

Meanwhile Bennett and the footman rowed hard and soon the boat pulled alongside the quay. Albert climbed out and tethered the boat while Bennett hoisted his son on to the quay. Caroline was making her way towards him when a high wave suddenly rocked the boat. Bennett struggled to keep his balance.

His wife might have recovered hers, too, if a rogue gust of

wind had not caught her parasol, sending her tumbling over-board with a splash that swamped Bennett's defences. The prospect of Caroline coming to harm opened a bottomless chasm of dread for which he was totally unprepared.

'Mama!' Wyn cried.

'Don't fret, son.' Bennett threw off his coat. 'I'll get her. Albert, watch him,' he called to the footman, then jumped into the water after his wife.

The coldness of it slammed into him, making every particle of his flesh scream with shock. It didn't help that he'd overheated himself with strenuous rowing.

As he bobbed to the surface, a surge of relief pulsed through him when he spotted Caroline's head above water. Strands of drenched hair were plastered over her face like seaweed. Her mouth opened and closed convulsively as she gasped for air. Her blue-green eyes were wide with terror as she flailed about in a desperate effort to keep from sinking beneath the surface again.

One vigorous kick propelled Bennett to her. He grabbed for her hand and tried to pull her close. She did not seem to realise he was trying to help her. Caught in the grip of panic, she struggled against him, writhing and kicking with surprising strength. The next thing he knew, she was forcing his head under water as she fought to keep afloat.

Bennett wished he'd ordered Albert to take Wyn and go for help. From what he'd seen, the young footman possessed little initiative. He might well stand there on the deserted quay and watch helplessly while his employers drowned. Bennett feared he might have to abandon Caroline to prevent her from dragging him down with her.

Though his lungs cried out for air and the water's chill

sapped his strength, Bennett knew he must get Caroline to safety as quickly as possible. After that, he could take care of himself. Rather than fighting her to get his head back above water, as every instinct urged, he concentrated on sinking as deep possible.

There! His feet made contact with solid ground.

Gathering his dwindling strength, he clutched Caroline by the legs and thrust her upwards with all his might. Then, as darkness closed in on his senses from all directions, he strained towards the light above him.

Chapter Thirteen

The moment Caroline felt that cold, dark water sucking her down, some savage creature seemed to take possession of her body. When her head broke the surface, she gasped for air, but her lungs could not seem to take it in. She twisted and thrashed like a wild thing with a single urgent purpose—to fight the relentless force dragging her to the depths.

Something caught at her arm, trying to still its raging movement. She could not let it. If she stopped struggling, she would sink and drown! As she fought against it, some instinct told her the solid object trying to hold her would give her a firm surface to push against. Rather than trying to shove the object away, she began to grapple with it, seeking any hand or foothold to lever herself up. For a terrifying instant, it fought back, thrusting her beneath the water again. Redoubling her frantic efforts, she managed to gain the advantage. The object sank beneath her.

Then suddenly it seized her by the legs, pressing them together with overpowering strength. She tried to resist, only to find herself hurtling upwards, propelled by a power not her own. She burst free of the water, briefly flying into the air.

An instant later she fell back, crashing down upon something hard that forced a spurt of water out of her mouth. Gasping for air, shivering violently, Caroline gradually realised she was hanging half-in, half-out of the row boat, not certain how she'd got there.

'Mama, are you all right?' Shrill with alarm, her son's voice penetrated her muddled thoughts. 'Where is Papa?'

Bennett! He must have been the *solid object* she'd fought against, pushing him underwater in her desperate effort to save herself.

'Can you move, my lady?' Albert called to her from the quay. 'Try to pull yourself into the boat so it doesn't tip over.'

Though her legs felt limp and useless, Caroline managed to drag them over the side of the boat and collapse on the middle plank. 'My...hus-band?'

If Bennett had drowned trying to save her after what she had done to him, she would never forgive herself.

'He's hanging on to the side of the quay, ma'am,' replied the footman. 'I'm going to help him out of the water now.'

Overcome with relief, Caroline gave a shaky nod.

Wyn was still calling out to her in an agitated tone. Raising her hand in a weak wave, she forced herself to smile. 'Just... give me a...moment to rest...dearest...then I'll...come to you.'

By the time she mustered the energy to try, Albert had helped Bennett out of the water. Turning their attention to her, the men took her by the arms and lifted her on to the quay. It felt so blessedly firm and steady beneath her feet she would have knelt and kissed it, except she feared she might never get back up again.

The moment she had her feet under her, Albert let go of her arm, but Bennett did not. He felt as firm and steady as the quay itself. Those were qualities she had never properly appreciated.

Not trusting her wobbly knees, she clung to him, though she had no right to. 'I—I'm sorry I dragged you under when you tried to help me. I didn't know what I was doing.'

'Don't concern yourself about that now.' Bennett sounded as if he cherished every breath he drew.

'Mama, Papa.' Wyn hung back. 'Why did you go in the water? I was frightened.'

'We're all right now, son,' Bennett tried to reassure the child. 'Though I must report the water is not yet warm enough for sea bathing. You were a good boy to stay on the quay with Albert.'

Taking his dry coat from the footman, he wrapped it around Caroline. It reminded her of that night at Almack's and how he'd given her his coat after she'd subjected him to the greatest humiliation a married man could suffer. Even at a time like that, he could not fail to consider another's comfort.

'Can you walk?' he asked her. 'We must get back to the house and out of these wet clothes as quickly as possible. I would do the manly thing and carry you, but I'm not certain I'm quite up to it just now.'

'No need. I can walk that far...I think.'

'Good.' He tugged her forwards. 'Walking should help warm you up.'

Leaning against one another for support, with Albert and Wyn leading the way, they staggered back to the house.

'My lord, my lady!' cried Parker when she caught sight of them. 'What happened to you?'

'What do you think happened?' Albert snapped before either Bennett or Caroline could muster breath to reply. 'Her ladyship fell into the water and his lordship fished her out. Both of them could have drowned.'

'Could you have drowned, Mama?' Wyn asked anxiously.

'I suppose I could,' she admitted, sensing he would not be satisfied with an evasive answer. 'But I did not, thanks to your brave papa.'

'You're a hero, Papa!' The child gazed at Bennett, as if he were one of King Arthur's knights come to life.

'So he is,' Caroline agreed before her husband could shrug off the praise as he always did. 'And to a great many more people than us.'

People who did not even know his name, or he theirs. Yet he strove with all his heart to save them from the living death of slavery. She had never fully embraced the cause that consumed so much of her father's time and attention. It had been the same after she married Bennett. Only now did she truly repent what she might have cost those he championed, with her thoughtless folly.

Her reference to his Abolition crusade seemed to take Bennett aback. 'There will be time enough to rest on my laurels later. First we need to get into dry clothes before we catch a chill. Parker, kindly take charge of Master Wyn and see that he gets his supper.'

'What about her ladyship? I should attend to her.'

'I can manage, thank you, Parker.' Caroline tried to sound stronger and more capable than she felt. After her near-drowning, the short walk to the house had quite exhausted her. 'It will ease my mind to know Wyn is being looked after. He's had quite a fright. Do your best to divert him while I change clothes.'

Her words seemed to remind the maid that there were more important things at stake than her jealously guarded position. 'Very well, my lady. Come along, Master Wyn. Let's see what Mrs Jenkins has prepared for supper. I heard her say she might make burnt cream for pudding since you're so fond of it.'

'I hope she did!' Wyn raced off toward the kitchen. 'Would you like to see the seashell I found on Little Cheese Island?'

As soon as their son was out of sight, Bennett nudged Caroline. 'He'll be fine, which is more than I can say for us if we stay in these sodden clothes much longer.'

Drawing strength from him, Caroline put one foot in front of the other to climb the stairs. The effort required the last dregs of her energy. By the time they reached her bedchamber, her legs were threatening to give way.

She sank on to the trunk that stood at the foot of her bed. 'I'll rest here a moment, then get changed.'

'You're sure?' Bennett seemed reluctant to leave her. Or perhaps that was only what she wanted to believe.

Not trusting her voice, she waved him away, though her arms felt like tubes of jelly.

'Very well, then.' Casting her a worried look, Bennett withdrew.

When he'd gone, Caroline tried to summon the strength to peal off her wet garments, but it eluded her. She kept telling herself she only needed another minute to rest, then she would begin. But one minute soon passed, followed by several more. She was still sitting there with water pooling on the floor beneath her feet, when a soft tapping sounded on her door.

'Caroline,' Bennett called, 'how are you getting along? Are you ready to come down for supper?'

She hesitated, trying to collect her scattered thoughts.

Before she could manage to, Bennett pushed open the door. 'Good Lord, Caro, you gave me a fright. I thought you'd swooned. I knew I should never have left you alone after such a shock.'

'I'll be all right,' she protested, though she felt better having him near. 'I just need another moment to get my strength back.'

'Of course you'll be fine.' Bennett spoke with calm, soothing assurance as he knelt in front of her and began to untie her slippers. 'But I believe it will take more than a few moments to recover your strength. Once I get you out of these wet clothes, I'll send for Mrs Hicks to look you over...as a precaution.'

Part of Caroline wanted to protest that she wasn't ill, only soaked and exhausted. But she could not resist his capable, caring ministrations. He had never touched her in quite that way before and her body had never responded with such complete immersion. Not only did it kindle welcome warmth in her chilled flesh that spread swiftly through her whole body, it also sank deep inside to caress her heart.

He pulled off her ruined slippers and set them aside. She wished he might reach up her thighs to unfasten the ribbons that held up her stockings, but all her thrashing in the water had already accomplished that. Her stockings sagged to her knees and Bennett had only to give them a gentle pull to slide them off.

All the while, he kept up a casual discourse about their excursion to the offshore islands. If he hoped to distract her from the fact that he was removing her clothes, his ploy did not succeed in the least. Though she nodded and murmured vague responses as if she were paying attention, his words simply washed over her. Meanwhile, the deep, mellow music of his voice played a fitting accompaniment to the slow, stirring dance of his hands over her body. Her gaze lingered upon his face, taking in every familiar feature with something more than admiration.

'Now, let's have this off.' He unwrapped his coat from around her.

She was sorry to part from its light, warming embrace, which carried a tantalising whiff of his bracing scent.

'I never thanked you,' she murmured as he moved behind her and began to unbutton her dress, 'for saving my life.'

'I couldn't very well let you drown.' His fingers fumbled over the last of her buttons.

Another disturbing thought occurred to her. 'Have I ever thanked you for *anything* you've done for me?'

He murmured some awkward response about there being no need. Threading his arm under her shoulder, he lifted her just high enough to hoist her skirts up to her waist. Then he eased her back down again.

'Heaven knows where I might have ended up if you hadn't married me,' she persisted. 'Living in very straitened circumstance, I imagine. Or more likely the mistress of some rich old man.'

She had never fully appreciated the favour he'd done her, never before considered the kind of life he might have spared her. Instead she'd been preoccupied with wanting more than he could give, feeling slighted and sorry for herself.

'I doubt you'd have had any difficulty finding another husband if I had not insisted you marry me.' He tugged down the short sleeves of her dress, eased the bodice away from her bosom and pulled the sodden garment off over her head.

'Perhaps not one so well to do, but one who might have been better suited to provide you with things you needed more.'

There was only her shift left now. The delicate Irish linen might hardly have been there for all it concealed. The dampness plastered it tight to her breasts and rendered the fabric all but invisible. The dusky pink of her nipples showed through quite clearly as they jutted out, stiffened by the chill of the air and the heat of her arousal.

When Bennett reached to untie the ribbon threaded around the low, scoop neck, his hands trembled. The tie resisted, then suddenly pulled loose, making his hand slip to graze her breast.

Caroline gave a violent start that sent her arms flying up to fasten around his neck. The next thing she knew, she was pulling him towards her. Her lips opened and closed as they had when she was in the water struggling for breath.

Now she was drowning in desire. She needed his kisses as urgently as she had ever needed air. She prayed Bennett would once again come to her rescue.

With the yearning fullness of her breast beneath his fingertips and the urgent pressure of her arms pulling him towards her, Bennett could not resist his wife's overture any more than he could break free of a powerful ocean current. Caution tried to warn him of the danger, but blood pulsed in his ears like a roaring surf, deafening him to everything but the siren call of desire.

Casting prudence aside, he plunged into the hot, velvet depths of Caroline's kiss, urgently seeking something he could not name. A faint taste of brine lingered in her mouth. He sought to scour it out with the dart and flick of his tongue.

His hand closed over her breast, first through the cool, damp linen, then beneath to the soft, yielding flesh.

She gave a delicious gurgle of pleasure, pressing into his caress with obvious enjoyment.

He was only too happy to oblige her. Cupping his palms around the inviting fullness of her breasts, he admired her womanly perfection. Swiping the pads of his thumbs over the yearning firmness of her nipples, he longed to taste their incomparable flavour once again. Her body felt so satisfyingly familiar, yet enticingly new. Damp and dishevelled as she was, he had never wanted her more.

She seemed to want him just as much, drinking in his kisses as if they were the sweetest nectar. Untwining her arms from around his neck, she ran her fingers through his damp hair. The fond intimacy of the gesture stirred feelings within him even more potent than desire.

A realisation rolled over him with the raw power of a tidal wave, sweeping him completely out to sea. He wanted more than her body—he wanted Caroline's heart as well.

Scavenging together the remnants of his shattered self-control, he gave her breasts a parting caress and disengaged his lips from hers.

'You should be in bed...resting.' His words emerged in a breathless rasp.

Caroline had almost drowned, he reminded himself, yet here he was taking advantage of her shock and weakness to gratify his desires.

She refused to let him go easily.

'By all means, take me to bed,' she whispered, her fingertips feathering over his face. 'But I need *you* more than I need rest. To warm me up and bring me back to life again.'

He understood what she meant. After their cold, dark brush with death, he also felt the need to reaffirm life by making their hearts pound and their breaths race, stirring all their senses to an intense pitch. Though he wished Caroline could want more than that from him, he knew he had no right to seek it from her now.

That would not stop him from offering it.

Drinking in the delicate beauty of her features, he raised his hand to graze her cheek with the backs of his fingers. Then he let his hands fall to grasp the hem of her shift and pull it up over her head. 'If it's warming you need, I am your man.'

He wished he'd had the strength to carry her all the way home from the quay, but he'd barely been able to stumble back under his own power. Now enough of his strength had returned that he was able to hoist his naked wife in his arms and carry her the last few steps to her bed. Laying her gently upon it, he paused to shed his clothes.

When he turned back towards her, a ridiculous feeling of bashfulness came over him. In the past, he and Caroline had never lain together in broad daylight. He wasn't certain his wife had ever got a clear view of his bare body, particularly the straining column that rose from the tuft of dark hair between his thighs. Might the sight alarm or disgust her?

Perhaps she guessed his uncertainty, for she held out her arms to him, her lips arched in a playful smile. 'I'm pleased to see you want me as much as I want you.'

For once he welcomed her teasing, which lightened an awkward moment and somehow deepened the intimacy between them. So much so that he was able to infuse his reply with a touch of wry wit. 'If you want me that badly, I wonder how you can stand it.'

Accepting the invitation of her extended arms, he crawled on to the bed where he knelt over her.

Caroline broke into a husky chuckle. 'What makes you think I can?'

Pulling him down on top of her, she rubbed her body against his with wanton abandon that taxed his physical control to the breaking point. A feral growl rose in his throat.

His mouth sought hers, hot and hungry. She returned his kiss with lusty passion that fed his desire even as it consumed him. Her hands ranged over his body with provocative, earthy boldness beyond anything he remembered from the early days of their marriage.

Everything about this encounter felt different than any they'd shared before, especially the nature of his desire. It was no longer enough to sate the need she whetted in his body, with only an afterthought to spare for *her* pleasure. Now he yearned to coax her to the heights of sweet, shuddering bliss, feel her writhe beneath him and grip around him. For once in their marriage, he wanted to be truly one with her, however briefly.

That intention communicated itself to their kiss, which grew warmer and deeper—less like scorching fire and more like a sun-drenched tidal pool. With his varied touch, Bennett sought to convey the approval and admiration she longed for. Not only of her generously rounded bosom, lush bottom and soft, silky thighs, but of her quicksilver wit, warm sympathy and quiet strength—the many qualities he had failed to appreciate until recently.

Slowly he inched downwards, kissing her long, graceful neck and elegant shoulders, on his way to the delectable perfection of her breasts. When his lips closed over one pert nipple while he stroked the other with his fingertips, Caroline arched towards him.

In spite of the blazing ache in his loins that demanded he take his pleasure swiftly, Bennett lingered over her breasts, determined to savour the sight, smell, touch and taste of them until his senses were altogether sated. He did not neglect his hearing either, greedily drinking in every faint expression of pleasure to escape her lips. Each sigh, each murmur, each catch in her breath further heightened his desire and assured him he was succeeding in his quest to delight her.

Gradually those sounds took on an edge of intensifying need that he understood all too well. Her legs parted slightly, then wider. Her hips flexed, pleading for his attention. He could not resist their compelling call indefinitely.

Ranging farther south, his tongue skimmed over the satin skin of her belly, relishing the delicate flavour of woman, seasoned with a hint of brine. Meanwhile, he extended his hand down to her knee and began working his way up to her thighs, delighting in the smoothness of her skin and the yielding softness of the flesh beneath.

Higher and higher he brought his fingers, altering their movement from a feathery, teasing graze to a voluptuous, liquid glide. When he flickered over the downy tuft of hair that crowned her loins, she gave a sharp gasp and a tremor rippled through her body. He wondered how much more of his amorous play she could endure before he drove her over the edge.

A spark of wicked mischief he'd never realised he possessed was eager to discover the answer to that question. Yet another part of him wanted to be quite certain he was inside her to experience the slick, pulsing caress of her climax. He sensed that the hotter he fuelled her anticipation, the more intense that final spasm would be for them both.

Gingerly, he trod the narrow path that scaled the heights of desire, even as his lips and tongue plumbed the hot, wet recesses of her womanhood, lapping, darting and gliding within her sweet, secret chasm. When at last the tension in her flesh grew so taut it must shatter and her breath reached a fevered, pleading pitch, his own tightly coiled need quivered on the knife edge between pleasure and pain.

Rising up like a powerful, cresting breaker, he plunged into her—his tongue deep into her soft mouth and his straining shaft into her slick, searing heat. In a wild, thrusting rhythm, they raced together towards the furthest extremity of pleasure, beyond any they had previously charted.

Then the swift, smooth movement of Caroline's hips erupted in powerful spasms that quaked through her body. The shuddering contractions wrung an answering release from him. It demolished the floodgates of his self-control, releasing a fierce torrent of ecstasy that flowed over and through him, drowning him in delight.

Chapter Fourteen

As she lay in Bennett's arms, her pulse and breath gradually slowing from their breakneck gallop, Caroline felt as if she'd been shattered into tiny pieces and magically put back together again. In the early days of their marriage, when she'd been so hopelessly infatuated with her handsome, enigmatic husband, they'd had many passionate encounters. None had overwhelmed her quite like this one.

Was it because their near-drowning had made her appreciate the wonder of raw, pulsing life in a whole new way? Or because it had been so long since Bennett touched her, held her and kissed her, and she knew this time would be the last? Or could it be on account of the new feelings for him that had taken stubborn root in her heart?

She'd once thought she loved him, but now she realised he had been right to accuse her of not knowing what love was. Looking back, she could see that shallow, self-involved fancy was not even close. It had not been the real Bennett she'd cared for. Rather it was a character she'd conjured out of her naïve, romantic imagination and attributed to him because he'd refused to let her see the flawed but good man he truly was at heart.

Later, when she discovered her husband bore little resemblance to her fancied ideal, she'd felt betrayed and deceived, refusing to acknowledge the truth—that she had wilfully deceived herself. For all that, she could not let it go. She'd been compelled to make him pay attention to her. His increasing indifference had only spurred her to more reckless lengths until her irresponsible behaviour threatened to destroy everything for which she'd claimed to care.

Yet, out of her folly and misery something good had emerged. Her destructive infatuation with Bennett had been broken at last. Over the past few weeks, her caustic resentment had slowly subsided, too. In its place had grown a sincere appreciation for the man he truly was. In spite of the painful events from his past, or perhaps because of them, he had become an honourable, tenacious champion of any who needed his assistance or protection. If only she had realised that before it was too late.

'Caro?' His whisper broke the intimate, fragile silence between them. 'There's something important I must ask you.'

'What?' Wary tension crept through her body. She knew by the sound of his voice that it could be nothing good.

'I know you've told me before.' His words gusted out like a sigh. 'At least you tried to. But this time I am prepared to listen and believe what you say.'

Could he mean...? She scarcely dared hope after his prolonged refusal to accept that she'd stopped short of committing that final betrayal. Somehow, he had grown to trust her. Even George Marlow's letter and those disgusting caricatures had not been enough to destroy his newfound faith in her.

Whether she deserved his trust, *that* question undermined Caroline's fragile hope.

'You never did take Astley as a lover, did you? Nor any other man? You have been faithful to me throughout our marriage?'

For weeks now Caroline had longed to protest her innocence at every opportunity. But she knew she would only be wasting her breath and perhaps provoking Bennett to leave the island with her son. Now, when she'd least expected it, she had the chance to tell her husband what had really happened, secure in the knowledge that he would believe her.

Caroline inhaled a deep breath to steady her. 'I swear you are the only man I have ever...given myself to in this way.'

That was all very well as far as it went, she realised, but it was only part of the truth. And perhaps not the most important part. 'I see now that all my foolish flirting was nearly as much a betrayal of our marriage as outright adultery. Yet somehow I knew I could never be satisfied with the sort of attentions from another man that I only ever wanted from you.'

At first her confession of both innocence and guilt met with nothing but bewildering silence from her husband.

'You do believe me, don't you?' she prompted him when she could bear the suspense no longer.

'Of course.' He sounded vexed at being made to acknowledge it. 'Deep down, I think I've known the truth all along. I refused to believe it because I wanted to punish you for that night at Almack's. And because I knew it would change everything.'

Muscles taut and unyielding, he pulled away from her and rose from the bed.

As he slipped into his drawers and breeches, Caroline sat up, pulling the sheet under her arms to conceal her bare breasts.

Suddenly, she felt acutely self-conscious of her naked body. 'What do you mean, it changes everything?'

Picking up her nightgown, which Parker had left folded over the headboard of the bed, Bennett handed it to her. 'Surely you know I cannot seek a divorce now.'

'Why shouldn't you?' Caroline pulled on her nightgown and huddled in the middle of the bed, hands clasped around her knees.

Bennett retrieved more of his scattered clothes from the floor and put them back on. 'I realise I have not behaved much like it of late, but I do possess some notion of honour. I can hardly seek a divorce on the grounds of adultery when I am satisfied you have committed no such act.'

Pushing back her lank, damp hair, Caroline shuddered to think what a fright she must look. Had Bennett only taken her to bed out of pity? It was clear he regretted that ill-considered impulse, just as he regretted losing the opportunity to break free of the millstone that would pull him down to destruction.

'You are too scrupulous.' She could not force him to continue their marriage when he wanted and needed to be free. 'You stood before a vicar and promised to love me when you did not. With the number of witnesses who saw Astley kiss me at Almack's, you should have no difficulty obtaining a divorce without ever having to speak a single untrue word.'

Something in what she said seemed to unsettle Bennett. Abruptly he stopped dressing. 'What about you, Caro? You stood before that vicar and promised to love me. Did you only marry me in a final bid to win your father's approval or was there more to it than that?'

His probing gaze demanded the whole, unvarnished truth. That might only make him feel a greater obligation to stand by their feeble excuse for a marriage, no matter what it cost them. In the end, he would grow to hate her even more than he had before. The way she'd come to feel about him, Caroline could not bear that.

'Yes!' she snapped, frightened by her vulnerability. 'Since you insist on knowing, I did fancy myself in love with you. What was worse, I persuaded myself you cared for me!'

Her revelation rendered Bennett incapable of concealing his emotions for perhaps the first time in their marriage. As plain as anything, Caroline saw the pity she'd expected, as well as remorse, regret and a futile yearning for something that could never be.

After a moment of stunned silence, he headed for the door. 'I must go see how Wyn is getting along. I will take charge of him so Parker can come tend to you.'

Without another word, he left the room as if making his escape from some terrible threat. With a sinking heart, Caroline watched him depart. She wondered if he regretted going to such perilous lengths to save her from drowning. His future would be far easier if he had not.

Somehow, she must make him see that divorce was the least painful alternative available to them.

He could not possibly divorce Caroline now. No matter how desperately she wanted him to.

That thought ran through Bennett's mind in a continuous, taunting refrain as he tried to keep his young son amused while Parker attended to his wife.

Did she not understand? It was a matter of honour. He could not bring suit for damages against Fitz Astley when the worst his enemy had done was to arrange an incriminating ambush to steal a kiss from his wife. It was despicable conduct to be sure, but hardly illegal. The comparison Caroline had made to his insincere wedding vows was not valid in the least. By marrying her, he had never intended to do anyone harm. Quite the contrary.

He might not have *meant* to harm Caroline by wedding her, his conscience reminded him, but he had just the same. After the first flush of infatuation had worn off, he'd made no effort to cultivate the kind of closeness that might have stood the test of time. He had never confided in her, never asked for her help, never tried to understand her. Looking back, Bennett wondered if perhaps he had been afraid to forge a deeper bond with his beautiful bride in case he might come to care for her more than he could afford.

All the while, she had loved him in her way, yearning for the kind of affection he was not capable of giving her, even if he'd wanted to. When he thought of all the things he had never taken the time to find out about her and all the things he had neglected to disclose about himself, he wondered if she'd sometimes felt more like a mistress than a wife. Perhaps even less than a mistress.

Bennett did not realise how deeply he'd fallen to brooding until Wyn looked up suddenly from the collection of seashells they had spread on the table. 'Are you angry with Mama for falling in the water and making you fish her out?'

The child's question troubled him. Far too often when he was preoccupied, Wyn assumed he must be vexed about something. Had Caroline also misinterpreted his frequent silences as stern disapproval, especially after their son was born and she'd struggled with the demands of new motherhood?

'Angry with your mama?' Bennett shook his head as he

reached to grasp the child's hand. Thanks to Caroline's tutelage he was becoming more comfortable conveying tender emotions with touch 'Not at all. I was worried about her and afraid what might happen if I didn't get her out. You probably felt that way, too, did you?'

Wyn responded with a grave nod and squeezed his father's hand.

They sat in silence for a minute or two, then the child spoke again. 'I'm glad you're not angry with Mama. You have been getting on so well together. Do you not have those differences any more that made you shout at each other?'

His son's observation made Bennett think. 'We still have plenty of differences. But we've come to see that the things we share are far more important. Besides, differences don't always have to cause problems.'

Wyn's features settled into a pensive frown as if he was trying to make sense of an idea it had taken Bennett decades to grasp. He was not certain he could explain it in terms a child might understand, but he sensed Wyn needed him to try.

'You see these shells?' He picked out two from among the small collection spread out on the table. 'They're quite different from one another, don't you think?'

Wyn nodded. 'That one's big and that one's small. That one's brown with spots and that one's all white. That one is long and thin. That one is almost the shape of a lady's fan.'

'Excellent observations.' Bennett offered his son a warm smile of approval and reassurance. 'You're very perceptive—that means you take notice of things other people might miss. It's a fine quality to have.'

More to himself than to the boy, he added, 'You must get

that from your mother, for my powers of perception are downright feeble.'

After all, he'd failed to notice any of the signs that might have indicated Caroline was once in love with him. Or had he deliberately ignored them, wary of anything that might make him care about her?

His praise provoked a proud smile that lit up Wyn's small face. It was Caroline's smile, Bennett realised with a pang. And his son's eyes were the identical shade of blue-green to hers.

'Even though these shells are so different,' Bennett returned to the point he was trying to make, 'you liked them both enough to pick them up.'

'Yes.' A glint of understanding quickened in those familiar, beloved eyes.

'Both those shells provided protection for the creatures that once lived inside them.' That notion made Bennett realise something else.

He and Caroline had both been hurt in the past—both had covered their vulnerable hearts with protective shells. Because those coverings had taken such different forms, neither had recognised the other's for what it was. When Caroline had dared to advance a soft feeler toward him, it had stubbed painfully against his hard, spiky carapace. No wonder she'd retreated deeper into her colourful, luminous bubble.

Was it too late to coax her back out and find the courage to emerge from his shell to give her the kind of love she needed and deserved? He feared so. But for their son's sake and Caroline's, and perhaps most of all for his own, Bennett knew he must try.

* * *

Once Parker had washed the salt water from her hair and combed it out to dry, Caroline had returned downstairs to be with her son. Since this might be the last evening she would spend with him in quite some time, she had not wanted to miss a moment of it. Not long after she joined Wyn and Bennett in the parlour, her husband excused himself and headed upstairs. After the past few weeks of pleasant companionship, his sudden reluctance to be in the same room with her made it clear that he believed bedding her had been a mistake.

Though her body still tingled with an echo of delight whenever she recalled the thrilling ways he had kissed and touched her, Caroline could not disagree. His ardent attentions had woken feelings within her that threatened to grow hungry and demanding, tempting her to cling to her marriage no matter what it cost Bennett or their son.

'Look, Mama.' Wyn glowed with pride as he showed her a basket brimming with seashells. 'Papa helped me clean the sand out of them. He says when we get back to London he is going to have a box made for me with a little nook to hold each shell. It will have a glass top so I can look at them and hinges so I can open it to add new ones.'

'Fancy that.' Caroline wrapped her arm around her son's shoulder, surprised to discover how much taller he'd grown during the past few weeks. Their time on the island had done him so much good. The child positively glowed with renewed health and happiness. 'Your papa has such clever ideas, doesn't he?'

Wyn nodded. 'Papa says he's not per-cep-tive, but I think he is.'

Caroline marvelled at her young son's proper use of such

a big word, proud yet dismayed by further evidence of how quickly he was growing up. The urge to cling to him was growing stronger than her good intentions.

'Your papa has a great many fine qualities,' she assured their son.

Bennett was clever and honourable, persistent and compassionate. He'd been trying very hard to be a more attentive, affectionate father. But she had to agree he was not the most perceptive of men. Only now had he realised how much she'd once yearned for him.

'Papa is good at explaining things.' Wyn began to pick through the shells in his basket. 'He told me it doesn't hurt to have differences, like these shells. They aren't all alike, but each one has something special about it.'

'He said that?' She picked up a shell that must once have held some sort of sea snail. The opening gradually spiralled inwards, deeper and deeper.

Wyn nodded. 'Papa said that's why you two are getting on so much better.'

'Perhaps it is.' Caroline turned the shell over in her hand, admiring its natural elegance of form.

She and Bennett were very different in the way they'd responded to past hurts. She'd become like a crab—scuttling here and there, seizing what she wanted in her relentless claws and clinging to it at all costs. By contrast, Bennett had retreated into his thick shell like a solitary oyster. Chafed by the grit of past pain, he had slowly transformed it into the priceless pearl of compassion for others.

Lately he'd begun to emerge from that shell, to show their son more overt affection and even to confide in her. But after bedding her, Bennett seemed poised to retreat back into himself once again, as if seeking refuge from some threat. Was that how he viewed the things she'd told him? When he had fled her bedchamber so abruptly, it was clear he resisted acknowledging her fidelity and the love she'd once felt for him.

Bennett had wed her in the throes of blind infatuation and perhaps out of a sense of obligation to her father. Too late, he'd come to his senses and realised she was not the kind of woman he wanted and needed. Now, just when he'd glimpsed an opportunity to be free of her, he found himself honour bound to maintain their irreparably damaged marriage.

As if summoned by Caroline's thoughts, her husband's firm footsteps sounded on the stairs. An instant later, he strode into the parlour. His mouth was set in a determined line, but his eyes held an uneasy look. 'Wyn, how would you like to go treasure-hunting with me tomorrow morning?'

'Where, Papa?' The child thrust his basket of shells into Caroline's hands and bolted towards his father. 'What sort of treasure?'

'I'm not certain what we'll find, but these islands were the haunt of pirates and smugglers in the past.' Bennett leaned down to gather the child in a fleeting but fond embrace.

Caroline could tell such gestures of affection still did not come easily for him, but he was becoming a little less self-conscious each time. That was one result of this whole sordid mess from which she could take comfort. It had made Bennett see the kind of warm, loving relationship their son needed.

'Look what I found behind one of the drawers in the old wardrobe.' He produced a rolled-up piece of paper that Caroline suspected had been fabricated for Wyn's amusement.

She wondered how long Bennett had also been planning this surprise treasure hunt. It was the sort of whimsical adventure she might have contrived if she'd thought of it. The whole thing seemed rather out of character for her solemn, practical husband, but she approved his willingness to try something different for the sake of their son.

Wyn's eyes widened as he unrolled the paper and looked it over. 'Do we have to wait until tomorrow, Papa? Can't we start now? Please!'

Not long ago Caroline would have been inclined to give in, but Bennett had made her see there was more to being a parent than treats and indulgence. 'The treasure will keep for one more night, dearest. It's almost your bedtime. Treasure hunters need a good night's sleep to keep their wits about them.'

Her husband looked at her in a way that made Caroline catch her breath. She told herself it was only gratitude for supporting his decision.

'I'll be too excited to sleep,' Wyn protested.

'Good things are worth waiting for, dearest.'

For a moment the child pouted over not getting his way. But when his parents stood firm, he seemed to accept the inevitable. 'Will you tell me a story at bedtime?'

'Of course, if you want me to.'

'About pirates?'

'I'm afraid that might give you bad dreams.' Searching for an alternative, Caroline recalled how intrigued Wyn had been by the notion that these islands might be the last remnant of drowned Lyonesse. 'What about a tale of King Arthur's knights?'

Too late she recalled how many of those stories glorified *courtly love,* a fancy name for adultery. When she'd been a girl on the cusp of womanhood, her heart had thrilled to those tales of fair ladies who'd risked everything for the chance of love. She'd pictured herself as Guinevere, Isolde or Ygraine, swept off her feet by a dashing hero. How could a man like Bennett Maitland have hoped to live up to that romantic ideal?

Chapter Fifteen

Later, as Bennett listened to his wife tell Wyn the story of Sir Gawain and the Loathly Lady, he was surprised and dismayed to discover how much the ancient legend related to their situation.

In her most dramatic tone, Caroline spun the tale for their enthralled little son. 'Once she had forced him to wed her, the hideous creature told Sir Gawain she was a fair damsel who had been placed under a terrible enchantment. By marrying her, he had broken half the curse. She could be beautiful by day so that all the world would honour and envy him for possessing so fine a wife. But alone with him at night she would be monstrous ugly. Or she could be repulsive by day and beautiful by night so that he alone could admire and love her.'

Bennett wondered which he would have chosen in Gawain's place. In a sense, he had been given a similar choice. Before that fateful night at Almack's, Caroline had been a charming hostess, elegant dance partner and glamorous trinket on his arm. Many men had envied him such a wife. But in the privacy of their home, she'd been nothing to him.

Since coming to the island, she had transformed into a woman of sense, sympathy and sweetness who had captured his heart. But if he took Caroline back to London now, all the men who'd once flirted with her and the women who'd sought to copy her style would shun her as if she were a hideous monstrosity. He might be content with that, but how could he expect her to endure it?

'Which one did Sir Gawain choose, Mama?' Wyn's question recalled Bennett from his musing.

'I'm glad you asked.' Caroline sounded a bit startled, as if she too had been lost in thought. 'It was not easy for Sir Gawain to decide. He considered how each of those choices would affect him. Then his heart was moved with pity for what the Loathly Lady had suffered. He said he would let the decision be *hers*.'

Bennett wasn't certain whether he pitied the knight's folly in surrendering control of the situation, or respected his courage.

'No sooner had Sir Gawain spoken those words,' Caroline continued, 'than there was a flash of sparking light and the Loathly Lady transformed into the most beautiful maiden he had ever beheld. She told him that by permitting her to choose her own fate he had freed her from the spell entirely. Now she would be beautiful all the time. Wasn't that lovely?'

Wyn nodded. 'Did Sir Gawain and the Lady live happily ever after?'

'Why, of course,' his mother assured him.

Bennett wished the problems of real life could be as easily solved as those in stories.

'Did they have any children?' Wyn asked.

Caroline smiled at the question. 'Yes indeed. Three strong, brave sons and three lovely, clever daughters.'

'What were their names?'

Bennett recognised his son's ploy to prolong the story and delay going to sleep. 'Your mama can tell you all that tomorrow. Now you need to get your rest for treasure hunting.'

Caroline did not seem offended by his interference. Leaning forwards, she dusted soft kisses over the child's forehead. 'Those are to sweeten your dreams. Goodnight, dearest!'

A few weeks ago, Bennett would have doubted the sincerity of such a gesture. Now he knew better than to question Caroline's love for their son. He only wished he had not denied *himself* the opportunity to experience the full bounty of her affection.

Wyn flung his small arms around her neck. 'Goodnight, Mama!'

Mother and son exchanged a fond embrace, then the child raised his arms to Bennett. 'Goodnight, Papa!'

'Goodnight, son.' He pulled Wyn tight to his chest, grateful to Caroline for making him realise what he'd been missing. 'Sleep well.'

Once they left Wyn's room, an awkward silence fell between them. Caroline seemed in a hurry to reach the stairs. Bennett wondered if she was afraid he might pull her into his bedchamber and ravish her again. Or was it her own physical desires she did not trust? Did she fear he might mistake that passion for a sign of deeper feelings she no longer had for him?

'Would you…care to take…a walk?' he asked, unsettled to find himself as tongue-tied as a schoolboy. 'There are…

matters we must settle tonight. I would rather not risk Wyn overhearing us.'

'No. I mean…it would be better if he did not.' She sounded every bit as skittish as he felt. 'Of course I will walk with you. Just let me fetch my wrap and bonnet.'

By the time Bennett donned his hat, she had returned, ready for their stroll.

They could not have picked a finer evening for it, Bennett reflected as he offered her his arm and they set off southwards, past the Old Blockhouse. With midsummer only a few weeks away, it was still quite light out. A soft breeze carried the perfume of flowers and the warm, wholesome scent of drying hay. A month from now the air would reek of burning seaweed, but by then they would be long gone. At least he and Wyn would be for certain. As for Caroline, her future was what they must settle.

'I shall be sorry to leave this island,' he ventured. 'The past few weeks have been the pleasantest I've spent since I used to come here as a boy.'

Caroline gave a slow nod. The brim of her bonnet concealed her expression from Bennett's curious glance. It did not help that she'd turned slightly away from him, as if captivated by the sight of the wide eastern horizon where the sky was gradually changing to a deeper, darker shade of blue.

'I have enjoyed our time here, too.' She spoke in a quiet, wistful tone. 'Mrs Hicks was right in claiming these islands are a good place to heal. I feel as if I have recovered from a sickness I've had all my life without ever knowing it.'

Had the folly of loving a man like him been one of the symptoms of her ailment? Bennett could not bring himself to ask.

'It isn't only the scenery I've enjoyed.' Bennett hoped he was not making this effort in vain. 'Or the healthful climate.'

He inhaled a deep breath of air sweetened with the smell of new life blossoming. 'It has been the opportunity to experience a happy family life. I now realise it is something I've longed for all my life.'

'It has been very pleasant.' Caroline stooped to pluck a wild rose from a thicket that clung to an old stone wall.

When she tucked her hand back into the crook of his elbow, Bennett reached over to cover it with his other hand. 'I wish we never had to leave. But I have received a letter from my friend Marlow summoning me back to London. He says there is to be an important vote soon and I am needed.'

'Then you must go, of course.' Caroline lifted the wildflower to her nose. 'How soon will you and Wyn be leaving?'

Was that a catch he heard in her voice? And if so, was it only caused by the prospect of her son's departure?

Bennett cleared his throat, which had suddenly developed a troublesome lump. 'I have given the matter a great deal of thought. For a great many reasons, I would like you to come back to London with Wyn and me.'

His words jolted Caroline from her earlier quiet pensiveness. Turning abruptly towards him, she sucked in a deep breath of air to fuel her rebuttal.

'Please.' He raised his hand to bid her hold her tongue. 'Let me have my say, then you are welcome to have yours. I know I have not been the kind of husband you wanted and needed. I let the experiences of my past blind me to your feelings and stifle my own. I have unjustly accused you of adultery, packed you off to this remote spot and threatened to take your child away. Though I am sorrier than you can ever know for all those things, I neither deserve nor expect your forgiveness.'

'Do you not?' Caroline cried, no longer able to restrain herself. 'Then surely I cannot hope for *your* pardon after the way I humiliated you in public and wreaked such terrible damage on your career and your cause.'

Put like that, it did sound impossible that they could hope to repair their poor wreck of a marriage. Yet that was what Bennett knew he wanted, more than he'd ever wanted anything.

Return to London? Go on with their marriage? Keep her child? A few weeks ago, Caroline would have given anything to gain what Bennett now offered. But lately she had learned some hard lessons about the ultimate meaning and measure of love.

It was not a matter of treats and indulgence. The substance of love involved putting the needs and desires of those she cared for ahead of her own. As enjoyable as the past few weeks had been, Caroline knew once her husband and son returned to London they would be better off without her.

She sensed Bennett knew it, too. It was clear from his pensive silence as he pondered her question about whether he could forgive the way she'd humiliated him and damaged his standing among the Abolitionists. He had only made this generous offer out of a sense of honour and possibly guilt for never having loved her. That was a perilously weak foundation on which to build a future together.

'I thought we agreed to put all that business behind us and not look back,' Bennett replied at last in a rather gruff tone.

Did it make him angry to be reminded of what she'd done?

Then how would he respond when he was forced to deal with the actual damaging consequences of her actions?

'It was one thing to forget the past while we've been on this island, away from anything that might remind us.' Caroline stared toward the dusky horizon. Out of sight lurked the mainland, like a powerful predator waiting to pounce if they dared venture back into its territory. 'In London everything will remind us of all our old grievances. All the same pressures and temptations will be waiting to draw us back into old habits. Before we knew it, we would be as miserable as ever. I don't want that. Do you?'

She chided herself for the yearning tone of her final question. It sounded as if she were pleading with him to contradict her. Or perhaps to provide her with a good enough excuse to do what the selfish side of her so desperately wanted.

In truth, there was only one reason that might persuade her to risk attempting a permanent reconciliation. But that was a reason Bennett could never give her.

'No. I wouldn't want that.' He heaved a deep sigh. 'I only wish…that is…we've been so happy these past few weeks.'

'You know that was only playacting for Wyn's benefit. We cannot maintain such a charade for the rest of our lives!' Caroline spoke more sharply than she'd intended to. She had to remind herself of the harsh truth so she would not fall back into her old pattern of believing Bennett felt more for her than he was capable of feeling.

'I know.'

She sensed the intensity of his gaze upon her, willing her to turn and look into his eyes. But she did not dare for fear of what she might see there and the vulnerability her eyes might betray.

'I cannot deny it began as playacting,' he continued, 'but...'

Bennett's hesitation made her turn towards him. 'But what?'

Now it was his turn to avoid her searching gaze. 'Never mind.'

'What were you going to say?' Caroline insisted.

'It doesn't matter.' He inhaled a deep breath of cool sea air. 'I think we should head back to the house before it gets any darker.'

What had she expected or hoped he might say? She tried to ignore a sharp little stab of disappointment. 'I suppose we ought to.'

She'd secretly hoped Bennett might tell her he loved her, Caroline admitted to herself as they began walking back the way they'd come. But that was never going to happen.

Bennett hadn't loved her when they were first married. How could he possibly have those kinds of feelings for her now, after all that had gone wrong in their marriage? She wasn't certain he *could* love anyone other than their son. From everything he'd grudgingly confessed about his past, she knew his heart was like a wounded limb, part amputated perhaps, that could not be expected to function as a sound one. If he was ever to have the opportunity to love a woman, he would need to start fresh, without all the mistakes and hurts they had accumulated over the years.

That was the other important reason why she did not dare return to London with Bennett and Wyn. She feared these powerful new feelings for her husband, knowing he could not return them. Because they were so much stronger and deeper than anything she'd felt for him before, Caroline knew she could not be content to live as his wife, craving what he could not give her. She would end up even more discontented than she'd been before.

'I know it would not be easy for you,' Bennett mused, 'to go back to London and face down all the gossip.'

Did he think that was what prevented her from returning to Sterling House with him and Wyn? All the wagging tongues in the Westminster would not have daunted her if she believed there was a chance Bennett could care for her as she did for him.

'No worse than for you,' she countered, 'to alienate all your followers in the Abolition Movement by refusing to divorce the wife who discredited you.'

Bennett gave a wry shrug. 'I suspect Mr Wilberforce would be gratified to see us reconcile. He is such a devoted family man himself. Besides, a whisper of scandal might be just what the movement needs to enliven it again. Too many people have grown complacent since the slave *trade* was outlawed. They forget that still leaves millions in bondage and more born into slavery with every passing year.'

The warmth with which he spoke of his cause made Caroline more conscious than ever of what her heedless behaviour might cost so many other people. Bennett had once accused her of never looking past the tip of her nose and he'd been right. Was it possible, in the years to come, that she might find a way to make productive use of her time to aid the Abolition cause in some way? The notion beckoned her with a soothing whisper of purpose and atonement.

'What matters most to me,' Bennett continued, 'is the welfare of our son. No matter how we try to explain it to him, I fear Wyn may still believe he is somehow to blame for the break up of our family. That was what I thought when I discovered my mother had left my father. It is only lately I have come to realise I was not the cause of my parents' failed marriage, but its victim. Looking back, I regret I made you its victim, too. I cannot bear to make Wyn pay the price for our mistakes. For *his* sake, can you not give our marriage another chance?'

Until very recently, Caroline would not have believed her cool, enigmatic husband capable of making such a heartfelt plea. Now his words seemed to reach into her chest and rend her heart in two.

She pulled away from Bennett, not trusting herself to be near him. If he tried to sway her with a kiss, she feared all her good intentions would be no match for the passionate yearning he would kindle within her. 'Do you think I *want* to give up my place in Wyn's life so soon after finally forming a true bond with him? It is *because* I love him that I cannot bear to see him tainted by my scandal. It is because I love him that I now understand he will be better off with you and Mrs McGregor.'

'Tainted by scandal?' Bennett shook his head. 'I do not believe that. Gossip may spread like wildfire for a time, but it soon consumes the fuel and moves on to new territory. My parents' separation was one of the most sordid scandals of its day, yet you had never heard so much as a whisper of it. By the time any of this would matter to Wyn, it will be long forgotten, I assure you.'

Her maternal instincts begged Caroline to give in. She might not have the kind of marriage she and Bennett had playacted for the past few weeks, but at least she would have the chance to be a real mother to her son.

Bennett must have sensed her resolve weakening for he

redoubled his efforts. 'I know you love our son, Caro. Your actions these past weeks speak louder than any words. You have worked so hard to be a more attentive mother and help me become a more affectionate father. Besides, Wyn thinks the world of you. Even with the progress I have made, the boy still needs his mother. I cannot understand why you are so reluctant suddenly. I thought this was what you would want.'

'I did.' Caroline's footsteps picked up speed as if she were being pursued by some powerful, hungry predator.

Bennett lengthened his stride to keep pace with her.

'What changed?' He sounded deeply and sincerely perplexed.

What had changed? Very little for him, clearly, or he would not have been obliged to ask. For her so much had changed that she scarcely knew where to begin, even if she dare tell him.

How could she explain, after all that had happened, knowing he could not care for her, that she had let him into her heart again—this time dangerously deep? He was willing to brave the scandal and take her back for Wyn's sake. If he discovered she still cared for him, might he try to pretend he returned her feelings? How long would he be able to keep up *that* charade?

Was it selfish of her to resist risking her heart for her son's sake? For once in her life she wanted to do the right thing for Wyn and Bennett. But he was making it hard for her to be certain which choice would be best for them.

'I fear not enough has changed!' She felt as if she were fighting for her life. 'We made a dreadful mess of our marriage the first time. Wyn will be the one to pay the heaviest price if we fail again. Now please do not tempt me to change my mind or I fear I will not have the strength to do what I must!'

Seeing the lights of the house a short way off, Caroline broke into a frantic run and did not stop until the door of her bedchamber swung shut behind her.

There was no use chasing after her. Bennett reluctantly accepted that fact as he watched the shadowy figure of his wife dash for the sanctuary of the house.

He could follow her and try to argue his case further. But that would only risk Wyn overhearing them, something Bennett did not want to happen again. Besides, it was evident Caroline had made up her mind. She was prepared to accept a divorce and give up her child rather than remain in a marriage she could no longer tolerate.

Turning away from the house where he'd been so happy, he headed for the lonely shore of Gimble Porth, summoned by the endless lament of the sea.

He treasured his memory of the day he and Caroline and Wyn had spent there, searching for seashells and building their stone cairn. He recalled pointing out the ancient stone buildings and field enclosures, lost long ago beneath the waves. As he paced the bluff overlooking the deserted beach, Bennett thought about his wife and son.

Was his marriage altogether lost, like those drowned farms? If so, he had no one to blame but himself. Caroline had made it clear he'd destroyed whatever tender feelings she once held for him. Though he wished she would give him the opportunity to make things right between them, he could hardly blame her for being afraid he would only hurt her again.

She might be right about one thing, he conceded to the restless questioning of the surf. Once back in London, the call of duty might draw him away from her and make it difficult to give her the attention she needed. He hoped he could keep that from happening with his son. He would need to work hard to fill the void left by Caroline's departure after she and Wyn had grown so close.

The longer he reflected on it, the more Bennett wondered how his wife could willingly give up their son after the lengths to which she had gone to keep Wyn with her. A few weeks ago, he might have assumed she'd grown bored with motherhood. Now he knew otherwise. During their time on the island, Caroline had learned the true meaning of love. By giving up Wyn, she was demonstrating that hard-won knowledge in the most selfless way possible.

From the star-studded sky above, the pale melancholy face of the maiden in the moon seemed to challenge Bennett. Did he have the courage to do the same?

Chapter Sixteen

After a restless night, Caroline woke with a start the next morning, uncertain what had roused her. When her eyelids fluttered open, she discovered Bennett sitting on the trunk at the foot of her bed. The shock of seeing him there brought a sharp enquiry to her lips. But the look of weary sadness on his face moved her to speak gently instead.

'How long have you been here?' she whispered. 'Did you get any sleep at all last night?'

She wondered if he had come to try winning her back by appealing to the passionate physical connection they'd lately revived. If so, he might succeed, for she was sorely tempted to open her arms and invite him into her bed. All that prevented her was fear of the regret she might glimpse in his eyes afterwards.

In reply to her question about sleep, Bennett slowly shook his head. 'I will have plenty of time to sleep on my journey back to London. I'm sorry I startled you, but I wanted a chance for a private word before Wyn wakes. I intend to take a boat to St Mary's after his treasure hunt, then catch the next ship back to the mainland.'

'That sounds like a good plan.' Caroline sat up. 'Wyn will be so excited about finding his treasure, I'm certain he won't mind leaving the island. You can take Parker and Albert along to help care for him on your journey. They will be glad to get back to London again.'

It required all her willpower to stifle a forlorn sigh. She could not afford to let Bennett guess how weak her resolve was. It would be best if her husband and son departed soon, before her good intentions gave way beneath her longing to remain part of their lives no matter what the cost.

Bennett rubbed his eyes. 'I spent the night walking and thinking about all the things we discussed and everything that has happened since we came to Tresco. I came to tell you I have reached a decision.'

That word made Caroline uneasy. Did he somehow intend to force her to return to London and go on with their marriage? The latter prospect made her heart flutter with a mixture of panic...and hope.

Reaching into the pocket of his coat, Bennett took something out. His fingers wrapped around the object so Caroline could not tell what it was. 'That story you told Wyn last night gave me a great deal to ponder.'

She thought back over the tale of the Loathly Lady. Though she recognised certain parallels to their blighted marriage, she was not certain what lesson Bennett could have drawn from it.

'Seven years ago, I gave you little choice but to marry me. Now I intend to leave the decision about your future—*our* future—in your hands.' Leaning over the footboard of the bed, he extended his arm towards her.

Instinctively, Caroline opened her hand to receive whatever he intended to give her. Just as the small rounded object dropped into her palm, she heard the faint thump of Wyn's feet hitting the floor. Her fingers closed around her wedding ring—the one she'd torn from her hand and flung at Bennett several weeks ago.

That day now seemed so long in the past. Recalling it, she scarcely recognised the frustrated, angry enemies she and her husband had been then. She could not risk any action that might turn them back into those people.

Bennett gave a visible start when he heard Wyn jump out of bed and scurry around his room. Eager as he was to begin the treasure hunt, the child must have decided to get dressed all on his own. He would not likely allow his parents many more minutes of privacy.

'If you cannot forgive me for the years of unhappiness you have endured as my wife and give me a chance to become the husband you deserve,' Bennett rattled off the words in his haste to get them out, 'then I will assist you to obtain a legal separation so you can keep Wyn. You will not have to remain on Tresco, though I hope you will settle close enough that I may see our son quite often.'

'Legal separation?' Caroline repeated in a bemused murmur as if she had no idea what those words meant. In fact, she understood them all too well.

For a fleeting instant when Bennett returned her wedding ring, she'd experienced a flicker of hope that he was about to make a heartfelt declaration in a final bid to win her back. His mention of a separation quashed that foolish dream so harshly that she'd paid little heed to anything else he said.

'That's right.' Bennett rose from his improvised seat on her trunk. 'A *mensa et thoro* it's called. It would allow you to be free of me, yet still keep Wyn. I know if you consented to return to me, it would only be because you could not bear to part with him. That is not what I want.'

What *did* he want, then? Caroline's brow furrowed.

Last night Bennett had pleaded with her to continue their marriage, for Wyn's sake. She'd assumed he finally recognised her genuine love for their son and remembered how the estrangement from his mother had blighted his childhood. Yet now he claimed he *didn't* want her to come back only for the good of their child. Indeed, he seemed to be going out of his way to give her no reason to remain in their marriage.

'I don't...understand.' Cradling her discarded wedding ring in her palm, she wondered what had possessed Bennett to keep it and why he'd chosen this moment to return it to her. Was it meant to be a symbol, to remind her of all the unhappiness they'd caused one another?

A fierce scowl gripped Bennett's features. Perhaps he was vexed by her bewilderment. 'I will not press my attentions upon you if they are unwelcome. But if you change your mind, you have only to place that ring back upon your finger...and I shall be—'

From out in the hallway came the sound of Wyn's door opening, followed by footsteps.

Bennett's hands clenched. 'That is...you shall make me—'

'Papa?' Wyn tapped softly on his father's door. 'Can we go hunt for that treasure now, before someone else beats us to it?'

'I shall make you what?' Caroline prompted her husband in a yearning whisper.

She had seldom seen him so discomposed, his gaze shifting from her to the door and back. He seemed to have trouble swallowing. 'You shall make me the...'

'Papa?' Wyn called again, his tone more insistent, becoming agitated.

'What's the use?' Bennett muttered as he spun away from her. 'I cannot do this, even if it would make a difference.'

Then he raised his voice to call out to the child, 'I'm coming, son.'

Without looking back, he strode off, leaving Caroline more perplexed than ever.

A moment later, she overheard him talking to Wyn out in the hallway.

'Is Mama coming with us to look for the treasure?' the child asked.

'Your mother is still in bed. We should let her rest,' replied Bennett without bothering to consult her. 'If we find some treasure, we can bring it back to show her.'

The next sound Caroline heard was their footsteps on the stairs.

The ring in her hand felt heavier than it ought to, as if it had absorbed the weight of all the old bitterness between them. She could not escape the superstitious fancy that if she put it on again, all those venomous old feelings would seep back into her heart. Rising from the bed, she hurried to the windowsill and placed the ring there. Then she backed away, as if from something dangerous that might follow her if she let down her guard.

What had Bennett meant last night, when he'd urged her to return to London and give their failed marriage another chance? she asked herself as she removed her nightgown. Had it only been a passing whim he'd repented almost immediately? Or had she deceived herself once again into hearing only what she wanted to hear?

Clearly whatever he'd said last night no longer signified, Caroline decided as she began to dress for the day. He must have seized upon this idea of a legal separation as a way to get rid of her without compromising his honour. As he had so often reminded her, actions spoke louder than words.

That thought gave Caroline pause. What could Bennett be trying to tell her by offering this choice between a legal separation and the wedding band she'd so violently discarded? It was a riddle as puzzling to her as the man himself. And yet, she'd made progress these past few weeks in beginning to grasp the contradictory enigma of her husband's nature.

The more she understood him, the more she'd come to care for him. Did she dare risk loving him even more with the final end of their marriage in sight?

As Caroline wandered down the stairs, lost in thought, she met Parker on her way up, carrying a tray. 'I thought you might like a bite of breakfast in your room, my lady, seeing as how his lordship and Master Wyn have gone out.'

'Have they left already?'

The maid nodded. 'Just headed off a moment ago, ma'am. Bolted their breakfast in a trice. Master Wyn's that excited. He said he'd let me have my pick of something from his treasure.'

The thought of her son's generosity brought a faint smile to Caroline's lips. 'Thank you for fetching me breakfast, Parker, but I haven't much appetite this morning.'

'Are you ill, my lady?' Parker sounded more concerned about her well-being than vexed at having gone to some effort for nothing. 'Should I go fetch that healer woman?'

Caroline shook her head. 'I'm not in need of any brew from

Mrs Hicks, but thank you for asking. A dose of sunshine and sea air is what I require now.'

'If you say so, ma'am.' Parker made a careful turn on the narrow stairs and headed back to the kitchen.

Caroline followed her as far as the parlour, where she donned her bonnet and set off on her walk.

A few minutes later, she paused at the top of the bluff that looked out over Gimble Porth and afforded such a fine view in all directions. To the west, across a strip of blue water studded with rocks and offshore islets, lay the island of St Martin's. Behind the bay stretched hummocks of windswept heath. To the south, the stone buildings of Dolphin Town clustered on the edge of the fertile, green downland. Tresco's varied landscape reminded Caroline how she'd once compared Bennett to this isolated island of contrasts.

Once again, she turned her thoughts to the choice he'd given her. Only this time, she tried to keep her self-doubt and defensiveness in check as she pondered how her choice would affect *him*.

She had never heard of a legal separation until a year ago when Lady Byron had obtained one from her husband, amid rumours of his cruelty and madness. Almack's had buzzed with scandalised whispers of a highly improper liaison with his half-sister. Almost overnight, society's favourite had become a vilified outcast, exiled to the Continent. In the years to come, would anyone remember the fine poetry he'd written or would his reputation always be tainted by the scandal of his failed marriage?

Caroline asked herself what it would mean for *her* husband if she sought such a separation. Would he be branded cruel, mad or wicked, like Lord Byron, and shunned from society?

The effect on his Abolition work would be disastrous, harming his reputation far worse even than her scandalous kiss with Fitz Astley. Yet, Bennett was willing to suffer all that so she might have her freedom without losing her child.

The notion struck her like a hard gust of wind off the sea, making her sway on knees suddenly gone weak. Could Bennett be trying to demonstrate with actions something he found impossible to convey in words?

She recalled his fumbling efforts to tell her the significance of putting her wedding ring on again. Other things he'd said came back to her as well, things she'd scarcely heeded in her dismay over the proposed separation. Something about forgiving *him* for the unhappiness of their marriage, the mention of a chance to become the kind of husband she deserved. If she understood him correctly, it seemed to be an opportunity he desired.

To think she'd been disappointed when Bennett made no effusive declaration of affection. Had she not watched him struggle these past weeks to demonstrate his deep love for their son? Had she not learned that deeds spoke louder and truer than words?

No words, no caresses, not even the most rapturous bliss of lovemaking could express his feelings with such poignant clarity as this choice he'd offered her.

Clearly Caroline had made her choice and she wanted to be free of him.

Bennett faced that harsh certainty as he and Wyn headed back to the house a few hours later. He had not left himself much time to catch the boat to St Mary's, but perhaps that was for the best. Quick farewells were less awkward, after all.

He and Wyn had spent such an enjoyable morning together, he'd been reluctant to see their treasure hunt end. Besides, if this was to be their last day together for quite some time, he wanted to make it one the boy would later recall with pleasure. Earlier in the day, he'd kept an anxious eye out for Caroline, glancing up expectantly at every little sound. But she had not joined them. As the hours wore on, Bennett came to the bitter realisation that she never would.

He made a determined effort to hide his dejection from Wyn and believed he'd succeeded. Of course, the child was so absorbed in their search for treasure that he might not have noticed anyway.

'What do you reckon Mama will think of all this?' Wyn clutched a small, battered wooden casket to his chest.

Bennett reached out to ruffle his son's hair. 'I'm certain she'll be most impressed with your treasure.'

The box was the one Caroline had discovered in the attic, containing some old coins and fragments of jewellery, and he knew she would make a suitable fuss over it for their son's benefit. She was a surprisingly good actress when she needed to be. The past few weeks, for example, when she'd made him hope she might feel something for him that ran deeper than physical desire.

He recalled a passage of Scripture he'd often heard quoted: 'For where your treasure is, there will your heart be also.' He now knew his treasure and his heart lay with his family.

At least he would have the memory of these special weeks on the island to cherish in the years to come.

As he and Wyn approached the house, Caroline suddenly appeared, running towards them. From the look of rapturous welcome that illuminated her face, one might have thought they'd been gone for months, rather than a few hours. 'There you are! I was afraid you'd run off with your booty to live the high life abroad.'

A burst of sweet, infectious laughter assured Bennett she was only teasing. It grieved him to recall his irrational fear that she had meant to run away abroad with their son.

His gaze lingered over her as she caught Wyn in a warm embrace. With her golden hair gleaming in the sunlight and her blue-green eyes dancing with delight, Caroline appeared as fresh and vibrant as when they'd first met. Yet there was an air of sweet ripeness about her that appealed to him far more that that frivolous girl. It seemed almost as if she'd been re-born. Could this be how Sir Gawain's Lady had looked when her spell was finally broken? He only wished she had not needed to be free of him to undergo such a transformation.

As he watched his wife and son with painful longing, Caroline suddenly reached out and pulled him into their embrace. A rogue spark of hope inside him ignited a blaze of elation and a pyre of fear. Was this only a gesture of gratitude for the freedom he'd offered her...or could it be something more?

Wyn was too excited to remain confined in his parents' arms very long. Far too soon for Bennett's liking, the lad wriggled free. 'Look what we found, Mama! It was just where the map showed it would be, down near Oliver's Battery.'

He thrust the box towards Caroline so she could examine his loot. 'Do you think it was left here by pirates? Or maybe the knights of Camelot?'

Just as Bennett had expected, she looked over Wyn's treasure with eager admiration. 'I imagine this is the treasure of a noble knight.'

As she spoke, Caroline cast Bennett a playful smile that

made his heart bound. This must be more than gratitude, surely. His gaze darted to her left hand, searching for a glint of gold at the base of her ring finger.

But in spite of how hard and hopefully he looked, her wedding band was not there. Disappointment struck him a hard blow in the pit of his stomach.

What had he expected? his conscience demanded. He had presented her with so many compelling reasons to leave him and not a single one to stay. He'd hoped she might recognise his willingness to sacrifice everything he valued to secure her happiness as the ultimate proof of his love.

But what if Caroline had mistaken his offer as a measure of how much he wanted to be rid of her? After all, she'd known far more cold rejection in the past than she had of open, effusive affection. But she needed that kind of love, just as the flowers around Tresco Abbey needed warm sunshine and shelter from the harsh sea wind to thrive.

'They are wonderful treasures.' Caroline returned a tarnished old necklace with a broken clasp to the box, handling it as carefully as one of the Crown Jewels. 'You and your papa were very clever to find them. Now, I'm certain Albert and Parker would like to see all this. Why don't you go show them? Mrs Jenkins has something for you to eat. You must be hungry after such a busy morning.'

The prospect of food and a fresh audience for his treasure sent Wyn scrambling towards the house without a backward glance. His parents watched him go with a mixture of fondness and pride. Then, all at once, it seemed to dawn on them that they were alone, without the familiar buffer of their son's presence.

Caroline was the first to break the awkward silence. 'I saw you looking at my hand. I want to explain about the ring.'

'There is no need of that.' Bennett shook his head vigorously. He could not let her speak of it until he'd had his say. If he was to have any hope of altering her choice, it must be before she had openly declared her decision. After that he must remain silent, or it would be as if he had not allowed her to choose freely at all. 'I beg your pardon for interrupting, but there is something most urgent I must tell you first.'

Caroline seemed to brace herself for what he was about to say. Was she reluctant to hear his clumsy declaration of his feelings? Did she fear it might move her to take him back out of pity?

With those thoughts plaguing him, Bennett had to force himself to continue. 'I know I said you would have a free choice and I mean to honour that offer. But I fear I may have left you with the wrong impression of my feelings in the matter.'

A bottomless pit seemed to open in the depths of his belly and all his other organs threatened to sink into it. 'I assumed you would understand my reasons…and thus my feelings.'

He groped for Caroline's hand, hoping his touch might convey more than his halting, self-conscious words. 'Now I fear that may have been asking too much, for you and I have never understood one another properly since we first met.'

Caroline seemed to understand better than he'd expected, for she gave his fingers a reassuring squeeze. 'I believe I do know what you meant by giving me this choice. Your generous gesture spoke louder than words.'

Tempted as he was to refrain, Bennett made himself continue. 'Actions may speak *louder* than words, dearest Caro, but not always *clearer*. Difficult as it is for me, I need to share what is in my heart. For my own sake as much as yours. In the past weeks, you have taught me so much about how to express love. It is only fair that you now receive the benefit of that tutelage.'

Her lower lip began to tremble and her beloved blue-green eyes sparkled with the suggestion of a tear.

In spite of what he feared those signs might mean, Bennett persisted. 'It was wrong of me to ask for your hand in marriage when I did not love you. But that is in the past and I cannot change it. All I can do is ask for your hand again. Only this time I do…love you, more than I can say.' His lips twisted into a wry grin. 'Obviously.'

Now that *the word* was out, like a tightly wedged cork pried from a bottle, others followed a little more easily. 'I fought hard to resist these feelings, for I was afraid they would leave me vulnerable to the kind of hurt I'd suffered as a child. The kind of hurt I later inflicted upon you. I cannot begin to tell you how much I regret that. Nor can I blame you if you are unable to forgive me or care for me as you once did.'

The reminder of that painful longing lent Caroline's features a look of heartbreaking beauty.

Bennett feared he might be persuading her to do the very opposite of what he wanted, but he felt compelled to make certain she knew how much he regretted the pain he'd caused her. 'Against my will, that love for you grew stronger and stronger until I could no longer deny or resist it. So I surrendered to it heart and soul. I love you, Caro! I will *always* love you, even if you choose to be free of me. What I tried to tell you this morning about your wedding ring was that if you will put it back on and give me the opportunity to win your love again, you will make me the very happiest of men.

'There.' He blew out a long breath. 'I have said my piece at last and the choice is still yours to make. Do not make it out of pity or duty, but only in the way you believe will secure your happiness. I will be content with that.'

'About the ring…' Caroline began hesitantly. 'I fear it holds too many unhappy memories for me ever to wear again. And I do not wish to revive the feelings I once had for you, because I now see they were not love, after all.'

His heart would not break, Bennett assured himself, though it pained him fiercely. His love for Caroline and their son was the binding that would hold it together. Neither did he regret the long-overdue declaration of his feelings. At least now he would know she had made her choice from a position of knowledge.

'What I feel for you now…' she continued. 'What I will feel for you for ever after, *that* is love. You have won it already. Or, perhaps, it has won us.'

Had he heard her correctly? A different kind of ache gripped Bennett's heart as it threatened to burst with joy. His look of bewilderment brought a smile of such transcendent bright-ness to Caroline's face that it was like staring directly at the rising sun. Certainly, it made Bennett's eyes sting.

Reaching up, she strove to smooth away any lingering fur-rows of distress from his countenance with the gentle balm of her caress. 'I would take a new ring, however, if you will give me one. As a symbol of our new feelings and our new marriage.'

The best answer he could give his darling wife was to sweep her into his arms for a lingering, joyful kiss.

'A new marriage,' he agreed, a few moments later, savouring the divine sweetness of those words. 'This time, a love match.'

Epilogue

London—August 1833

For perhaps the twentieth time in as many minutes, Caroline pulled back the curtain of her dressing-room window and peered out.

On this occasion, she was rewarded by the sight of her husband riding up the broad drive. Though her heart always beat a little faster when she saw Bennett again after even a brief absence, today she had an additional reason for excitement.

Leaving her maid to continue packing for the family's annual holiday on the Isles of Scilly, Caroline headed for the door. Out in the hallway, she started for the staircase, only to meet her daughters.

The elder one flashed Caroline an ingratiating smile that usually managed to secure whatever she requested from her doting father. 'Mama, I've been giving some thought to my début. After all, I will be seventeen by next Season.'

'Don't remind me.' Caroline looked from Hannah to her younger sister, Elizabeth. 'You are both growing up far too quickly.'

After so many years devoted to raising her children, she wished she could keep them with her a little longer. Wyn had already completed his studies at Cambridge and was hard at work on a book about the natural history of his beloved Isles of Scilly. All too soon, her pretty, accomplished daughters would be out in society. Thank goodness ten-year-old Thomas was not in such a tearing hurry to grow up.

'I was hoping,' continued Hannah in a wheedling tone, 'that you and Papa might host a ball for me at Almack's to make my début.'

The mention of Almack's brought a faint blush to Caroline's cheeks. She had not set foot in the place since that fateful night all those years ago. Finally happy in her marriage and busy with her growing family, she had not missed it in the least. But now, her daughter's request raised an awkward matter.

'Surely that old place is not still in fashion, is it?' She started down the stairs. 'The Lady Patronesses must all be in their dotage by now.'

'Please, Mama,' Hannah implored as both girls followed her. 'Almack's may not be quite as exclusive as it was in your day, but I assure you, it is still a most desirable establishment for a young lady of distinction to come out in society.'

Caroline chuckled, 'You sound as if you've swallowed a copy of *The Court Journal,* dearest.'

'Mama!' Hannah protested. 'Just because you and Papa are such notorious homebodies, it is not fair that I should be denied a fashionable début.'

Though her elder daughter might look a great deal like her, Caroline knew young Hannah had inherited her father's tenacity. She would keep bringing up the subject of Almack's until she got her way...or learned the truth.

'Don't fret, my dear. You'll be presented at Court and we will host a lovely ball for you.'

'At Almack's?'

Caroline shook her head decisively. 'I'm afraid your papa and I have not been welcome there for many years, even if we'd wished to attend, which we do not. Now pray excuse me. Your father is home and I must speak with him.'

Her revelation seemed to render Hannah speechless. But not Elizabeth. 'Why are you unwelcome at Almack's, Mama? Is it because of your Abolition work?'

In recent years, Caroline had been involved with the Ladies' Abolition Society and found far greater satisfaction in that work than she had in her former amusements.

'Abolition had nothing to do with it, dearest.' If she'd been less anxious to get away, Caroline might have found a more discreet manner to discourage her daughter's question. But today she wanted a few minutes alone with her husband before the children swarmed all over him. 'I'm afraid we caused something of a scandal.'

The girls' mouths fell open and their eyebrows flew up to such comical heights it made Caroline chuckle as she descended the last few stairs.

She emerged a moment later from the imposing front entrance, just in time to see Bennett dismounting. His bearing was as straight and proud as ever, though he now found it easier to bend down to embrace his wife and children.

As a stable boy led his horse away, Caroline hurried towards her husband. 'Welcome home, dearest! How was your day in the House?'

'Long, as usual,' replied Bennett, though he did not look tired. 'I happened upon an old friend of ours today at Westminster.'

That was not what Caroline wanted to hear about, but since her husband clearly wished to tell her, she was prepared to listen. 'Which old friend might that be?'

'None other that Fitz Astley. I scarcely recognised him. He's gotten all jowly and crippled up with the gout.'

'You sound almost sorry for him.' Caroline shook her head in amazement.

'Astley did play a part in bringing us back together.' Bennett caught her hand and raised it to his lips. 'I cannot help but feel that singular service cancels much of the trouble he made for me when we were younger.'

The warm pressure of his kiss upon her fingers stirred feelings of desire in Caroline that had not cooled from the earlier years of their marriage. 'I suppose you can afford to be charitable since you have prevailed over him in the long run. Now tell me what business was transacted in the Lords today?'

'Let me think.' Bennett pretended to search his memory. 'After a great deal of tiresome debate, the Catholic Marriages Bill passed second reading. And the China Trade Bill was sent into committee with several amendments.'

'Anything else?' Caroline knew perfectly well there must have been. But if Bennett chose to tease her a little today, he surely deserved to be humoured.

'Oh, yes, now I remember. The Ministerial Plan for the Abolition of Slavery passed third reading.' As he spoke those words, his voice grew husky with emotion. 'All it needs now is his Majesty's signature to make it law.'

'At last!' Unable to contain her elation, Caroline threw her arms around her husband and embraced him warmly.

Everyone had known the bill would be endorsed by the Lords once it passed the House of Commons. The outpouring of popular feeling over the recent death of William Wilberforce had only made its passage more certain. Yet Caroline knew her husband considered *this* day the crowning fulfilment of his long and distinguished career.

That scandalous night at Almack's had been a setback for the cause, but only one of many over the years. She doubted it had delayed today's sweet victory. The whole matter had surely been long forgotten...except by them. Looking back, Caroline often gave thanks that she and Bennett had been given a second chance at happiness and found the courage to take it.

'I would not have had the heart to persevere without your support, my angel,' Bennett murmured, holding her close. 'And this triumph would mean far less to me without you and our children to share it.'

A volley of giggles made them look up to see their mischievous daughters spying on them from the drawing-room window. Laughing back at the girls, Bennett kissed his wife on the lips with barely restrained passion.

As they headed back into their happy home, arm in arm, Caroline glanced down at her wedding ring with a smile of radiant joy. Though she had never taken it off in the past sixteen years, she had no trouble recalling the inscription Bennett had shown her before placing it upon her finger.

'In case I ever have difficulty telling you,' he'd whispered, 'this will be your reminder.'

Treasure...cherish...love.

Since then, a day had seldom gone by that he did not show or tell her of the devotion that grew deeper with each passing year. A devotion she amply returned.

* * * * *

UNTAMED ROGUE, SCANDALOUS MISTRESS
Bronwyn Scott

Notorious Crispin Ramsden is captivated when faced with self-made Miss, Aurora Calhoun. She's a woman whose impetuous nature ignites a passion that is as uncontrollable as it is scandalous! Can these two wild hearts find a place to belong?

HONOURABLE DOCTOR, IMPROPER ARRANGEMENT
Mary Nichols

Dr Simon Redfern has risked his heart once before and is shocked when he longs to make the compassionate young widow Kate his wife. Faced with family disapproval, Kate must fight her growing attraction to the man she can't have but so desperately wants.

THE EARL PLAYS WITH FIRE
Isabelle Goddard

Bitter Richard Veryan was left heartbroken after beautiful Christabel Tallis jilted him before their wedding. But when he and Christabel meet again, years later, temptation hangs in the air. He wants to prove he can still command her body and soul—then *he'll* be the one to walk away...

HIS BORDER BRIDE
Blythe Gifford

Clare, daughter of a Scottish lord, can recite the laws of chivalry. She knows dark rebel Gavin, illegitimate son of an English prince, has broken every one. Clare is gripped by desire for this royal rogue. Could he be the one to unleash everything she's tried so hard to hide?

Mills & Boon® Hardback
Historical

Another exciting novel available this month:

THE SCANDALOUS LORD LANCHESTER

Anne Herries

The wayward widow

With her wealth, beauty and playful nature, young widow Mariah Fanshawe is not short of suitors. Yet the only man she wants to marry is immune to her obvious charms! Upright Andrew, Lord Lanchester has always seemed determined to resist, but Mariah has a new plan to win him over…

Andrew is thrown when Mariah asks him to help her find a husband. The truth is he'd like nothing more than to make the wild Mariah his own obedient wife! But Andrew is living in the shadow of a scandal...

SECRETS AND SCANDALS
Nothing stays secret for long in Regency Society

HIS0112 HB TSLL

Mills & Boon® Hardback Historical

Another exciting novel available this month:

DESTITUTE ON HIS DOORSTEP

Helen Dickson

The Homeless Miss Lucas

Destitute and desperate, Jane Lucas knows there is one place where she can find refuge—her childhood home.

Landing on the doorstep, Jane is confronted with a new Lord of the Manor! Devilish Colonel Francis Russell is known for his fierce reputation in battle. The Civil War may be ended but, by stepping over the threshold, Jane fears she's crossing enemy lines…

She will use every weapon in her arsenal to claim back the home that's rightfully hers, starting with her bewitching charm… and then she goes and falls under the Colonel's spell!

0112 HB DOHD

*Mills & Boon® Hardback
Historical*

*Another exciting novel available
this month:*

THE DRAGON
AND THE PEARL

Jeannie Lin

The most beautiful courtesan of them all...

Former Emperor's consort Ling Suyin is renowned for
her beauty, the ultimate seductress. Now she lives quietly
alone—until the most ruthless warlord in the region
comes and steals her away...

Li Tao lives life by the sword, and is trapped in the treacherous
world of politics. The alluring Ling Suyin is at the centre of the
web. He must uncover her mystery without falling under her
spell—yet her innocence calls out to him. How cruel if she,
of all women, can entrance the man behind the legend...